Concrete Rose Publication Presents

Ghetto Rose

Nisha Lanae

GHETTO ROSE
By
Nisha Lanae

This novel is a work of fiction. Any references to real people, events, establishments, or locales are intended only to give the fiction a sense of reality and authenticity. Other names, characters, and incidents occurring in the work are either the product of the author's imagination or are used fictitiously, as those fictionalized events and incidents that involve real persons. Any character that happens to share the name of a person who is an acquaintance of the author, past or present, is purely coincidental and is in no way intended to be an actual account involving that person.

ISBN 13: 978-0998127507
ISBN 10: 0998127507

CONCRETE

P.O Box 16207
Long Beach, CA 90806

Dedication

*A **rose** can never be a **sunflower**, and a sunflower can never be a rose. All **flowers** are beautiful in their own way, and that's like **women** too.*

-Meranda Kerr

To every woman reading this: This is for you—for those women who suffer in silence; the women looking for acceptance from a man; the ones who look in the mirror and don't understand or love the reflection looking back at them because of what a man has told them; the women struggling with fitting into their clothes and not liking being overweight but too scared to change because of what someone is going to say or make them feel—I do this for you. I do this to give you the strength to say fuck what they say. Do whatever sets your soul on fire. You are beautiful no matter what color the pigment of your skin or the size of your jeans. Beauty doesn't have a color or a shape. You are beautiful.

Acknowledgement

I have to give all praise to my Heavenly Father above for all of the blessings He has bestowed in my life. I serve a mighty God. I have to give thanks and praise to my readers. I have readers that have been riding with me since 2012 and are still riding with me for this release of my fourth novel. I can never tell you how appreciated you are to me.

To my Lit sistahs who keep me motivated, in line, and push me to continue on this journey even when I feel defeated. Words could never justify how grateful I have been blessed to have encountered you ladies.

#BlackGirlmagic
#authorssupportingauthors
#womeninurbanlit

Aleta Williams, Marynette Beal, Sequaia Reed, Crystal Alexis, and Tameeka Mo'Nique. Greatness is around us, and with God's mercy, greatness will stay around and evolve into whatever our hearts desire.

To my family: I don't have to even name you. Everyone I have in my life currently knows the roles they play in my life because the love, support, and motivation go beyond words.

Chapter 1

The wind was blowing hard, making the tree brush up against Dahlia's living room as she lay watching *Love Jones* for the umpteenth time in the last month since her break up with Antonio. She only wished she could find a man to admire her like the men in the movies admired women.

Everything between Dahlia and Antonio had been going great, until a few weeks ago. Just out of the blue, he stopped spending the night and answering her calls and text messages. When Dahlia finally did speak with him, he dropped the bomb that he was no longer interested in her. Dahlia was crushed by the news and also at a loss as to what had caused the sudden change. The week prior to that he had been talking long-term goals.

The loud ringing of her cellphone brought her from pondering over Antonio once again.

"Hello?" Dahlia spoke into the phone, annoyed with the unknown caller who had been calling all into the wee hours for the last week. They never spoke, just listened to Dahlia's background.

"What is it? This is the second time tonight and the tenth time this week. Antonio, is this you? I thought we were over? Are you getting some kind of kick out of this? If you want to talk, then say it," she snarled.

"This ain't no-damn-Antonio," a female's voice replied.

"Well, who are you? And what can I possibly do for you?" Dahlia questioned.

The caller just sat on the other end of the phone breathing heavily and listening.

"Well, since you seem to have gotten tongue-tied, do me a favor: STOP! CALLING! MY! DAMN! PHONE!" Dahlia yelled before ending the call.

"People are really-fuckin'-crazy," Dahlia said out loud to herself, turning back to the movie. The phone rang again. This time her phone displayed 'private caller'.

"GET A LIFE, SHIT!" Dahlia yelled into the phone. "Didn't I tell you to stop calling my phone? I don't know what kind of childish-shit you're into, but I'm grown and I don't have time for this crap!"

"Child, who-in-the-hell you yelling and cursing at?"

"Oh, hey, Granny. I'm sorry about that. Someone has been playing on my phone all week."

"Who's playing on your phone?"

"I don't know, but I wish they'd stop. It's so annoying."

"Maybe it's Antonio calling to hear your voice. That boy knows he loves you. I told you he would come around. Sometimes men get scared when things began to get too serious in their eyes."

"It was a woman's voice, Granny," Dahlia informed her.

"Oh shit. Well, I don't know about that one. You don't have a crazy woman after your stuff do you?"

"What?" Dahlia questioned, not understanding what her grandmother was really trying to say.

"You know, those girls who like girls. What are they called?"

"Lesbians?"

"Yeah; you don't have a lesbian after you, do you?"

"No, Granny."

"Well, I just had to ask. You know Celia's granddaughter?"

"Keisha or Shante?" Dahlia questioned, prepared to hear the gossip her grandmother was about to share.

"Which one is the pretty one with all that nice, long hair?"

"Shante."

"Well, that one. Celia couldn't understand why that girl's almost thirty and she doesn't have any kids. Nor can she keep a man."

"Maybe she's focused on achieving her goals in life and not having kids right now, and she hasn't found the right man. Not everyone wants to be a man's baby's mother. I sure don't," Dahlia spoke, trying to quickly dismiss the conversation because she knew her grandmother wanted to know when she was going to have kids and get married.

"Dahlia, please. You know damn-well that child's a stripper down there at that club where all those rappers go on Sundays. Celia came home from church early on Sunday and found that child in bed with another woman. She told Celia that was her girlfriend. They're in love and plan on getting married."

"Well, if that's what she likes; it's her life and her choices."

"Well, I'm not gon catch you in my bed with a woman, am I?"

"No! Granny, I'm not a lesbian," Dahlia gasped. "I don't like women. I love men and everything that comes with them. I just haven't found the right one for me. That doesn't mean I'm going to turn to women."

"I just had to ask, sweetie. I would love you anyway because you are my granddaughter. I just don't want to catch you being another woman's evening snack."

"Ewww, Granny, that's just nasty."

"I'm just saying."

"What can I do for you, Granny? And why is your number showing up private anyway? Are you at home?" Dahlia questioned, changing the subject.

"Yes, I'm at home. That's a new feature I added to my phone. I'm tired of your brother calling all these floozies, then they get my number and start calling back, trying to sound all sexy, talking about 'Hello, is Desman there?'" her grandmother mimicked.

"Tell Desman not to give out your number, since he can't pay a-damn-bill over there," Dahlia snarled.

She was fed-up with her older brother. He didn't work nor did he have an income. He still lived with their grandparents, who only received SSI, leaving Dahlia to foot any bills her grandparents couldn't afford, which were the bills he ran up.

"You know that boy don't have a job and nowhere else to go."

"See there you go, Granny, taking up for him. Desman is dang-near thirty-four years old and still lives with his grandparents. He doesn't have a job and has three kids, so the only woman who should be calling, looking for his ass, is an employer," Dahlia scoffed. "I'm sorry for being disrespectful and cursing, Granny, I'm just tired of Desman. He is lazy and just living off you and Grandpa," Dahlia expressed.

"Don't be so hard on him. You know he's been through a lot."

"We all have, Granny, but when will you stop using that tired excuse for Desman? You're enabling him to be a deadbeat. Yes, our mother was killed right in front of our eyes. Yes, our father will be in prison for the rest of his life. I know what Desman has been through. I witnessed it; Daniel witnessed it. We've all been through it. That's still no excuse for Desman not doing anything. That should motivate him to do more, be more, for his own children.

"He'll get it right one day. Just be patient with your brother."

Dahlia huffed on the other end of the phone. The unknown caller had called three times since she had been on the phone with her grandmother, leaving voicemails every time. Between the caller and her grandmother and the tired excuses she made for Desman, Dahlia thought she would go insane.

"I hope that doesn't take another thirty-four years."

"But that's not what I called you for. I want to give the old geezer a surprise birthday party next Saturday and I need your help."

"What geezer?" Dahlia questioned, confused.

"Your grandfather. He will be seventy-five next Friday, and I want to give him a little gathering. Nothing too big, just a few friends and family."

"What do you need me to pay for, Granny?" Dahlia questioned, already knowing, like always, her grandmother would need her to pay for her grandfather's party, which she didn't mind because she loved her grandparents.

When Dahlia's mother was killed, her grandparents had helped their father do his best to raise them without his wife. When his lifestyle finally caught up with him and he was sent off to prison, her grandparents had taken full responsibility for raising Dahlia and her two brothers, Desman and Daniel, without a complaint.

"Just some tables and chairs. Oh, we need some decorations. Sham said she'll get the food with her food stamps, but you know that daughter of mine be lying, so I'm gon need help with that, too. I'll try to gather up some money from them cans and bottles around back."

"Don't worry, Granny, I'll be over there tomorrow to take you to the store to get the stuff you need," Dahlia assured her, knowing her aunt. She would be missing in action and not have anything for the party.

"Okay; what time you need me to be ready?"

"Around noon. I have a client at nine a.m. and an errand to run for a client. I'll come over there after that."

"Okay, I'll be ready. This old lady is about to lay it down; it's way past my bedtime. I'll see you tomorrow, and thank you, Dahlia; I can always count on you."

"Good night, Granny. I love you."

"I love you, too. Good night, sweetie."

Dahlia hung up the phone with her grandmother just as the credits were rolling on the screen.

"DAMN, I MISSED MY FAVORITE PART," Dahlia yelled, fishing around for the remote control to restart the movie, when she heard the ding from her voicemail signaling another voicemail message.

Dahlia checked the voicemails and was even more annoyed with the unknown caller. Three of the messages were the caller just sitting on the phone, and the fourth was of someone engaging in sex. Dahlia listened over and over again, and sure enough, it was a woman and man having sex. She didn't know if it was porn, or the actual caller having sex and intentionally leaving it on her voicemail. Either way, Dahlia couldn't deny it if she'd wanted to. It turned her on and had her hormones going. It hit her that she hadn't had her honey pot tampered with in over a month. It was around the time her ex-boyfriend Antonio had gone missing in action.

Removing the throw-blanket from over her, she went into her room in search of her small self-pleasure stash. Dahlia selected the Rabbit and made her way around to her bed. Lying back, ready to release some pent-up tension, Dahlia hit the power button, but didn't hear anything. She tried it again, but still no luck. It was dead.

"Shit!" Dahlia spoke, rushing to the bathroom closet in search of batteries. It had been so long since she'd needed any because Antonio had always been there to handle her every sexual need. After searching several places, no luck. There wasn't a spare battery in the house, and Dahlia was no longer in the mood, opting for a quick shower to see what it would do for her.

Dahlia showered quickly and slid into a long T-shirt left behind by Antonio that reeked of her favorite scent on him. Dahlia made her way around the house, making sure all the windows and doors were closed, before slugging up in her bed. Dahlia prepared to drift off to sleep. The flash of her phone shined in her face. Getting up to grab it off the dresser, she glanced down at the message from a number she didn't recognize.

562-222-7223: I HOPE YOU LIKED THAT, BITCH!!!

Dahlia clicked on the number to see who was playing on her phone, only to be hit with a text-only app message. Climbing back into her bed, Dahlia vowed not to answer another call from the caller. *'They must have the wrong number or have me confused with someone else,'* Dahlia thought as she pulled the cover over her face and let sleep invade.

Chapter 2

Dahlia pulled the covers from over her face as she heard the sound of her alarm going off. The morning sunrise peeked through the cracks of the blinds, shining bright in her face. Heading to the bathroom to relieve her morning urine and wash her face, she passed her phone and saw more missed calls from the unknown caller, and one from Antonio. She was surprised, but didn't have any intention of returning his call. If he really wanted to speak to her, he would have to try harder.

'Well, I could use him to handle this issue I'm having. He does lay the pipe down well,' she thought, then quickly dismissed the thought.

That was probably what he wanted—sex without the commitment. Dahlia wasn't settling for that ever again. Making her way to the bathroom, she showered, threw on some clothes, and made her way out the door to meet her client.

Dahlia was a hairstylist and personal stylist; she only worked with D-list celebrities and mostly people around Los Angeles. It paid enough money to keep up the house her father had purchased for her before he was sentenced to life in prison, and keep her dressed fly and pushing a big-body Benz.

It had been her dream since she was young to be the owner of her own salon, but life had its ups and downs. When she'd had the money to purchase a salon and even had a location picked out, her grandmother needed the money to pay off the loan on her house. She couldn't see her grandparents losing the house they'd worked so hard for and held so many memories for her growing up because Desman had decided to jump bail. So until she saved the money up again, she worked hard to keep a steady, regular clientele. She promised herself that, one day, she would be the proud owner of her very own hair salon.

Dahlia made it to her car and noticed her back tires were flat.

"What-in-the-hell?" she questioned, sitting her bags down to inspect her tires and noticed they had been slit. "UGH!" Dahlia yelled, pissed.

It was already past eight a.m., and it would take roadside assistance at least fifteen-to-forty-five minutes to make it to her home to change her tires. Dahlia phoned them, hoping someone was already in the area and could get to her fast. Twelve minutes later, a truck pulled behind her car. A pudgy man jumped down from the front seat.

"Dahlia Willowbrook?" he asked, approaching her.

"Yes, that's me."

"What can I do for you this morning?" He smiled, showing teeth so yellow and rotten they looked like they hadn't seen a dentist in years.

"I need my back tires changed. They have been slit open. I have a spare in my truck and an extra one in my garage."

After showing him her AAA card, the technician got to work quickly changing her tires out.

"Thank you so much for being so fast," Dahlia said, handing the man a twenty when he'd finished before jumping in her car. She had twenty minutes to get to the shop to meet her client. She prayed the 101 and 110 freeways weren't crowed. Dahlia sped off as soon as the technician pulled out her driveway.

"Good morning," Dahlia spoke to everyone as she rushed through the salon to her workstation toward the back of the salon.

"Good morning," Chandra, the owner, spoke as she French-rolled her client's hair.

Dahlia briskly began unpacking her bag and setting up so she would be ready by the time her client arrived. She had mange to get to the salon at ten after nine and hadn't seen her client sitting in the waiting area.

"Dahlia, can I talk to you for a quick minute?"

Dahlia heard the familiar male's voice as he approached. Dahlia stood still for a moment before she turned around to face Antonio. She couldn't believe he'd shown up to her place of business. He knew her place of employment was off limits. It had always been.

"What are you doing here, Antonio?" Dahlia whispered with a slight smile on her face. She knew everyone was either watching or listening to their conversation.

Dahlia had come into the salon fresh from the State board and had worked there for the last four years. Many people who currently worked in the shop had witnessed the violent relationship with her ex. Since then, Dahlia didn't involve them in her relationships. She had learned everyone was not a shoulder to cry on. Some people only used it to gossip to the next. They had only seen Antonio on occasion. That was how Dahlia wanted to keep it. She didn't want them prying into her relationship dealings.

"I need to talk to you," Antonio said, looking over his shoulder at the women who occupied the shop. Sweat trickled down his forehead like he had been running.

"You could've called me. I told you before not to come to my place of employment."

"You do hair, Dahlia. This isn't a real job. This isn't a corporate job I'm coming to," Antonio said, looking over his shoulder once more. He seemed jittery, like someone was waiting on him, or after him.

"It may not be a corporate job like your job down at the bank, but it's what pays my bills and my client is here. So if you want to talk to me, call me later." Dahlia gritted her teeth, pissed that Antonio wanted to downplay what she did for a living.

"How long will it take you to finish? I really need to speak with you."

"So you can talk all of a sudden? I don't know how long it will take me and I am not going to rush my client's hair. What is going on with you and why do you keep looking over your shoulder? Are you okay?" Dahlia questioned, looking behind him outside the shop to see if anyone was out there with him.

"Yeah, I'm good. I'll give you a call in about two hours. That should be a good enough time," Antonio said, walking off before Dahlia could get anything else out.

Dahlia watched him climb into his truck and pull off. She didn't know what was going on with him. He was acting weird.

"Hey, D," Sondra, her client, said, taking a seat in her chair.

"Hey, girl; what are we doing with this hair today?" Dahlia spoke, looking through her hair to check if any of her tracks needed to be tightened.

"I need some tracks tightened and a wash; then I want you to cut this into a real nice, layered bob," Sondra spoke, using her hands to describe how she wanted the bob to be cut.

"I got you," Dahlia told her as she wrapped the cape around her and began to sort through the tracks that needed tightening.

Sondra talked about her new boyfriend while Dahlia worked, tuning her out and thinking about Antonio and what he wanted. He seemed paranoid about something. Two hours later, Dahlia had tightened, washed, dried, highlighted, cut, and straightened Sondra's hair and had her smiling from one ear to the other at the outcome of her hair.

"Damn, girl, you are good. You hooked me up, as usual. I don't know why you don't have your own shop, instead of in here with all these hating-bitches," Sondra spoke, handing Dahlia her money. "I can't wait to go home and let this nigga see me," Sondra chuckled.

"In due time, I will. Don't be sweating your hair out in one night." Dahlia smiled as she retrieved her money from Sondra.

"He'll just be paying for a bitch to get her shit done again." She laughed.

Sondra was Dahlia's only client for the day; her other client had canceled. Dahlia packed her tools back into her travel bag and cleaned her area so she could head to her grandmother's to spend the rest of the day with her.

Just as Dahlia got into her car, her phone rang.

"WHAT DO YOU WANT? YOU HAVE CALLED ME FIVE TIMES IN TWENTY MINUTES?" Dahlia yelled into the phone harshly. Antonio had managed to work every nerve in her body for the day. "What is it you want from me, Antonio? Because just a few weeks ago, you told me loud and clear that you didn't want shit to do with me. So what do you want that you keep blowing my-damn-phone up?"

"Are you done with your client?" he questioned, getting right down to the point. "I need to speak with you and it's important to me."

"Meet me at my house in forty-five minutes. If you aren't there when I get there, I'm leaving," she uttered, pulling out the shop parking lot.

It took Dahlia a little over thirty minutes to make it to her house. When she pulled into her driveway, Antonio was sitting on her front porch waiting, like he had been there the whole time.

"What is it you want, Antonio? And make it quick; I have to go pick up my grandmother and take her somewhere," Dahlia spoke as she walked in the house, Antonio following close behind.

"How is your grandmother?" he questioned.

"She's fine."

"How is your grandfather?"

"My family is fine. Everyone is doing just marvelous," Dahlia replied, taking a seat on the couch.

"You look nice today," Antonio said, admiring her legs in the mini-dress she had on.

"So this is what you needed to speak with me about? I look the same as I did a month ago. There is nothing that has changed. You could've done this over the phone, asking about my grandparents. So what do you want to talk about? I thought we were over and done with?"

"I didn't mean that. I've just been going through a lot. You want more from me than I can give right now."

"All I asked for was a commitment. I have never asked you for money because I have my own. I was raised to always count only on my own."

"And that's more than I have to give."

"So, what'd you think: We're supposed to just be friends with no titles and fuck on the regular?" Dahlia questioned, slightly pissed she'd asked the questioned because she didn't want to hear the answer she already knew.

"Something like that."

"Well, if that's what you came here to ask, let me save you some time. The answer is hell-fuckin'-no."

"That was a thought, but not the reason I came here to talk to you."

"What is it? I'm not good enough to wake up to a man every morning? All you think I deserve is a fuck every now and then when you're horny?" Dahlia questioned.

"Dahlia, it isn't that. You're a gorgeous woman and any man would love for you to be his woman," Antonio spoke, kneeling in front of her and taking her into his arms. "I didn't mean to hurt you in any way. I'm just going through a lot in my life and you don't deserve to go through the bullshit with me," Antonio spoke, his hands sliding up Dahlia thighs. "I do care about you, and me not being with you right now is me really caring for you. I don't want you to get caught-up in this shit I have going on."

"Get your-damn-hands off me!" Dahlia pushed his hands back down her thighs. "Don't start trying to run-that-shit on me. It sounds like game, the whole 'it's me, not you'. What have you been listening to, Toni Braxton?"

"Let me make you feel good. I know something that makes you feel real good," Antonio spoke, his hands slowly creeping up her thighs again as he looked her in the eye. "Let me help ease that build up. I know you ain't had nobody sucking this honey of mine."

Antonio knew Dahlia wouldn't hear him out unless she was in a good mood, and he knew just the way to put her into a good mood. He just needed to get her panties off. The rest would be a done deal once his tongue hit her spot.

Dahlia wanted to protest, but his soft hands rubbing up against her thighs and the pleasure she wanted to feel so bad caused her to sit there as Antonio rubbed on her vagina. Leaning her head back, she spread her legs apart, waiting for him to explore her honey pot with his long, thick tongue. Antonio grinned wide as Dahlia spread her legs.

"You want me to make you feel good, huh?" he questioned, sliding her panties over. "Just tell me you want me to make you feel good."

He wanted to hear her beg for him to please her. He wanted to hear she still wanted him to suck all of the honey her pot had to give.

"Just shut up and eat my pussy!" Dahlia scolded, pushing his head down between her thick thighs.

Antonio smiled. He had her just where he wanted her: horny with her emotions on a roller coaster. Within minutes of Antonio letting his tongue wander around Dahlia's honey pot, she was squirming and pushing his head in deeper.

"Yeeesss!" she moaned as her bottom lip quivered. A sharp voltage pulsated through her vagina. Antonio knew how to hit her spot like he would win a prize every time. Today was no exception.

"Come ride my face," Antonio suggested, getting up from the floor where he kneeled in front of Dahlia and lying flat on the couch.

Dahlia and Antonio switched positions. Once Dahlia removed her panties, she made sure her pussy was eye-level. Antonio gripped her thighs and went back to work, darting his tongue in and out. Dahlia twisted her hips in rotation. She made sure his face was deep between her thighs, then she gripped the armrest of the couch. She felt her brewing orgasm was right at its peak. She was about to cum, then Antonio stopped.

"Why'd you stop?" Dahlia questioned, opening her eyes.

"Get off me," Antonio yelled, pushing Dahlia off him.

"WHAT-IN-THE-HELL?" Dahlia yelled, catching herself before she hit the floor face-first the way Antonio had flung her off him.

"Hello?" Antonio jumped up to answer his phone that was nestled in the front pocket of the button-down shirt he wore.

Dahlia watched him as he balanced the phone and tried to lick up her juices that were creeping down his chin. His phone had been vibrating for five minutes straight. She'd felt it every time. Someone was persistent about reaching him.

"I'm on my way. Don't leave. Please!" he pleaded into the phone before hanging up.

"D, I'm gon have to get with you later to finish this little thing." He grinned, moving in closer to her. "Because daddy long leg needs to feel them insides. I still need to talk to you about what I really came over here for. I have to handle something real fast and this is real important," he spoke, halfway out the door.

Dahlia didn't even try to wrap her mind around what was up with Antonio. She was upset she had fallen prey to him and even let him touch her. Grabbing her panties from the floor, she took a quick shower, changed her clothes, and was back out the door to pick up her grandmother.

Chapter 3

Dahlia pulled up to her grandparents' three-story home and was upset the lawn hadn't been taken care of. When she came last week, she'd reminded him it needed to be cut. Here it was a week later, and the grass still hadn't been cut. She had canceled the Saturday-morning lawn service when Desman agreed to the upkeep of their grandparents' lawn.

"This nigga don't do shit right," she huffed, checking her grandparents' mailbox.

Dahlia sorted through the mail and threw out all the junk mail. She came across the phone bill. She decided to open it since her grandmother had complained about it. Dahlia instantly was pissed at all the long distance and collect calls on her grandmother's phone bill.

"DESMAN!" Dahlia yelled, coming through the door, bypassing her grandfather, who sat in his favorite recliner in the family room watching reruns of *Walker, Texas Ranger*.

"Hello to you, too, Dahlia," James, Dahlia's grandfather, spoke, still looking at the screen.

"Hey, Granddaddy; where is that sorry-excuse-of-a-man you call grandson?"

"He should be up there in his room. He doesn't have anything else to do," he spoke, knowing Dahlia was about to let Desman have it.

Dahlia marched up the two flights of stairs to the room her brother occupied. Pushing the room door open without knocking, Dahlia stormed inside.

"DESMAN!" she yelled, shaking him hard, trying to wake him. "Wake yo' ass up. What happened to you keeping the lawn cut and watered?" she questioned. "Last week you said you were going to do it."

"I'LL DO IT LATER; I'M SLEEP!" Desman shouted, pulling the pillow over his head.

"Get your ass up! You don't have a job; why-in-the-hell are you so-damn-tired? And where-in-the-hell are you calling? Or getting calls from? Why-in-the-hell is Granny's house phone bill four-hundred-damn-dollars? You calling bitches collect like you're in jail or something."

"Dahlia, get the fuck out! I'm trying to sleep. Shit!" Desman scoffed, glancing up at his little sister.

"That's all your lazy-ass does is sleep—eat, shit, and sleep—and you don't earn a-damn-dime."

"Whatever, Dahlia; just get-the-fuck-out before I put your fat-ass out."

"You can't put me out. You don't pay any bills here; you have no right to put anyone out. So why haven't you cut the grass?"

"How much you gon pay me to cut the grass?"

"Pay you? I'm not gon pay you shit. You should do it without a problem. You do live here rent-free. You don't buy food. Hell, Granny still washes your-damn-clothes."

"But you pay those Mexicans," Desman chuckled.

"They don't live here. They provide a service. This is our grandparents' home. The least you could do is help out around here since you can't contribute to the bills."

"If they want me to do something, they'll ask. I don't need you bringing your fat-ass with that loud mouth in here talking shit. SO GET-THE-FUCK-OUT BEFORE I PUSH YOU THE-FUCK-OUT!" Desman shouted, jumping up from the bed into Dahlia's face.

"What you gon do? Hit me? As long as my grandparents live here and I'm helping them, I can say what-the-fuck I want. Like get a-fuckin'-job! You're thirty-four with three kids. Be a man for once in your life."

"What you know about a man? You can't even keep one."

"Because there're too many men walking around here like you—weak and broke-as-shit."

"Fuck you, Dahlia!" Desman snarled, balling his fist up. Dahlia was pissing him off.

"You'd better not hit her!" their grandfather spoke, coming up behind them. "Now, Desman, your grandmother and I allow you to stay here without asking for anything because we love you. It wouldn't hurt to at least help out around here. Like your sister said, we shouldn't have to ask you. Your sister helps us out a lot, and I can understand why she is upset that you don't do anything."

"Granddaddy, you're taking her side?"

"There are no sides here. All I am saying is try to help out around here more, or you may have to find somewhere else to go."

"You saying I have to leave, Granddaddy?"

"What I am saying is help out, son, or you gon have to leave. No grown-ass-man will lay up in my house, besides me, and do nothing, and my woman is cooking and cleaning. That's what I'm saying and that's final. And I'd better not ever catch you calling your sister out of her name again, let alone you trying to lay hands on her. I will personally kick yo' ass!

"Now come on down these stairs, Dahlia; your grandmother is waiting on you," James spoke sternly, waiting for Dahlia to walk out the room first.

Dahlia gave Desman a dirty look over her shoulder before leaving the room.

"Thanks, Granddaddy, but I didn't need any help with that loser. I can handle myself," Dahlia uttered when she'd made it down the stairs.

"I know you can, child. You're my grandchild and just as stubborn as your father." James chuckled, retreating back to his recliner.

"HEY, HEY!" Sham, Dahlia's auntie, yelled, coming through the door with her grandmother following behind.

"Sham, don't come in here with all that noise today," James scolded.

"Aww, Daddy, stop with the fussing, old man. I'm not even that loud," Sham spoke, lightly tapping her father on the shoulder as she passed.

"Hey, niece. I haven't seen you in a long time. When you gon whip Auntie Sham's hair up? I'm always seeing everyone whipped all up by you, and you letting yo' auntie walk around here looking all crazy about the head."

"Auntie Sham, you don't even keep still; you're always out running them streets. Where're the kids?"

"You ain't never lied," James cosigned with a chuckled.

"They're with their fathers. When you gon have some babies of your own? You're always asking me about mine. Dahlia, you are young, beautiful, and have a lot going for yourself. You need to get out there. You not gon find Mister Right in your living room."

"I'm not looking for a man. I'm focused on me and trying to get my own shop. I'm thinking of going back to school to get my master's."

"Find the right man and you'll have that shop in no time—if you know how to handle yours—if you know what I mean." Sham laughed, winking at Dahlia. "I think I found me a new little boo," Sham smiled. "He's flying into town this weekend for business and promised to take me shopping."

"Sham, I love you, baby, I do, but don't you ever try to give this child any advice about men. You're supposed to lead by example, and seeing that you have four kids, three baby daddies, and have never been married, I don't see you being able to give Dahlia good advice. This is coming from my heart, as your father and a man who will always love you no matter what you do."

"Damn, Daddy, did you really have to break me down like that?" Sham questioned, rolling her eyes. "I know I've made a few mistakes in life, but I am trying, and this one, he might be the one to sweep me off my feet and take care of me and my kids," she beamed. "He just might be the one to come and change my mind about marriage."

"James, just hush yo' mouth," Mabel, Dahlia's grandmother, interjected.

"That's my-damn-daughter; I can say what I want to her. Sham ain't a child," James scoffed, looking at Mabel then back to Sham.

"I love you, but you need to do better. You were raised . . ." James just stared at his only daughter and wondered where he and Mabel had gone wrong. He'd worked two jobs to provide for his family and had made sure they had everything they needed. Somehow, they'd still wondered into the streets. "You were raised better than this. If I offended you, I'm sorry, but you needed to hear it. When you were a young girl, I made a promise to you. I promised to always tell you nothing but the truth, and I will uphold that promise until I shut my eyes," James said.

"IT'S OKAY FOR DESMAN TO LAY UP IN HERE AND NOT DO SHIT, BUT YOU RIDE ME SUPER HARD? HE'S JUST YOUR GRANDSON; I'M YOUR CHILD!" Sham yelled out of hurt. It seemed like he rode her harder than anyone else.

"Desman is thirty-four and going through a tough time, but that doesn't mean I don't ride him. You don't see what I do on a daily. Shamera, you are fifty years old and you have four kids, two who are still in elementary. You have a daughter who needs to see better in life, so she can be better and achieve more. Ask yourself this: Do you want your daughter to date the kind of men you date? Because she will. Because she sees you doing it. I always wanted you to date men who were better than me. There is only one man I would have loved for you as my daughter to marry."

"Who, Zack?" Sham questioned.

"Yes; that is a good man. He loved you. He loved you like a father wants to see a man love his daughter."

"Zack is weak."

"I don't know where we went wrong." James shook his head.

"Whatever, Daddy." Sham rolled her eyes, walking out the living room.

"Let's go, Dahlia. I know you have better things to do then listen to all this bullshit," Mabel said, grabbing her purse and walking out the door.

"We'll be back in a few hours, Granddaddy. You told her the truth, but you were a little harsh." Dahlia kissed her grandfather on his cheek before heading outside.

Mabel was leaning on Dahlia's car with a cigarette dangling from her mouth. Dahlia knew her grandmother was pissed. It was written all over her face.

"Granny, she needed to hear it. You're always trying to save her."

"James just works my-damn-nerves! Always running his-damn-mouth," Mabel snarled as she put her cigarette out.

"Let's go grab something to eat. Then we can go pick up the things for the party."

"There isn't going to be a party. I'm not giving him shit."

Dahlia burst out laughing at her grandmother. "Don't be mean, Granny. We're still going to give the old geezer a surprise party. Granddaddy was just telling Sham something she needed to hear. We don't know how he feels to see his only daughter act how Sham be out here acting."

Dahlia tried to smooth out her grandfather's outburst. She agreed with her grandfather. Her auntie had two grown kids—twenty-two and eighteen—then a ten and a five-year-old. The kids spent most days with James and Mabel, or their fathers, because Sham was too busy in the streets. Dahlia was about to pull out her grandparents' driveway when Sham came running out the front door calling her name.

"DAHLIA, WAIT!" she yelled, rushing to the car.

"What's up?" Dahlia questioned.

"Where y'all going?"

"I told you yesterday Dahlia was taking me to get stuff for your daddy's surprise party. Where're those food stamps you said you were going to give me?"

"I spent them; the kids needed some food. But don't trip; I'm going to get some money from my man to get the food for the party."

"Don't worry about it, Sham. Dahlia's going to make sure I get what I need for the party. Just make sure you have time to show up for your dad's birthday party, and *please* don't bring any extra guests with you either."

"I'll be there.

"Dahlia, you have twenty I can borrow until later? I'll give it back once my man gives me some money. He'll be here in a few hours."

"That's what you always say. If I counted every time you've borrowed from me and have yet to pay me back, I'd have a few thousand in my account. Or maybe that shop you say I should have," Dahlia expressed.

"For real, Dahlia; Auntie's gon give it right back to you," Sham pleaded. "My new man is paid and he don't mind spending." Sham smiled.

Sham didn't look like she was fifty. She was giving women half her age a run for their money. Sham had never had a problem getting a man. It was just the type of men she craved: the dope dealers, hustlers, and even married men.

Mabel sat in the passenger seat and shook her head as she watched Dahlia looking in her purse for some money. She knew what James was telling Sham was true. She just thought he could have done a better job at expressing his thoughts to her. She'd always spoke empowerment to her child; she didn't know what had happened.

Dahlia fished in her purse, pulling out a ten-dollar bill. "Here; this is all I have on me."

"Thanks, niece; I love you," Sham responded, rushing off down the street.

Dahlia knew she was headed to the liquor store to get a blunt wrap and a Lime-A-Rita.

"Where do you want to get something to eat?"

"That deli over there on Slauson, then we can go into that party store in the shopping center next to it. I don't want to take up too much of your day. I know you have clients."

Dahlia and her grandmother made small talk the short drive to the small eatery located not too far from her grandparents' house.

"Has Granddaddy ate anything yet, Granny?" Dahlia questioned as they neared the restaurant's entrance.

"Hell if I know, or care right about now. He's grown; he can fix himself something or go get him something to eat," Mabel exhaled.

"You don't have to be so mean to my grand . . ."

Dahlia paused mid-sentence when she saw him sitting at the table with a woman—a very gorgeous woman, dressed in a form-fitting dress that revealed the top of her ample breasts and stopped right at her knees. Her long, honey-brown legs seem to be ongoing, resting with Louboutins on her feet. She had good taste. She looked like she had been handpicked off some exotic island. Dahlia studied the woman's stern face. Her makeup was flawless.

The way she delicately moved her hands when drinking her bottle of water. How she seemed to be extremely pissed, yet she never raised her voice. She was beautiful. Was she the reason he was no longer interested in her? She was a classic classy woman, a woman who Chanel, Gucci, and Cartier knew by name. Unlike Dahlia, who was rough around the edges. Although she shopped in those same stores, they didn't know her name. Just the name on her money.

"What's wrong with you?" Mabel questioned, noticing the disruption in Dahlia's sentence. Her eyes followed to where her granddaughter's eyes were fixated. "Is that Antonio?"

"Yes; I guess he's moved on," Dahlia spoke, trying not to sound crushed that she was still dealing with him breaking things off with her.

A small jolt of anger lay in the pit of her stomach. He had been blowing her up all day and had even had her legs spread wide no more than a little over two hours ago, and here he was sitting with another woman, her juices probably still fresh on his breath.

"Well, let's go say hello then," Mabel spoke, bypassing Dahlia.

"GRANNY, NO!" Dahlia yelled, but it was too late.

Mabel was inches away from the table where Antonio sat. Just as Mabel approached the table, Antonio turned and locked eyes with Dahlia. Gathering her bearings, Dahlia exhaled and made her way over.

"Antonio?" Mabel questioned, as if she wasn't sure it was him.

"Hey, Mrs. Willowbrook. How are you?" Antonio asked nervously, watching Dahlia approach.

"I'm good. I haven't seen you since the two of you broke up. Just because you two aren't together any more doesn't mean you can't stop by and check on an old woman."

The woman at the table cleared her throat, never taking her eyes off Dahlia, whose eyes never left the woman's.

"C'mon, Granny; let Antonio enjoy his date," Dahlia spoke harshly. She was upset that he didn't even acknowledge her presence.

"Antonio, you aren't going to introduce me to your friend?" The woman smiled, glaring at Dahlia.

"This is Dahlia and her grandmother, Mrs. Willowbrook," Antonio spoke; the nervousness and panic could be heard in his voice.

"Hello, Dahlia and Mrs. Willowbrook; nice to meet you ladies. I'm Sharron, Antonio's wife." She smiled.

"WIFE?" Dahlia blurted loudly, almost choking on her own saliva.

"Yes, his wife," she spoke sarcastically. "Antonio, you didn't tell your little friend, Ms. Dahlia, you were married?"

"It's not like that, Dahlia; I was going to tell you. I just needed to find the right time," Antonio pleaded, facing Dahlia. "I will explain everything to you later on. Just . . . please . . . go."

"She's prettier than the other bitches you cheated with," Sharron spoke, casually looking Dahlia up and down. "You must like her, you're in here pleading for her to leave. You don't want her to know the truth about you." The woman chuckled.

"Are you the one playing on my phone? Leaving voicemails of you two fuckin'?" Dahlia questioned angrily.

"Wait one-damn-minute! My granddaughter is beautiful; what-the-fuck are you talking about?"

"Girl, please. I am way too classy to be playing on another woman's phone over a man, especially a cheating man at that. Trust me, I no longer want him. He hasn't been in these goods in a very long time. It must be that young, crazy baby's mother of his.

"Mrs. Willowbrook, I never said she was ugly. She's actually beautiful—the best one I've seen in all the years I've been married to his cheating-ass," the woman informed.

"So you have more than one baby's mother?" Dahlia questioned.

"Girl, does he!" Sharon laughed. "Antonio, you didn't tell her you have three baby's mothers amongst your six kids?"

"Antonio, did you forget to mention that? You told me you had two kids that you hardly saw because your babies' mother was a bitch and mad you'd left her after finding out she'd cheated with her boss, who was also your friend."

"That bitch would be me." The woman laughed with a raised hand. "But in no way am I mad, because I left him for cheating. He doesn't see the three kids we have because he chooses not to. He always makes up excuses why he can't visit them. I only fucked his frat brother to make him feel half of the pain I'd endured from him. It was him who was fuckin' his boss' side-bitch."

"Sharron, just shut your mouth and mind your-fuckin'-business. I'm giving you what you want, signing the divorce papers," Antonio said through clenched teeth.

"Oh, now you want me to shut up and you're ready for the divorce? Just a few minutes ago you were trying to work it out, begging to slide between my legs. Telling me how much you love me and weren't going to give me a divorce because you wanted your family back. Admitting how you'd messed up time and time again, that you are finally ready to be a family. How you'd taken me for granted for so many years. What happened to all of that? Oh, I see. You need your job back. This girl deserves to know the truth about you, since all you can do is tell lies all over town. I'll tell her.

"Antonio, use to work for my father, but he was fired. He wants me to help him get his job back, so he thought he could sweet-talk my panties off, like I was the young girl he met over twenty-something-odd years ago. Then I would convince my father he needed his job and all that good stuff."

"It isn't your place to tell the woman I'm-fuckin'-anything!" Antonio grabbed the papers sitting on the table and quickly scribbled his signature on them. "Here; isn't this what you want? Well, you got it. Fuck that job. I can find another one. Your father can't run that bank without me. Now stay-the-fuck out my life. If it doesn't involve my children, I don't want to hear from you, you stuck-up-bitch!" Antonio snarled.

"That's fine with me. Shit, I've been asking for it to be like this for years. And my father's company was running *before* you and is still running *without* you," Sharron said, checking the papers before she stuffed them into her purse.

"Dahlia, doll, save yourself some time and the hassle of dealing with that crazy, ghetto baby's mother of his. Just leave his ass alone. The bitch should be at home bonding with their newborn, instead of following his ass all around town with that childish bullshit."

"New . . . newborn?" Dahlia questioned, her voice was shaky. "You have a newborn?"

"She's three months," Antonio spoke, his head held down.

He couldn't bear looking at Dahlia. He knew he had hurt her to the core. She'd thought he was the one, that her search for true love had come to an end with him. Antonio always knew it wouldn't happen. She was only supposed to be a quick-fuck and rebound chick, but she was different. He had feelings for her.

"It's all starting to make sense now." Dahlia peered at Antonio; the hurt was written on her face. "Were you ever going to tell me?" she questioned.

"Eventually; I was going to tell you when the time was right." Antonio stood to face Dahlia for the very first time. "Just let me talk to you, just us. I will tell you the truth about everything," he pleaded.

"When the time was right, huh?" Dahlia questioned, glaring at Antonio like he was filthy.

At that moment he was. Just like nasty, used gum on the bottom of her designer pumps. He was like dirt on the dirtiest ground she had ever laid eyes on. There was so much rage in the pit of her stomach, she felt like she would vomit just looking at him.

"The right time would have been a year ago when you found your black ass in my bed. Or maybe today when you showed up to my job and begged me to talk to you. Or maybe even after you sucked the juices from my pussy."

"It's not—"

WHOP! Dahlia smacked Antonio. "SAVE IT. I DON'T WANT SHIT TO DO WITH YOU. KEEP YOUR-FUCKIN'-LIES!" Dahlia yelled, rushing toward the exit.

She was hurt and embarrassed. The customers occupying the small establishment looked on in amazement, offering a few chuckles at the fiasco occurring.

"WHAT-THE-FUCK Y'ALL LAUGHING AT?" Mabel yelled. "There isn't anything to see. Turn around and mind your own-damn-business."

Mabel turned to face Antonio just as he was grabbing his coat to leave. "I told you I didn't want her to go through any more bullshit from a man. I will make sure her grandfather hears about this. Stay away from my granddaughter. If I find out you've been by her house, I'm going to send my goons after you. Trust me, I have some loyal young ones who are always locked-and-loaded."

"Despite what has happened, I really did care about your granddaughter. I'm sorry I wasn't and couldn't be the man she needed," Antonio confessed, brushing past the customers who still looked on and walking out the deli.

He glanced at Dahlia's car, knowing she was sitting behind the tinted windows crying her eyes out. Antonio was about to approach Dahlia's car when Mabel came out the restaurant.

"What do you think you're doing? I don't see your car over here," Mabel said, looking around the small parking lot for Antonio's truck.

Antonio didn't speak. He just turned and walked to the other end of the parking lot where his truck was parked. Mabel watched Antonio drive away before she got into Dahlia's car, where she found her sitting with a face wet with tears.

"I thought he was the one. I feel so stupid. Here I thought he was my man, only my man, only to find out I was just a pawn in his sea of woman."

"I'm sorry you had to experience that, baby. Antonio isn't a man; he's a little boy dressed in grown-men clothes, running around town portraying to be something he knows nothing about."

"Why do I keep falling for all the wrong men? Who use me, beat me, disrespect me, treat me like I'm not worthy of being loved?" Dahlia cried like a baby. "What's wrong with me, Granny? Am I not good enough to be loved? Am I only good enough to take to bed and be around *sometimes*? I don't understand. Why can't I find someone to treat me like a queen? Like Granddaddy treats you? Like my daddy treated my mother?" Dahlia rambled as the tears poured from her eyes.

"Listen to me, Dahlia, and listen to me good: You are worthy of love, respect, and to be treated like the queen you are, but love starts with self. You have to love yourself more than anything else first. You can't expect a man to love you more than you love yourself. Every day you need to look in the mirror and feel that you are worthy. Words have no meaning if the actions don't match. You are a beautiful woman, inside and out. You have experienced your share of heartache—we all have— but don't let that stop you from flourishing. When the time is right, a man who sees your full potential will come along and sweep you off your feet and cherish every ounce of the beautiful rose you are. Don't ever let anyone dim the light that shines bright within you."

"I hope you're right, Granny," Dahlia spoke, wiping the few tears that lingered on her face away.

"I know so. I have been in your shoes before, trust me. One monkey don't stop no show. You have to experience heartache and pain to know what true love really feels like. True love is waiting for you, my beautiful granddaughter. Now let's finish our day." Mabel smiled, forcing Dahlia to smile weakly.

Dahlia put on a smile for her grandmother as they went in and out of stores, getting all the items needed to put on the best surprise birthday party her grandfather ever had. Inside, she was crushed. Love had played her once again. She just wanted to go home, climb in her bed with a gallon of rocky road ice cream, and watch reruns of *Martin*.

"All we need now is the food," Mabel said, loading the last few bags of party decorations into Dahlia's car.

"Why don't I just pay for catering? That way, you won't have to be up early, cooking or worrying your little pretty self with anything, and you can enjoy Grandpa's party."

"No, that's okay, baby. You've already done enough. I can't ask you to spend all of your hard-earned money. I can just get a few items and whip up something in the kitchen. The old woman's still got it." Mabel chuckled.

"I insist on it, Granny. I've got it. You just make sure you're dressed to impressed, and I'll make sure your hair is laid."

"Okay, and I have the perfect outfit. Before you drop me off back at the house, can you run me by Smart & Final to pick up some chicken for dinner?"

"Okay," Dahlia said, making her way toward the store.

Chapter 4

After dropping her grandmother off, Dahlia swung by the local grocery store for a bottle of wine. The day had left her emotionally-drained and in need of something to calm her nerves. She wanted to sit on the beach and watch the sunset, but didn't feel like being around people. Plus, she couldn't wait to speak to Traci. Traci was her best friend who'd introduced her to Antonio. Dahlia put the wine in the freezer, slid out of her shoes, and went to wash the stress of the day away.

When she was done, she flopped down on the couch with the bottle of wine in hand and dialed Traci's number. As she waited for Traci to answer, the events of the day flashed before her eyes, making her even more upset and hurt.

"Hey, girl?" Traci said all bubbly in the phone.

"Did you know Antonio was married?" Dahlia blurted out, getting right to the point.

"Well, hello to you, too, Dahlia. As for Antonio, I did know he had a wife, but they're separated," Traci confessed.

"And you didn't think to tell me that when you hooked us up?"

"I didn't think it was a big deal. He was separated and you were desperate. I didn't expect for y'all to fall all in love and shit. I thought you were going to let him knock the cobwebs off the pussy, or keep him around for a little booty call every now and then. You said you weren't looking for a man."

"You still should have told me and let me make the decision if I still wanted to see him," Dahlia bellowed out of frustration.

"You're right, I should have told you from the beginning, and I'm sorry about that. But what's going on, girl? You sound stressed."

"Stressed isn't even the word. Today has been one long, fucked-up day. For the last month, I have been racking my brain on why Antonio just broke it off with me. Today I found out why. Not only is this man married, he has six kids, not two like he told me in the beginning. His youngest . . ." She paused. "The man has a-damn-three-month-old baby."

"WHAT?" Traci yelled into the phone. "Hold on, you gon have to start from the beginning because I'm lost-as-hell. A baby?"

Dahlia reclined on the couch, taking sip after sip as she filled Traci in on what had being going on, bit by bit, leaving Traci lost for words.

"Wow, I didn't know that man had all that going on. Girl, I'm sorry. I guess I should never play matchmaker."

Traci laughed, trying to lighten the mood up for her best friend. She knew Dahlia was taking it hard with all the drama she'd endured in her last relationship.

"I feel like a-damn-fool. Either I'm the dumbest bitch in the world not to see the signs, or his ass was a really good liar."

"I think he was just a good-ass-liar. You are not dumb. You just gave someone your trust who didn't deserve it. You can't beat yourself up about it. It happens."

"This kind of makes me wonder what else this man has lied about. This was just what she blurted out. Something tells me there's more."

"Hell, this was enough. What else could he be hiding?"

"I don't know, but it explains all the crazy phone calls I've been getting. Now I'm curious if his baby's mother knows where I live. I forgot to mention someone slashed my tires this morning. I want to talk to his wife. I just have a feeling he's hiding more. He became so defensive when she started to air out his business."

"Yeah, that sounds like some crazy-baby-mama-type shit, but if you're done with him, which I hope like hell you are, then it shouldn't matter what else he's lying about. That's another bitch's problem to deal with.

"Oh, I am done with him, trust me on that. I just feel like this whole year I've been living a lie. I just want some closure and to know the truth about everything. I've invested time into the man."

"Did you love him?

"I have love for him, but I wasn't in love with him. I found myself falling in love with him, which means I was falling for something that wasn't even real. I just want to know why and have closure— like, is it me?"

"You know you may never get that from him, and you can't trust everything this wife says. What if she's putting extras on it? Because she doesn't want to see his cheating-ass happy. I know, like hell, if Charles' ass did some shit like that, I would make his life a living, fuckin'-hell."

"That may be true, but he didn't deny anything she said."

"So, what, you gon look the woman up and try to have a sit-down with her?"

"Maybe," Dahlia said, thinking of actually doing it.

She knew she shouldn't care, but she did. She'd fallen in love with Antonio, and to know almost everything he'd told her was a lie, hurt. He didn't respect her enough to tell her the truth.

"I know you're sitting over there, thinking of really doing it, too," Traci said, knowing Dahlia.

They had been friends since middle school. Traci knew how hard Dahlia loved and how she wanted to be loved back hard by a man but always stumbled across the wrong men.

"I just don't want you to go back through that dark space like you went through after that last situation," Traci spoke, referring to Dahlia's last relationship with her high school sweetheart.

"I'm not going to go back to that space. This relationship isn't like that one. Even though his lies hurt me, nothing can compare to that relationship and all the bullshit I allowed myself to go through," Dahlia spoke. "I actually loved the ground that bastard walked on."

"Okay; I just don't want you to give up on yourself, or on finding love. There is going to be a man who will treat you like royalty. Sometimes, it just takes time for two hearts that are meant to be together to find each other."

"Hopefully; if not, I'll just be an old woman with a dog because I hate cats." Dahlia laughed, starting to feel the effects of the half of bottle of wine she had drank so far.

"I'd play matchmaker again before I let that happen."

"Thank You, Jesus. We may have to conduct full-length background checks because Lord knows I can't deal with this shit. Hold on; it sounds like someone is pulling into my driveway. I see lights."

"Who is it? Don't tell me it's Antonio?" Traci questioned.

"I can't see who it is," Dahlia spoke. She could see a figure approaching her front porch.

"Dahlia, I see you in the window. Can you open the door? I just want to explain. After this, I promise to leave you alone. I just think you deserve to know the truth about everything and to hear it from me."

"Is that him?

"Yes."

"Tell his ass to get away from your door. Hell, give me his number; I'll tell his ass to get-the-fuck away," Traci ranted.

"Please; open the door so we can talk like two adults," he pleaded.

"Dahlia, no; don't fall for it. Don't let him in. Tell him to get-the-fuck-off your porch," Traci urged over the phone. She knew if Dahlia let him in, there was a possibility he would do what he'd done earlier to her. He knew she was vulnerable.

"Traci, let me call you back. I need to do this for me. I don't want him, but I want to hear the truth, and from him."

Dahlia hung up the phone before Traci could say another word. Dahlia held her hand on the door as she inhaled deeply. She knew there was more to the story and she didn't know if she would be able to digest any more lies, but she needed to know all of it. Dahlia opened the door.

"You have five minutes to explain and I want all of it in those five minutes. I don't want to hear you tell me how much you care about me, how you didn't want this, because I don't give-a-fuck. All I want is the truth and the whole truth," Dahlia blurted.

"I don't even know where to start?" he spoke, coming inside the house, his hands tucked in his pants pockets.

"You can start at you being married and why you failed to mention that to me over a-damn-year ago!" Dahlia hissed, slamming the front door behind him.

"I didn't see it as a problem because she and I were separated and not even on speaking terms. When Traci mentioned she had a friend, she said you were just looking for someone to keep you company. When I first saw you, I liked you and knew you wouldn't give me a chance if you knew I was married. Women like you don't want to hear it, nor do you trust a guy who says he's married. But I'm separated. All you would have thought was I was just cheating on my wife and trying to make you some side-chick."

"What about your children? Why did you lie about how many kids you had? Did you cheat on this baby's mother who has your newborn? Or did you cheat on me?" Dahlia questioned without thinking.

She was torn between wanting to know the answer and not being able to digest what she already knew the answers to be by the way his wife had talked. The baby's mother had been in the picture for some time now.

"I've been with Jasmine on and off for the last six years. When I first met you, we weren't together. I didn't know she was pregnant until after things between you and I got real serious. One night, you were busy doing something for your grandparents, and I was horny and ended up at her house. One thing led to another, and well, she ended up pregnant. I knew if I told you my ex-girlfriend was expecting you would have ended what we had built and I wasn't ready for that. Was it selfish of me? Of course, but as men, sometimes we want things the way we want them. Can you sit here and say if I had come over and said my ex-girlfriend called and told me she was pregnant with my baby, you would've been cool with it?"

Dahlia sat and pondered his questioned. "You're right, I wouldn't have been cool with it, but you didn't even give me that option."

"I didn't because I can honestly say I was only thinking of myself at the time. I was only worried about keeping everything I wanted in order. I never intend to hurt you; I'm sorry. You were so happy and I wanted to keep it that way. I didn't want to put you through the stuff I knew the last nigga had done to you. I wanted to treat you better. Hell, in my opinion, I did. I never disrespected you nor put my hands on you."

"Wow, what a fuckin'-low-blow. Yeah, give yourself a pat on the back. You didn't beat my ass like my ex did. Nah, you just ripped my heart out and stepped on it. Good for you!"

"I didn't mean it like that."

"You meant it just like you said it. Is there anything else you're hiding? Am I going to run across your wife and find out some more lies you've hidden?" Dahlia questioned.

Antonio put his head down and exhaled loudly before running his hands up and down his face, then over his head. "Just hear me out. I lied about my age. I'm not thirty-five; I'm actually fifty-two, and as you know already, I have six kids with three baby's mothers. I have three children with my wife—twenty-five, twenty-two, and fifteen. I also have a fifteen-year-old with another woman, who is a family friend of my wife's who was also sleeping with my father-in-law. Then there's Jasmine, who has my two youngest children—a five-year-old, and as you know, the newborn, who's three months old."

Dahlia was lost for words as she replayed what he'd just told her, over and over again in her mind so fast her head was spinning. For the last year, she'd been with a man who was the same age as her father. Almost everything he'd told her was a lie. Dahlia felt sick. She couldn't believe this was happening to her. This was something crazy, like a Lifetime movie, only she was the main star in the movie called her life.

"Was that your baby's mother who played on my phone last night and slashed my tires this morning?"

"More than likely it was. She found out about you a few weeks ago. One night when I didn't come home, she checked my call log and found your number and some text messages. Do you see why I had to break it off with you?"

"Wait, you live with her?"

"Yes; I lost my job six months ago when I told my father-in-law I wouldn't divorce my wife. Shortly after, I lost my apartment. I knew I couldn't ask you to move in here; plus, I wanted to be closer to my kids, so I spent some nights here with you and the rest with Jasmine at her apartment. She told me I had to move all the way in or stay out. I want to be there for my kids; I made a lot of mistakes with my older kids. Jasmine took me back, so I had to break it off with you. It was the right thing to do."

"I don't want to hear any more," Dahlia spoke, with a raised hand. She had heard enough. "Please just leave my house and never come back. When you see me in the streets, just pass me by like we've never met," Dahlia spoke, opening the front door for him to leave.

"I'm sorry if I hurt you. I promise that was never my intent; I just got caught up."

"Yeah, well, it's done now. Please leave."

Antonio prepared to walk out the front door. He stopped on the porch and looked back at Dahlia.

"I told you I was no longer interested in you because my children's mother and I are back together. Letting you go was something I had to do to make that work. I knew you weren't that clingy girl and wouldn't come after me looking for answers. I love her too much to just let her go, so I had to let you go. Don't beat yourself up about it, Dahlia. You're a beautiful woman with a good head on your shoulders. Some man will come along and cherish that; I just couldn't be that man," Antonio spoke, walking past Dahlia.

"Was I even a choice?" Dahlia thought out loud.

"No; I've got love for you, but I'm not in love with you. She is where I always wanted to be. You were just supposed to be fun, but I fell for you. That was until she wanted me back, and it was where I needed and wanted to be," Antonio spoke, walking out the door, not looking back. He knew his words would hurt, but he felt she needed to hear it so she could get herself together.

"ANTONIO!" a female's voice yelled, as she charged at him. "I knew you wouldn't stay away from this fat-bitch. I hope she's worth losing your family, you big-fuckin'-dummy."

"Antonio, please take your drama away from my house or I will call the police," Dahlia said calmly.

"Not before I whup yo' fat-ass, bitch! You need to leave my man alone. He don't want yo' ass, so stop blowing up his phone, fat-bitch. I don't see what he even saw in your ass. You must be a cash cow. There's nothing attractive about you. Yeah, bitch, I've been watching you!" she spat, glaring at Dahlia.

"You need to speak with Antonio. The only one blowing up a phone is, what'd you called him? Your man?" Dahlia chuckled. "Well, tell yo' man he should go brush his teeth. My pussy juices probably still reeking off his breath from when he sucked the juices out this fat pussy, bitch!" Dahlia spoke with a smile, not once raising her voice.

"You were fuckin' this bitch today?" the woman questioned, turning to face Antonio, who stood a few feet behind her.

"Nah, she's a-fuckin'-lie. I came over here to tell her to stop calling me, that I was done with her fat-ass. I don't need her any more," Antonio lied.

"You're a professional liar. I think he's been filling your head up with lies and your silly-ass must be hanging on to his every word. I promise you don't want any of this fat-bitch, so I think you'd better get off my property NOW! And take your lame-ass baby-daddy with you!" Dahlia barked, slamming her front door.

She could hear them yelling back and forth with each other. She wanted to cry, the scars on her heart hadn't even healed yet, and now her stitches were bursting open yet again. Dahlia had to laugh to keep from crying. She stood at the window, watching Antonio's baby's mother throw punches at him. It made Dahlia laugh at the sight of Antonio's six-foot frame ducking punches from the much-shorter Jasmine. Dahlia was about to go lie down for the night and let her neighbors call the police on them when she heard the loud sound of glass shattering. Running to the living room's big picture window, Dahlia turned on her porch light and looked out the window. Antonio's baby's mother was taking a bat to his truck.

"BITCH, I SEE YOU IN THE WINDOW. BRING YO' ASS OUT HERE AND GET SOME OF THIS ASS-WHUPPING, TOO, WITH HIS ASS. SINCE YOU WERE BRAGGING HOW HE WAS LICKIN' BETWEEN THEM FAT, FUNKY THIGHS," she yelled, waving the bat in the air.

Dahlia just stared at her from the window. She wasn't scared at all. She just saw no point in fighting over a man, especially a lying, cheating man.

"SINCE YOU DON'T WANT TO BRING YOUR ASS OUTSIDE, BITCH, I'LL JUST FUCK-UP YOUR CAR. HE PROBABLY HELPED YOU BUY THIS MUTHAFUCKA!" she yelled, rushing to Dahlia's car parked in her driveway, bringing the bat down on Dahlia's car front window.

"COME ON OUT, FAT-BITCH!" she taunted, making her way around to the driver's side, swinging the bat, shattering first the front then the back windows. "I see you got those tires fixed, huh?" The woman laughed. "You move fast. Let's see how much damage I can do this time."

"THIS BITCH IS TRIPPING. YOU HAVE LOST YOUR RABBIT-ASS-MIND!" Dahlia yelled, rushing outside without shoes on her feet. "Bitch, you must be crazy!" Dahlia spoke, rushing up on the woman, throwing strong punches. "You should have just left my-fuckin'-house, you stupid-little-bitch!"

Dahlia threw a punch to the side of Jasmine's head, pushing her weight up against the woman on her car so she couldn't swing the bat that was still in her hand. She constantly threw blows at the woman's face until she dropped the bat. Jasmine yelled in agony from the blows to her face.

"You wanted some of this fat-bitch, well here she goes. I told you to just-fuckin'-leave," Dahlia spoke, through clenched teeth. "I'm not to be fucked-with."

"C'mon, Dahlia, that's enough now. She's bleeding," Antonio pleaded from afar.

"Fuck you and this bitch. I was over here minding my own business and you decided to bring your lying, dirty-dick-ass over here and this bitch followed, talking a bunch of shit. This is what she gets. Remember, I'm the woman you don't want, so why-in-the-fuck would I give two shits about the bitch you do want? You just treated me like shit in front of this hoe. Do you think I give-a-fuck what you're saying? Fuck no!" Dahlia spat with a fist full of Jasmine's hair.

"You made your point; now let her go."

"I'll let her go when I am good and ready, just like you fucked me until you were good and done with me. Well, I'm going to beat yo' bitch's ass until I'm done. What you gon do?" Dahlia snapped.

"DAHLIA, GET OFF HER!" Antonio yelled, trying to pull Dahlia off of Jasmine. She had beat her enough.

"GET YOUR HANDS OFF HER!" Traci yelled, jumping out her car.

Traci didn't live that far from Dahlia. Something told her something wasn't right when she'd called Dahlia back several times and didn't get an answer.

"Traci, it isn't even like that, but this-bitch is tripping. She needs to get up off my girl like that. All this shit is uncalled for. She got her point across," Antonio said, backing away from Dahlia. He saw the Taser in Traci's hand.

"Bitch? Oh, I got your bitch!" Dahlia scoffed, gripping tighter on the woman's hair. Using an open hand, she struck her face repeatedly until her cinnamon-colored skin was beet red. "This is what you wanted, right?" Dahlia questioned, slapping the girl once more with an open hand before she let her limp body slide down the car. "You and this-bitch get away from my house before I fuck-you-up next!" Dahlia spat, pushing Antonio.

"This was real childish of you, Dahlia. I thought better of you, but you're just like the rest of these ghetto-ass-bitches out here. Then you wonder why a nigga cheats and beats on you," Antonio blurted out.

"What did you say?" Dahlia questioned

"You're getting too-damn-disrespectful now, Antonio; you need to leave," Traci interjected, trying to block Dahlia from getting to Antonio.

"No, Traci, let his ass keep talking because I'm at the point of no return. He can get his ass beat, too." Dahlia was fuming.

"You heard me. You're just like the rest of these-bitches out here," he repeated.

Dahlia paused for a moment and let his words seek in.

"Did this nigga, who think he's a-fuckin'-man, just call me a bitch? Not once, but twice?" Dahlia questioned herself.

"This is probably why the last nigga was beating yo' ass. You're extra."

"Let's go in the house while they leave before someone calls the police," Traci spoke, trying to get Dahlia in the house. She knew Dahlia had to be extremely upset to act such way. She hadn't seen Dahlia act like this in a long time.

"That's what you're acting like. I thought you were classier than this. I guess I was wrong."

"YOU AND THIS CHILDISH-ASS-WOMAN OF YOURS ARE THE ONLY BITCHES I SEE AROUND HERE, BITCH!" Dahlia barked, pushing Traci out the way.

She leaped, striking Antonio in his face with a right-left combo. She waited to see if he was going to try to hit her back. Traci stood next to Dahlia, waiting to see if Antonio flinched. She was waiting because they were going to jump him had he thought he was going to hit Dahlia.

"Fuck you, Dahlia," he spoke, picking Jasmine up off the ground.

"Antonio, would you and your woman just leave before someone calls the police?" Traci spoke, trying to be the voice of reason.

"Too late," Dahlia informed, seeing the patrol car pull in front of her house.

Two officers got out and made their way down the pathway.

"We received a call about a disturbance at this address," an officer spoke, approaching them.

"It's nothing, Officer. Just a little disagreement that got out of hand. Everyone is going home now," Traci spoke up, looking at Antonio and Jasmine for them to agree.

"Bullshit! She attacked my girl. Look at her face," Antonio whined.

"Is that true?" the officer questioned.

"She came to my residence and damaged my property, and we got into a fight," Dahlia responded, pointing toward her car. "I have a right to defend my property," Dahlia hissed, glaring at Antonio and his girlfriend. "Officer, would you please escort them off my property. You can run the address. I own this house we're standing in front of."

"I'm not going anywhere. I would like to press charges for assault," Jasmine spoke, holding her bleeding nose she glared at Dahlia.

"Yes, we would like to press charges, Officer. I am a witness to the brutal attack on my girlfriend. Her name is Dahlia Willowbrook," Antonio added. "And this is her residence and that's her friend, Traci."

Dahlia just stared at Antonio as she laughed hysterically. He was a straight-punk.

"Really, Antonio?" Traci asked with a light chuckle. She couldn't believe this man, after all he'd put her friend through, was trying to send her to jail.

"Really, Traci. Dahlia needs to deal with the consequences for her actions. She went way overboard. It didn't have to come to this."

"Dude, you're a joke. You brought all this bullshit to my front door and now you can't handle the aftermath. You shouldn't have come here. I told you earlier to leave me the-fuck-alone. Yet, you showed up to my door with Raggedy Ann following you. So if I went too far, it's because all your lies pushed me there."

"Are you sure you want to press charges?" the officer questioned, looking at Jasmine then to Antonio. "Because if what she's telling me is true, I'm going to have to take both ladies to jail, since this is her home and I can clearly see her car has been damaged.

"Officer, I don't want to press charges; I just want them off of my property. That's all I want.

"Look, it's late. I don't want to have to take you ladies to jail, so why don't we just consider the beef squashed here? Sir, you can take your woman home and just don't come back here," the officer spoke, looking at Antonio and Jasmine.

"And you, young lady," the officer spoke, turning his attention to Dahlia, "I know you're pissed she destroyed your luxury car, but don't retaliate. Just leave it alone. Sound like a plan? Then we can all go on about our business."

The officer looked at everyone.

"I'm cool with it," Dahlia replied dryly.

"Fuck that! I want to press charges," Jasmine groaned. "I think she broke my nose."

"Do you need medical attention?" the officer questioned.

"Yes. It feels like my tooth is loose, too, and my eye hurts," Jasmine whined. She had gone into full-acting mode. She was performing like she was up for an Oscar.

"Well, I'm going to have to take both of you ladies down to the station. Ma'am, you will be looked at once you're booked."

"They came to her house with all this bullshit and you're arresting her? This is some real bullshit!" Traci exploded. "I hope you're charging her with property damage."

"It's good, Traci. Would you just lock up my house and call my grandparents so they can come bail me out? Can she go inside and get me some shoes?" Dahlia asked the officer.

"Yes," the officer replied, looking at Traci.

Traci returned with a pair of sandals for Dahlia. Jasmine was taken away in the car that was already there. Minutes later, a car pulled up to take Dahlia.

"I hope she has her brother Desman come beat yo' ass. You are so bitch-made for sending that girl to jail because that bitch of yours got her ass whupped!" Traci snapped on Antonio once the police left.

"Yeah, whatever. She went overboard."

"OVERBOARD? YOU AND YOUR-FUCKIN'-LIES ARE OVERBOARD. THAT BITCH COMING HERE AND BUSTING OUT DAHLIA WINDOWS IS OVERBOARD. THAT ASS-WHUPPING SHE GAVE HER WAS WELL-DESERVED. I HOPE YOUR DIRTY-DICK-ASS GETS A WELL-DESERVED ASS-WHUPPING, TOO. I WISH I'D NEVER INTRODUCED HER TO YOUR SORRY-ASS!" Traci yelled as Antonio walked towards his truck. "THERE'S SOMETHING SPECIAL CALLED KARMA FOR MEN LIKE YOU. REMEMBER, YOU HAVE DAUGHTERS. A TRIFLING MAN'S GON COME AROUND AND FUCK-YOUR-DAUGHTERS' WHOLE WORLD UP."

"I'll kill a nigga," Antonio replied.

"Well, consider yourself a murderer. Mark my words," Traci replied.

She knew if Dahlia's father was home, he would have beat Antonio's ass all over Los Angeles for this bullshit he'd pulled.

"Whatever," Antonio hissed, getting in his truck and speeding down the street.

Traci locked up the house as Dahlia had asked and left to drive to Dahlia's grandparents' home to let them know what had happened.

Chapter 5

Dahlia sat on the dirty bench in the holding cell with six other women. Once they booked both ladies, they took Jasmine to have her wounds looked at. The cell reeked and was dirty and cold. Every time Dahlia thought about where she was at that moment, she wanted to fuck Jasmine and Antonio up again.

"Willowbrook?" the officer called out as he approached the holding cell.

"That's me."

"Let's go. You bonded out," he said.

Those words were like music to Dahlia ears. Dahlia followed the officer into the reception area where she was given a Summons to appear in court. She was then led to a larger waiting room where she saw her grandfather camped out on a chair.

"Thanks, Granddaddy, for coming to get me," Dahlia spoke, walking out the station with her grandfather.

"You know it isn't a problem, but what happened? I couldn't believe that child when she came knocking on my door, talking about I had to go get you out of jail. I couldn't believe my baby had been arrested."

On the ride to her grandparents' house to pick up her grandmother, who her grandfather had refused to bring to the station with him, Dahlia filled him in on what happened.

"He seemed like a nice guy, but even a wolf wears sheep's clothing sometimes. You can't go to someone's house and not think he or she isn't gon kick your ass. If he didn't know, now his ass does, fuckin' with a Willowbrook. Wait until I see his narrow ass," her grandfather uttered. He was pissed.

It was well after two in the morning when Dahlia and her grandfather made it to her grandparents' house. Mabel sat on the front porch smoking a cigarette. She was ready to fight. She didn't play about her family, her man, and her money.

"What-in-the-hell happened? Where's that-nigga Antonio live?" Mabel questioned with her gun sitting fully-loaded and cleaned in her lap.

"Granny, what are you doing with that gun? Go put that away," Dahlia pleaded. She didn't even know her grandmother owned a gun.

"Did you know she has that?" Dahlia questioned her grandfather.

"Yeah, we have a few around here," he spoke, pulling a shotgun from behind the front door. "We're old and we live in South Central. These young kids don't have any morals, and if they run in mine, they're going to get hit with a surprise. I'm gon kill 'em dead right in that living room."

"I don't know what I'm going to do with you two."

"We're good, but how are you, baby? They didn't hurt you, did they? Let me check you out," Mabel said, inspecting Dahlia.

"I'm fine, Granny. I just can't believe he told them to arrest me. I know I went crazy last night and let my anger take me overboard, but I was hurt. Drinking half a bottle of wine didn't help. When I saw her messing up my car, my emotions were all over the place and I just lost it. You know I don't like violence and try to keep it out my life as much as I can but, last night, I was pro-violence." Dahlia chuckled a little. "I can no longer just sit around and let people do whatever they want to me. Do you know that man lied about his age? He is the same age as my daddy. He knew how old I was. I'm beyond disgusted."

"I know, baby; sometimes the heart lashes out. That man hurt you, and when I get to him, just say my name is karma, and she is one bad bitch."

"Now I may have a criminal record. She said I broke her nose and she has a loose tooth, but that could all be an act. She didn't start all that until the police showed up. I took all my anger out on her. It should have been directed towards him. He was the one who made me believe he loved me, that he wanted to spend the rest of our lives together. And to think he told me last night he had love for me, then he called me a common b-word and said he couldn't believe he'd messed with me."

"Don't you start crying and shit! Look at me!" Mabel demanded, grabbing Dahlia by her chin. "What did I tell you yesterday? You are beautiful! You don't need a man to define you. There is another lover out there for you, maybe out there going through a tough love situation with someone else, getting prepared for you, so when you meet, you two can learn from your mistakes and have something so beautiful those old memories will be far from your mind. Focus on you, baby. You want your own shop and to travel. Worry about that, and when God is ready, He will send that man to you. Trust me. More than anything, trust God and his timing. What have I always told you?"

"God, may not come when you want Him to, but He's always on time. Everything is according to His plan," Dahlia spoke.

"That's right, so trust His timing."

"I hear you, Granny," Dahlia responded, trying to hold back the tears that threatened to fall.

"You hear me, but do you understand me?"

"I hear and understand what you're saying, Granny."

"You hungry? I can whip you up some bacon, eggs, and grits."

"No, I'm good, Granny. Thank you anyway. I just want to go home, take a bath, and get some rest. I have a few clients today. I still need to call the insurance company to report the damages to my car. I also need to get a rental car for the time my car is being fixed."

"Okay, let me go get your keys Traci dropped off. She said call her. She was here with me waiting, but her husband called. She left not too long ago," Mabel said, retreating into the house.

"Okay."

Dahlia sat on her grandparents' front porch like she'd done so many times when she was a young girl and watched the cars drive past. She wished she could turn back the hands of time to have her mother back in her life and her father freed from prison. Something about her grandparents' home made her think of what her family use to be.

"Come on, baby," James spoke, handing Dahlia her house keys.

Dahlia climbed into her grandfather's pickup alongside her grandmother. She couldn't wait to just bathe and lie down. She hadn't received any major bruises from the fight, just a few scratches.

Her body was beyond sore and her head was spinning.

When they arrived at Dahlia's house, Dahlia just shook her head looking at all the glass on the ground from Antonio's truck and all the damages to her car.

"Go on inside and call the insurance people. Take some pictures of all this mess, and Granddaddy will clean it up and deal with them. Get you some rest, then I'll take you to get a car or to work, whatever you want," James said, inspecting Dahlia's car.

Jasmine had shattered Dahlia's front and back windows and banged up her driver's door badly with the bat.

"Come on; Granny will draw you some water and make something for you to eat when you wake up," Mabel spoke, leading the way in the house.

Dahlia called her insurance company while she waited for her bath water to finish running. She sent Traci a text thanking her for being a friend and letting her know she had bailed out and was home safely. She promised to get with her later. The insurance company was sending a claims adjustor out within the next few hours to inspect the car. With her insurance, they would provide a rental car while they worked on getting her car fixed.

"That water should be ready, Dahlia. Go soak in it and relax your mind, child," Mabel said, coming into the room and seeing Dahlia lost in a daze.

"Okay, Granny; thank you so much."

"Girl, hush it; that's what I'm here for."

Dahlia retreated to the bathroom, dropping two rose petal bath bombs in the steaming hot water, and climbed in. The intoxicating smell of the bath bombs mixed with the bath liqueur filled the room. Lying back, Dahlia closed her eyes and tried to enjoy the bath, but all she could do was think about her life.

In the last year, she'd felt joy and happiness she hadn't felt in a while. She'd thought Antonio was heaven-sent. He had comforted her during the times she'd felt low, times when she'd felt lost and couldn't talk to anyone. He'd been her shoulder to cry on. It didn't hurt that he'd wined and dined her around the city at places she'd known nothing about. The way he fucked her body had made her dizzy from the pleasure.

Dahlia kept her eyes closed so the tears wouldn't fall. Was she just not enough for men? What was it other woman had that she didn't? She tried not to seem jealous, too needy, or overbearing. She tried to hide her insecurities. She'd answered his every call and text. She had done almost everything he'd asked of her.

The questions swarmed around her head. Then she heard his voice: *"You were never a choice."*

Dahlia opened her eyes to let the tears release. She sat in the tub until her fingers and toes became wrinkled and the once-steaming-hot water was now chilled. Powering her cellphone off and setting the alarm on the clock sitting on her nightstand next to her bed, she climbed in her bed. As soon as her head hit the pillow, she was out.

When Dahlia finally awoke, the sun was peeking through the blinds. She was feeling much better. Her grandparents were gone. Her grandfather had gotten her car off to the shop. Enterprise had dropped off a rental car. Her grandmother had cooked her a meal and left it in the microwave. Dahlia smiled, packing up the baked turkey chops, garlic-cheese mashed potatoes, and steamed broccoli. She didn't know how her grandmother had made all of this and she hadn't smelled it at all.

Dahlia found something to throw on and was out the door headed to the shop. She had a few clients today, which was good. She wanted to keep her mind off her personal life and focus on her career. Being in the shop took her mind off all the bullshit in her life.

Dahlia pulled into the shop's parking lot, which was packed like always on a Friday. Parking in her assigned stall, Dahlia grabbed her bags and made her way into the shop.

"Hello, everyone," Dahlia said bubbly as she walked past the stations, making her way to hers.

"Hey," Chandra spoke as she bobbed her head to the music playing in the shop.

Dahlia set up her workstation and focused on what was ahead of her. She had been booked to do the hair of a Los Angeles up-and-coming female rapper by the name of Keisha Kane. Though Keisha was only an up-and-coming artist, it was big for Dahlia. Keisha had a big following on social media, which was what Dahlia was looking for. She wanted to build her clientele up before she ventured off on her own.

Dahlia saw her first client headed her way—a little girl who came faithfully every two weeks for two ponytails with baby doll curls.

"Hi, Miss D; I have a new hairstyle I want this week," the ten-year-old, bushy-eyebrow, chocolate girl spoke.

"Hi, Ari; what did you have in mind?" Dahlia smiled, glancing up at Monica, Ari's mother, as Ari told her how she wanted her hair.

"Sure, I can do that. Did you mother give the okay?"

"Girl, yes," Monica chimed. "She has been bugging me to call you all week so she could tell you how she wanted her hair." Monica chuckled. "Do you; I'm going to sit down and read my book."

"Okay," Ari said, taking a seat in Dahlia's chair. She knew the routine.

As Dahlia washed her hair, they made small talk about school and Ari asked questions about everything she had questions about. Dahlia smiled as she tried to provide the best answers to Ari's questions. She couldn't wait to have a daughter and share moments like this with a child of her own. It didn't take long for Dahlia to do the hairstyle Ari had requested. A fishtail braid in the front and the back of her hair pulled into a ponytail with baby-doll soft curls coming out the ponytail.

"All done," Dahlia said, turning Ari around to face the mirror. "Is this what you wanted?"

"Oh my gosh! Yes! This is just how I pictured it. I told my mom you would know what I was talking about. Mom!" Ari called out, trying to gain her mother's attention. "Look! Miss D slayed it." She smiled.

"Thank you, Dahlia." Monica smiled as she paid Dahlia for Ari's hair. "I'll see you on Sunday for my hair. Miss Thang here has two birthday parties tomorrow."

"Have fun, Ari."

"Thank you, Miss D." Ari smiled, giving Dahlia a hug.

"You're welcome," Dahlia replied.

"See you later, Dahlia," Monica said as she and Ari left the shop.

Just as Dahlia finished cleaning around her station, her next client was walking in.

The time had flown past. Before Dahlia realized it, she was finishing up the last client she had booked for the day.

"How do you like it?" Dahlia asked as she pulled the cape from around the woman's neck.

"Girl, you know you're good with the hands. I love it." She smiled, checking herself in the mirror. "I'll see you in a month," the woman said, handing Dahlia the money to cover her hair and a tip.

Dahlia took the money, stuffing it in her apron. Once the woman left, Dahlia took a seat in her chair; her feet were hurting. Dahlia was preparing herself to head home to relax for a little bit, then meet Keisha at her hotel room to do her hair.

"D, I know you're about to get out of here, but we have a walk-in and I'm booked. Do you mind doing her hair? It's an older woman and today is her seventy-fifth birthday."

"Yeah, I'll do it," Dahlia agreed.

She really didn't want to do it—she wanted to have some time to chill before her night appointment—but her grandmother's face popped into her head when Chandra said it was an older woman.

"It's a simple press-and-curl."

"Okay."

Chandra walked off and returned with a woman who didn't look over fifty.

"Mrs. Janice, this here is Dahlia. She'll be doing your hair today."

"Hello, Mrs. Janice. I hear it's your birthday today? How old are you, forty?" Dahlia laughed.

"Chile, please; I wish. Forty has been long gone." She smiled. "I am a proud, seventy-five-year-old, black woman." She shook her hips. "Black don't crack, and the only thing that gets old is clothes and men. And even clothes come back around every other decade. Now men, chile, that's another story in itself. It is nice to meet you. Dahlia is a pretty name. Now, all an old woman wants is for you to straighten my hair and give me some tight curls so tomorrow I can feather them out."

"Okay, I can do that for you."

"My ex-husband and I have the same birthday, and for some-damn-reason, our kids and grandkids thought it was a good idea to give us a party together. You know I have to be the finest-old-thang in that building, especially since he has a new girlfriend who's younger than me. Hell, I can't tell; she looks old."

"Oh, I'll make sure you're the best thing in that building, that even he'll be questioning himself."

Dahlia laughed. Mrs. Janice reminded her of her own grandmother.

"That's what I'm talking about. I like you already, Dahlia."

Mrs. Janice and Dahlia chatted for the next hour as Dahlia did her hair. Dahlia turned Mrs. Janice to face the mirror to check out her hair. "All done," Dahlia spoke.

"Oh, honey! I love it. Dahlia, thank you so much. I know it was last-minute and you looked like you were on your way out the door."

"It's okay; I'm just glad you like it. I hope you have a wonderful day tomorrow and enjoy the night to the fullest."

"How much I owe you?"

"It's just twenty-five for you. Happy birthday!"

"Thanks; let me just go get the money from my grandson. He's treating his nana to get her hair and nails done." She smiled.

"Aren't you a lucky lady? I'll be right here, packing up my stuff," Dahlia said as she began to pack all the items she would need tonight as she waited for Mrs. Janice to return.

"Dahlia?" a male's voice spoke.

"Yes, I'm Dahlia," she replied, looking up at the man standing before her.

He didn't look familiar, but he had every woman in the shop practically drooling.

"How may I help you?"

"Here you go," he said, handing her a fifty-dollar bill. "My grandmother sent me in to give you this. She said she loves her hair. I want to thank you for taking her so last-minute and giving her just what she wanted."

"Oh, it wasn't a problem. Let me get you some change."

"No need; keep it. Like I said, thanks for doing her hair last-minute. Her day wouldn't have been right had she not gotten her hair done. You made that happened for her. She also told me to tell you she'll see you in two weeks."

"Okay, thanks. Here's my card. Tell her to call me to let me know the date and time. Tell her I said have a fabulous time at the party tomorrow." Dahlia smiled.

"I will," the man said as he turned and left.

"Who's that sexy-ass-nigga?" a stylist who worked in the shop with Dahlia questioned.

"My new client's grandson," Dahlia replied.

"When's he coming back in here? He's fine and I need a taste."

"You're a mess. For all we know, that man could be married with children. Or worse . . . gay." Dahlia chuckled.

"It's okay; I can be his mistress. Now gay, honey, he can keep it. He doesn't look like the gay type. I ping him as the playboy type, and I like to play, boy." Jesse moved her hips in a circular motion.

"I can't play with you. You're way too much for me," Dahlia said, packing up the last few items in her hair caddy.

Even though she'd smiled, Jesse's comment about being a man's mistress pissed her off. She hated those kind of women—too quick to settle for another woman's man. Dahlia finished sweeping the floor around her station, grabbed her bag, and headed for the door.

"Chandra, girl, I'm out of here for the night. Have a good night, ladies."

"Good night, D," the ladies chimed as Dahlia made her way out the shop for the night.

Dahlia made it home to rest and received a text from Keisha Kane's manager that the show had been canceled and she would need to re-book her hair appointment. Dahlia was a little sad, she'd wanted to slay Keisha's hair, but it worked in her favor because she wanted to lie down and forget the day had actually happened. Taking a quick shower, Dahlia settled with the half-empty bottle of wine from the night before. She climbed into her bed and watched *Love Jones*, once again.

Chapter 6

Dahlia hadn't seen her grandparents since they had come to her rescue her several nights before from jail. She had been straight going home from work for the last few nights. She hadn't been up to being bothered by anyone, but she needed to go over the last few details for her grandfather's upcoming surprise birthday party.

When Dahlia pulled into her grandparents' driveway, she noticed Desman's baby's mother, Sarah's, car parked in front of the house. She noticed her grandfather's truck was gone. She shut off her car to call her grandmother's cellphone, then remembered they were going to a friend's party. She was about to start her car back up when she heard loud yelling coming from her grandparents' home.

"What-the-fuck is going on?" Dahlia thought out loud, grabbing her cellphone to check out what was going on. From the front door Dahlia could hear Desman loud voice. She struggled with her key to unlock the door.

"I CAN'T BELIEVE I EVEN FUCKED-WITH-YO'-ASS FOR AS LONG AS I DID, LET ALONE HAD KIDS BY YOU," Sarah yelled, throwing blows at Desman.

"Keep yo'-fuckin'-hands off me!" Desman snapped, grabbing Sarah by her throat. "Don't make me fuckin'-hurt you," he whispered.

"DESMAN, DON'T HIT HER!" Dahlia yelled, finally getting the door open.

"Nah, let him hit me, so I can send his black-ass right back to jail. He don't do shit anyway."

"Desman, let her go. Now!" Dahlia demanded.

Desman released the grip he had around Sarah's neck and backed up. He didn't want to be too close if she decided to swing on him again.

"Sorry-ass-nigga," Sarah hissed, turning her nose up at Desman.

"What is going on around here?" Dahlia questioned. "And you two do know your children are standing here watching this?" Dahlia gritted pissed that Desman and Sarah both were acting so childish.

"She came over here tripping," Desman admitted.

"TRIPPING? HOW ABOUT IF YOU CALLED YOUR CHILDREN EVERY ONCE IN A WHILE? SPENT A LITTLE TIME WITH THEM? HELL, I'M NOT EVEN BEGGING YOU TO PAY THE-DAMN-CHILD SUPPORT YOU HAVEN'T PAID IN FOREVER, SO I HAVE EVERY-FUCKIN'-REASON TO BE TRIPPING."

"Sarah, please lower your voice. You are in my grandparents' home and I could hear you two from the street, so I know everyone else can hear. We don't do all of this drama. It is not needed nor is it welcome. I understand you're upset; I get it. Desman isn't doing what he needs to do for his children, but coming here, doing all this hollering in front of the kids, Sarah, isn't cool. What does it solve, you coming here putting your hands on him?"

"That's his problem now. Every time I turn around, you and your grandparents are making an excuse for his sorry-ass, straight babying his grown-ass. How about y'all help him take care of his kids?"

"First off, as their auntie, I've already told you to call me if there is anything they need. It was never a problem in the past, so why is it now?" Dahlia questioned. "I don't baby him. I have expressed to him a countless number of times that he needs to step up, and so have my grandparents. So, all that mess you're talking, save it for the next one. And I'm not feeling you coming here to my grandparents' house, being all disrespectful."

"Let me tell you something. At this point, I don't give-a-fuck how anybody's feeling! I'm tired of raising these kids by myself. I didn't make them by myself, and from here on out, I'm not gon raise them by myself. You can start by helping your brother's deadbeat-ass watch the kids tonight. I have something to do," Sarah spoke.

"I'm trying to not act a fool in front of these kids, because you and Desman have already done enough, but you're pushing my patience," Dahlia whispered.

"Whatever," Sarah replied, making her way to the front door without even saying bye to her children.

Dahlia followed Sarah to the door and swung the door open for her to leave. "Sarah, don't come back here. Send your mother or your sister to come get the kids. You aren't welcome in this home," Dahlia spoke.

"Girl, I don't care about coming here. This house ain't all that. I'll also send someone to pick up my child-support check or send the police to pick up my baby-daddy." Sarah laughed.

"Get-the-fuck-out!" Dahlia said, slamming the door behind Sarah.

Dahlia could hear Sarah outside laughing and talking shit. Dahlia was pissed and wanted to let Sarah's ass have it. But when she looked at her niece and nephew's somber faces, she decided to let Sarah have this one. They had seen so much in just that little time, Dahlia didn't want them to see any more. She didn't know what else they'd seen in Sarah's care.

"So what do you say I order some pizza, and we can have a pizza-and-movie night?" Dahlia questioned the kids.

"I want cheese pizza, Auntie," Devin spoke, his hand raised, showing his deep dimples and toothless grin.

"Desman, turn on the TV in the living room while I order the kids some pizza."

"C'mon, let's go watch some cartoons while Auntie Dahlia orders some food. Dahlia order some wings," Desman said.

"You got some money?" Dahlia questioned, turning to look at Desman.

"Never mind."

"I know," Dahlia replied.

"Daddy, can we watch the Disney channel?" Desman's only daughter, Kia, asked, grabbing her father's hand as they made their way into the living room, hand-in-hand. She was Desman's twin. She looked just like her father. Kia was only a shade lighter.

Dahlia smiled. It wasn't that Desman was a bad father, he'd just let his bitterness toward Sarah cause him to lack being there for his kids because he choose not to deal with their mother. Desman was too busy sitting in his own sorrow to notice how his kids were suffering.

Dahlia called and ordered the pizza, then joined Desman and the kids in the living room for a night of movies.

❦•❧

After several hours and countless movies, everyone was stuffed on pizza and breadsticks. They all were on the couch in a food coma. Dahlia got up to use the restroom when she heard her grandfather's truck pulling into the driveway. She glanced at the grandfather clock hanging in her grandmother's kitchen and noticed it was well past two o'clock in the morning. Dahlia was coming out the bathroom just as Mabel and James were coming through the door.

"What're you doing out so late?" James questioned. "I know you weren't waiting on us to get home?" James chuckled.

"I came over here to check on you two when I realized tonight was the party. How was it?"

"It was really nice and fun, other than me having to tell that ugly-bitch Deloris to stay out of your grandfather's face. Every time I turned around, her big-tooth-ass was just grinning, showing off all them-damn-gums," Mabel fussed.

"Nobody was paying that-damn-woman any mind. Your grandmother is just crazy and feisty-as-hell." James laughed. "I love my baby though."

"I may be crazy, but I'm not blind. I know what the clean-up woman looks like. She ain't gon get shit anyway. I've got papers on his ass."

"You two are a mess." Dahlia laughed, admiring her grandparents.

"I didn't know Desman was going to have the kids today. I wanted to see my babies. Sarah must have pulled her head out her ass," Mabel spoke, looking at the kids.

"Well, that's why I'm still here. I was about to leave when I realized you two where gone to the party, until I heard yelling. I walked in on Sarah throwing blows at Desman, and Desman damn-near choking the girl. She's upset that he isn't providing for the kids and helping her raise them. Like I told her, I understand that, but she was being super disrespectful, calling him all sorts of names and hitting on him, and all of this was happening in front of the kids. That wasn't cool. I informed her she isn't allowed here, and she needs to send her mother or sister to pick up the kids. I told her not to bring that drama to this doorstep.

"I'm gon kick Desman's ass. I've told him to at least try to spend time with the kids. They don't know his ass is broke. All they'd know and understand is Daddy was there and they had fun with Daddy. This boy acts like he lives under a rock."

"Well, it's way past these kids' bedtime. They don't need to be leaving here. Wake his ass up and tell him to take them kids upstairs and lay them down until the morning," James instructed.

"Desman," Mabel called out, shaking his leg, trying not to wake Kia, who lay across her father's chest.

"Huh?" Desman replied groggily, focusing his eyes to look at his grandmother.

"Go lay them kids down upstairs. It's too late for that girl to be trying to come get these kids."

"All right," Desman said. Cradling Kia in his arms, he lifted off the couch and carried her upstairs to Dahlia's old room.

The house phone began to ring, causing them all to look at the cordless headset on the living room table.

"Who-in-the-hell's calling my house at this time in the morning?" Mabel spoke.

"One of Desman's little chicks," Dahlia put in her two cents.

"His-ass needs to get a cellphone, having people calling my-damn-phone in the wee hours and shit,' Mabel spoke.

"Who is this and why you calling here this late?" Mabel questioned, until she heard the voice. "The kids are sleep, Sarah. It's almost three o'clock in the morning. Wait 'til daylight to come get them."

"No disrespect, Mrs. Mabel, but I'm sending someone for my kids now. They're outside, so would you send my kids out? Your granddaughter made it clear I'm not welcome at your home," Sarah said from the other end of the receiver.

"If that's what she said, that's what goes. I heard you were over here being disrespectful? Go home, Sarah, and come back once the sun comes up to get these kids. They're sleep."

"Mrs. Mabel, would you just get my kids? Their ride is outside."

Just as the words left Sarah mouth, there was a knock at the door.

"Is she really trying to drag these kids out the house at this time of the night?" Dahlia questioned as she made her way to the front door. When Dahlia opened the door, she was surprised to see a man standing there. "How can I help you?"

"I'm here to pick up Sarah's kids."

"Yeah, that's not going to happen. I don't know you. Tell Sarah to send someone we know."

"Look, I ain't with all the drama. Would you just go get the little shorties so we can be on our way?" the man said.

Dahlia could tell from his Timberland boots, his North Face coat, and how he talked, he wasn't from California.

"No disrespect, but my niece and nephew aren't going anywhere. I don't know you; I've never seen you before. You think I'm just gon trust their lives in your hands? Boy, bye!" Dahlia said, closing the door.

"Sarah must be on some drugs to think I'm just going to let the kids go with this strange dude," Dahlia spoke, getting more and more pissed with Sarah as the night went on.

"What dude?" Desman questioned.

"Some man your babies' mother sent to pick up your kids."

"Word?"

"Yeah." Dahlia frowned.

"Desman, just take a seat and let us handle it," James spoke, seeing his grandson getting worked up.

"My kids aren't going anywhere unless their mama comes to get them. Where's the phone?" Desman questioned.

"That girl knows what she's doing. She sent that nigga over here knowing it was going to get Desman all riled up," Mabel said.

Desman paced the floor as he waited for Sarah to answer. He was hotter than fish grease. The veins in his neck pulsated as he breathed in and out of his nostrils.

"You're really on some petty-shit, huh? You gon send some random dude to my grandparents' house? Is that how we gon play it now, Sarah?" Desman questioned. "It's three in the-damn-morning."

"You're calling my phone like you're telling me to pick up a check. I sent my man to get my kids, but yo' fat-ass-sister's playing Captain Save-A-Deadbeat. Since your family refused to give me my kids, have them ready at nine o'clock in the morning. If my kids aren't ready when I get there, I'm calling the police and telling them you're a felon and you're holding my kids hostage." Sarah hung up.

"I can't stand her," Desman admitted, laying the phone down.

"Y'all good?" Dahlia questioned, looking at her grandparents.

"I'm fine. Sarah knows I'm not the one. I'll beat her white-ass like I was her mother," Mabel spoke.

"Okay. Well, I'm about to leave. I had a busy day today."

"It's too late for you to be driving by yourself," James spoke.

"Granddaddy, I'm good."

"Call us when you make it home," Mabel said as James walked Dahlia out to her car.

Dahlia made it home in no time since there were only a few cars on the freeway. She still couldn't believe Sarah had sent some random dude she was fuckin' to her grandparents' home. She prayed she wouldn't be so petty and bring the dude back when she did pick up the kids. Dahlia called her grandparents to let them know she had made it home safely before she jumped in the shower for a quick shower, then to bed and she was out.

Chapter 7

Dahlia shifted in her bed as the rays from the sun peeked through the cracks of the blinds. She desperately wanted to stay in bed after having to deal with all of Desman's bullshit. She didn't have any clients booked for the day. She knew if she tried to ditch the lunch date she'd set with Traci, she wouldn't hear the last of it.

Dahlia had closed her eyes for just a few more minutes of sleep when she heard her phone buzzing on the nightstand next to her bed. Reaching over, Dahlia picked up the phone to see Traci already calling.

"I'm up, Traci," she spoke into the phone, still half asleep.

"You're a lie and the truth isn't in you. Wake yo' ass up! I know you, Dahlia Willowbrook. Yo' ass is still nestled under the covers with your eyes closed as we speak."

"Traci Malcolm, *I am awake.*"

"Dahlia, I thought we agreed to meet at noon?"

"We did. What time is it?"

"That means you're late, dear. It's noon," Traci spoke sarcastically.

"I'm getting up right now, smart ass," Dahlia replied, hearing the sarcasm in Traci's voice.

"See you in two hours, slow ass."

"All right."

Dahlia hung up the phone and threw the covers off her body. She rambled through her clothes for something to wear. Although the sun was out, it was still slightly cold. Dahlia settled on leggings, an oversized sweater, and knee-high riding boots. She pulled her hair into a high bun and lightly touched her face with some makeup.

An hour later, she was cruising down Hollywood Boulevard, listening to the sounds of Chrisette Michelle as she made it through the mid-day traffic. Dahlia pulled in front of the small shrimp place just as she hit the two-hour mark.

"Do you always have to be late?" Traci asked, waiting for Dahlia at the door.

"I'm not always late. Traffic was crazy on the 101 freeway."

"Table for two, please."

"Right this way, ladies," the host spoke, showing Dahlia and Traci the way to seats close by the bar area.

"Thank you," the ladies spoke.

"So what's been going on, lady? I haven't seen you in a few days, since that last ordeal went down?" Traci questioned, looking Dahlia over.

"I'm good, taking it one day at a time. You know me, trying to save the world and everybody." Dahlia laughed.

"Oh, Lawd, what's going on now?" Traci questioned.

"Girl, last night, I went to check on my grandparents, and walked into Desman and that-bitch-Sarah fighting in front of the kids. I agreed to help watch the kids last night. Do you know this-bitch sent some random-ass-dude to pick up the kids well after two in the morning? And, she was talking all kinds of shit."

"I told Desman's-ass long time ago to leave that white-bitch alone."

"I was so pissed I wanted to punch her and Desman."

"I know Desman is your brother, but let him handle his own shit. Stop trying to always fix everyone else's bullshit. I don't like the white-bitch—never have—but as a woman and a mother, I understand why she's mad. I would be pissed if Charles said fuck it and didn't help me with the kids he didn't have a problem fuckin' to make. That's between them. Not you."

"I hear you. Last night, I did it for my niece and nephews. I didn't do it for Sarah or Desman. You should have seen their sad faces watching their parents cursing and fighting."

Dahlia paused, hearing her cellphone vibrate on the table. "Hey, Granny?"

"Hey, Dahlia," Mabel huffed.

"What's wrong?"

"It's your brother. He's been arrested."

"What's new, Granny?" Dahlia questioned, rolling her eyes.

Every few months, Desman was in jail. She was so use to it. It was like the county jail was his home away from home.

"That damn-white-bitch-Sarah. She brought that man from last night back over here, talking about she wants Desman to sign over all his rights. Of course he told her hell-no and to get-the-hell away from here. Her boyfriend added his two cents and things escalated from there. Desman started whupping on the man and Sarah's-ass called the police. They arrested Desman and the man," Mabel said.

"I'll be on my way in a little bit, Granny. We'll talk when I get there," Dahlia said, ending the call and throwing her phone in her purse.

"Duty calls for Superwoman," Traci joked.

"Let me go handle this issue. I didn't even get to get me any shrimp or crab legs. This is some bullshit!" Dahlia spoke.

"Okay. Well, shit, I'm going to order me something to go. I'm not about to sit in here by myself. Call me and tell me how everything goes."

"All right." Dahlia grabbed her purse and headed out the restaurant.

"This nigga's always in need of some help," Dahlia mumbled, making her way out to her car.

Dahlia took her time getting to her grandparents' house, giving her time to collect her thoughts. So much had occurred in her life in the space of a week. She hadn't taken the time to process everything.

When Dahlia made it to her grandparents', she could tell her grandmother was pissed and had probably smoked half the pack of cigarettes that sat next to her.

"So what happened?"

"I know you think your brother is a fuck-up, which isn't too far off. This time, Dahlia he really tried, but the dude provoked Desman. Him and Sarah were calling him punks and all kinds of shit. Desman snapped. She keeps worrying about Desman, but I can't wait to catch her ass!" Mabel ranted.

Dahlia didn't talk; she just let her grandmother rant.

"You've gotta bail him out, Dahlia."

"I don't have any extra money to bail him out, Granny, and neither do you. I am dealing with my own legal issues after being arrested a few days ago," Dahlia reminded her grandmother. "Plus, Desman doesn't like to do what he needs to do."

"I'll make sure he does whatever it is he needs to do; just get the boy out. You can use my house."

"Granny, we just paid off the house from the last time you used your house to bail him out. What did he do? Jump bail and went on the run. It took me three years to get that loan paid off," Dahlia expressed.

"I KNOW, DAHLIA!" Mabel shouted. "IS IT TOO-DAMN-HARD FOR YOU TO JUST DO WHAT I ASK OF YOU? THIS IS MY HOUSE. I KNOW YOU HELP ME OUT AROUND HERE."

"No, it isn't. I will put your house up to bail Desman out. They haven't booked him yet, so there is no bail," Dahlia spoke.

She was hurt her grandmother didn't care she had spent so much of her own money to save her house when Desman didn't even seem to care.

"I didn't mean to yell at you, Dahlia. I know you spent a lot of your own money to help me out. This time, your brother wasn't in the wrong, that's all I'm saying. I get what you're saying. You put out a lot of your own money to save my house. I appreciate everything you do to help me around here; I do. I just wouldn't feel right leaving my grandson in there, knowing this time he truly didn't do anything but stand up for himself."

"It's cool, Granny," Dahlia replied, even though deep down inside she was hurt.

She sat and listened to what her grandmother had to say. She didn't understand it. When it came to Desman, she didn't understand anything her grandmother did. Dahlia had learned long ago, out of respect, to never question her grandmother's orders.

Dahlia took a seat on the couch in the family room. She scrolled through her phone finding the number to the bail bondsman they had used to bail her out and on several occasions to bail Desman out. She informed him of what was going on and had him start the paperwork. He advised he would call her once bail was posted and all the paperwork was done.

Dahlia laid back and flipped through the channels on the TV, looking for something to watch, but nothing caught her eye. Turning the TV back off, she scrolled through the dozens of books she hadn't read that she had downloaded on her Kindle app on her phone. Dahlia settled on a book and curled up on the couch, engrossed in her new read.

BUZZ! BUZZ! Dahlia's phone vibrated against her cheek. She hadn't even realized she'd fallen asleep.

"Hello," she answered, still half sleep. She didn't even check to see who was calling.

"Sorry to wake you. It took some time, but we were finally able to locate Desman and get bail for him. Everything is set. We just need your grandmother's signature."

"Thanks, Tony. We'll be there shortly," Dahlia said, ending the call and pulling herself together.

The aroma filling the air made Dahlia's stomach rumble. She hadn't eaten all day. She knew her grandmother had gone into the kitchen and put her foot in the food she'd cooked. Anytime Mabel got mad, she either cleaned or cooked. Today it was cooking. Dahlia let her nose lead her to where she knew she could find her grandmother hovering over a hot pan.

"You hungry? I can fix you a plate."

"I'm starving," Dahlia admitted, taking a seat at the small breakfast nook. "Tony just called me and said he has all the paperwork done and ready for us. What did you cook?"

"I made some smothered turkey wings, collard greens, baked mac-and-cheese, and hot water cornbread. Once you eat, we can be on our way to get that child out of jail."

"Okay," Dahlia replied, waiting to get her hands on the food she knew her grandmother had put her foot and elbows in. Dahlia washed her hands and wasted no time grubbing on the food as soon as her grandmother sat it in front of her.

"Dahlia, if you don't slow yo' ass down, you gonna choke, stuffing that food in your mouth like that. How can you enjoy it if it's going straight down your throat?" Mabel fussed.

"I haven't ate all day. I'm starving and this food is on-point."

"Well, there's more. You can take your time and enjoy the food *and* the flavor of the food."

Dahlia just smiled as she watched her grandmother from the corner of her eye watching her eat her food. Dahlia slowed down and took her time until she finished her plate.

"Thank you," Mabel said, picking up Dahlia's plate.

"You're welcome, Mrs. Willowbrook." Dahlia laughed.

"Don't make me slap you, child, in here acting like you're some-damn-homeless person. Let's go get this boy out this jail so I can come sit my old ass down."

✷•✷

Dahlia and Mabel stopped by the bail bonds place so Mabel could sign the bail bond paperwork. Due to them doing plenty of business with Tony and having just been there bailing Dahlia out, Tony had already given the jail the okay to release Desman.

Dahlia and Mabel went over to the courthouse and sat in the lobby, waiting for him to be released.

"Awww shit," Dahlia mumbled when she saw Antonio and Jasmine walk into the station.

"What'd you say?" Mabel questioned.

"I'm sorry; that slipped out. Antonio and his girlfriend just walked in here."

Mabel looked around the police station until she laid eyes on Antonio standing alongside Jasmine as she talked to the on-duty officer.

"Men always seem to downgrade. She isn't pretty at all."

"Grandma, be nice."

"Fuck being nice. You'd better not be nice to his ass."

"I have no desire to talk to that man."

"Good; keep it that way! I have a few choice words for Antonio. I told his-ass something at that-damn-place, and he went and did the opposite—just like a boy."

"Granny, please don't."

"I sure am going to say something. I'll wait until all the legal bullshit's over, but trust I am going to say something to him," Mabel spoke, watching Antonio and Jasmine.

Dahlia made sure to stay occupied with her phone the best she could so she wouldn't make eye contact with either of them. They had been waiting longer than they were told it would take. Dahlia was about to go ask the desk sergeant how much longer it would be when she looked up to see Desman engaging in a brotherly hug with Antonio. She wanted to slap the shit out of Desman.

"Look at your grandson, over there having a good ol' conversation with Antonio." Dahlia chuckled.

"DESMAN!" Mabel shouted, causing everyone in the station to turn their attention to them. "BRING YOUR BLACK-ASS ON HERE!"

"I'm coming."

"NOW!" Mabel snapped.

"Granny, I was just speaking to Antonio. Why you in here yelling like you're crazy?"

"Fuck Antonio and that ugly-bitch standing next to him. You know he just had your sister arrested and you're all smiling in his face like you're some kind of faggot. You should have been letting his-ass know to leave your sister the-fuck-alone and questioning why he had her arrested!" Mabel fussed, pissed that Desman wasn't acting like Dahlia's older brother.

Dahlia had walked off when she saw Desman engaging in conversation with Antonio. She couldn't believe Desman. She was ready to beat the brakes off Sarah's-ass last night and here he was grinning in the man's face who had just had her arrested. When Mabel and Desman made it outside, Dahlia was already in her car waiting for them with it running.

The ride back to her grandparents was silent, which was fine with Dahlia. She wanted to chew Desman's head off, but it would only go in one ear and out the other, like always. He didn't care how anyone felt but himself. He was selfish.

"I'm giving you a warning now: Don't show up to court this time, I'm turning you in. I refuse to allow our grandparents to lose their home trying to save you from your foolish acts. So, Desman, it's in your best interests to attend court. I have enough of my own legal issues to worry about, but I know you don't care what I have going on."

"Damn-snitch! I'll be in court," Desman said, getting out the car, "because it's the right thing to do, not because you told me so."

"I can't stand him!"

"I apologize for his rudeness. Thank you for helping me get his rude-ass out. I'm about to go in here and give his-ass an earful. Call me when you make it home."

"Okay."

Dahlia watched her grandmother make it in the house. Desman stood by the door, smoking a cigarette. She wanted to let him have it now that their grandmother wasn't around, but she knew it would be a waste of breath and time. Dahlia backed out the driveway and dialed Traci's number.

"What's good, D? Did you get that-fool Desman out?" Traci questioned as soon as she answered the phone.

"Yeah, we got his-ungrateful-ass out."

"What's wrong?" Traci asked, hearing the sadness in Dahlia tone.

"I ran into Antonio and Jasmine—well, I saw them. I looked up to see what was taking so long for Desman to come out. He was standing there having a conversation with Antonio, then he embraced him in a brotherly hug. Yet, this-nigga didn't even thank me for coming to get his-black-ass out of jail, once again," Dahlia expressed, angered.

"Check his-ass. Better yet, next time—because we know there will be a next time—leave his-ass in there. I know you do it for your grandmother, but sometimes, you just have to follow your heart and let Grandma Mabel be mad for a little bit. She'll get over it. Stop trying to save everybody. How are you feeling about running into Mister Man and his-bitch?"

"Seeing him with her makes me want to hurt him, hurt him like he hurt me. Seeing them makes it a reality, that for this last year of my life, I was sharing my bed, myself, with a man I didn't even know," Dahlia spoke.

"It fucks-me-up to even hear the hurt in your voice. Deep down, I have to deal with the fact I brought that-man into your life."

"You can't beat yourself up about it. Hell, you didn't know all of that about him either."

"True, but I did know he was married and I withheld that information from you."

"To be honest, I could've dealt with the fact he was married and separated. It's all the other bullshit that's hard to digest."

"If nobody else knows, I know. You're a warrior. This is only spilled milk to the woman you are. You will bounce back. I really wish you would come to this party with me next week. You need to get out, forget about all this bullshit, and just have a good time with your girl."

"I'll think about it, Traci. I really don't want to be around people right now. I just want to take some time out for me, you know. I wish I could take my-ass on a trip somewhere, but with all this legal bullshit, I don't have the extra money."

"Bitch, take a staycation, where you stay yo'-ass right here and breathe and take a break."

"You are so silly." Dahlia laughed, pulling into her driveway. "Well, Traci, I made it home. I'll see you tomorrow at my grandfather's surprise birthday party, right?"

"Yes, I'll be there. Do you need me to help with anything?"

"Nah, I think I have everything together. I just have to do my grandmother's hair in the morning. I ordered food and already paid for it, and we got all the decorations last week."

"Well, I'll see you tomorrow. I'm about to go in here and prepare Charles' lunch; less I have to do in the morning. A bitch be tryna sleep in all she can." Traci laughed.

"All right; good night," Dahlia said as she walked in her house and flopped down on the couch. She was drained.

Dahlia drew her a nice, hot bath. She turned the lights down, put on some music, and climbed in the tub. She just wanted to relax. Tomorrow was going to be busy and she had to mentally prepare herself for it.

Chapter 8

Dahlia stood behind her grandmother as she applied the finishing touches on her hair. They had spent most of the early morning getting everything ready while James went on his weekly fishing trip with some of his church members.

"What else needs to be done, Granny?" Dahlia questioned.

"Nothing. You said the food would be here by two, which is just around the corner. I have already pressed and laid out your grandfather's clothes. All he will need to do is shower and put those clothes on once he gets here."

"Does Sham and that-grandson-of-yours know what time to be here? Since they didn't show up to help us do anything."

"I told Sham yesterday and Desman this morning before he left here, but you know neither one of them knows how to follow directions unless they're making them, or want you to do something for them. Have you talked to Daniel? I talked to him yesterday. He was so sad he would miss the party and he misses us."

"My brother texted me the other day to put some money in his account for a book he needed for school. I know he's homesick. I told him to stick the rest of the year out, and once it's done, if he still wants to come home, he can. I told him the rules for coming home are: He goes to a university and it must be full time. I don't want him to come home, get with his friends, and forget what he needs to do. I just know it can be hard being young and away from the family you were always with, but I also know being away from family can make you stay focused so you can get back to them. Sometimes family can be a major distraction."

"I hear your point of view. With all this-shit going on and all this-damn-killing, I'd prefer for him to be here, close to us. I know it's selfish, because he's at school getting his education. I just want to see him, hug him, and know he's okay. I know he's there, but I want him here," Mabel expressed.

She was truly proud of Daniel. He was the very first male in their family to go off to college. Mabel and James had three children. James Jr. had been killed while working at a construction site by a disgruntled employee. Desman Sr. was Dahlia and her brothers' father. He was serving a life sentence in prison. Their only daughter was Sham, who Mabel often felt was on the fast-track to hell.

"He'll be here in a few months. We know he's your favorite," Dahlia teased.

"He isn't my favorite. I love all my grandchildren equally. I am very proud of Daniel and you. I can't forget Lil Zack. He called me last night to tell me he got an A+ on his spelling test. He said, 'Granny, guess who's going to be a genius?' I said, 'Who, baby?' He said, 'Me, Granny. I aced my test with no worries. I was the only student in my class who didn't get any words wrong.'" Mabel laughed, speaking of Sham's youngest son.

Mabel had tried talking to Sham's older kids, Shane and Shana, about life and how making bad choices can affect your life forever. It always went in one ear and out the other. Sham and their father allowed them to do whatever they pleased and made excuses for them. Mabel never made excuses for her children's poor choices in life. She wouldn't do it for her grandchildren.

Most thought Dahlia and Daniel were Mabel's favorites, often because they had labeled their father as her favorite child, but it was far from the truth. She just knew they were destined to be something better than their parents ever were and not because someone had told them they had to be. They wanted better for themselves. Mabel supported that one hundred percent and would if it was any of her grandchildren. She wanted them all to be better than their parents, just as she wanted her children to be better than she and James ever were.

"I haven't seen Lil Zack in a while," Dahlia said.

"He's going to be here today. I talked to his daddy last night. He told me he'll bring him by. I don't know why Sham didn't stay with him. He works, owns his own home, and he has a good head on his shoulders."

"Granny, you know your daughter doesn't want anything that's good for her. She said Zack was too boring for her."

"A damn-shame."

"It's life, Granny. Isn't that what you always tell me? You know Sham is going to live her life the way she wants and doesn't care what anyone has to say about it."

"It still pisses me off. She's running around town like she wasn't raised better than half-the-shit her-ass is out there doing. Zack wanted to marry her. He proposed to her and she laughed in his face, in front of a crowd of people. I was so embarrassed. He treated her damn-good, and she treated him worse than a crackhead in search of their next high. Just wrong and trifling."

"Old lady, you are a mess." Dahlia laughed at her grandmother's choice of words. "Everyone who knows us knows Sham was raised well. I don't know what to say about that daughter of yours. She is a mess—always has been—and, at Sham's age, she's likely going to stay that way. You are all done, pretty lady."

Mabel checked herself out in the mirror hanging on the wall. "Thanks, baby; you really have a talent with this hair stuff," Mabel said with a smile on her face. "I'll be happy when you get your own shop."

"Thanks; you like it?"

"Yes; I love it," Mabel replied.

Dahlia had given her grandmother a French braid to the front of her head. She curled the ends and brought them down as bangs.

"Okay; well I am going to go get myself washed up and dressed."

"Go ahead; you know you're slow. Once the food gets here, I'm going to change into my shirt."

Dahlia walked into her old room and her heart almost stopped. It looked like time had stood still. It had been so long since she had actually stepped foot in the room. She hadn't realized nothing had changed. Dahlia walked inside and even the vibe of the room made her emotional. She took a seat on the day bed and glanced around the walls. They were covered with pictures. There were pictures of her mother, her father, her grandparents, and even pictures of her with her high school sweetheart, Shad.

Nothing about the room had changed since high school. The woman who was now sitting in the room was only a reflection of the girl in the photos all around the room. She was no longer the carefree girl she use to be with a wide grin on her face, with no worries or cares about love because she was surrounded with it. She had been surrounded by love and protection. Before Dahlia knew it, tears had welled in the corners of her eyes and threatened to fall on her plump checks. This wasn't the life she'd thought would be hers. She had planned by now on having her own shop, being married, and a mother to a few kids.

She walked to the vanity set and grabbed a picture that was stuck to the mirror. It was the last family photo they'd all taken together. Dahlia remembered the day like it was yesterday. It was summer and the heat was torture that day. Dahlia and Desman had begged their parents to take them to the Orange County Fair. It was the last day of the fair. Because they wanted to please their kids, Dahlia's parents had agreed to allow them to go to the fair for three hours. The fair was crowded with people, turning that three hours to a full day out in the heat.

Dahlia remembered, right before the picture was taken, she'd told her mother she was sorry for begging to come to the fair because her mother's freshly-pressed hair was ruined. Her mother smiled, pulling her hair into a ponytail, and told her it was just hair, it could be done again, but the smile on her children's face was priceless, and she enjoyed making them happy more than having nice hair. Everyone was smiling brightly in the photo, even Daniel, who'd complained the whole day because it was hot and his feet were hot in the Air Jordans their parents had dressed him in.

"I wish you were here, pretty lady. I need you. We all need you," Dahlia spoke as tears cascaded down her cheeks.

She missed her mother so much. The long talks about marriage and kids as they took turns wrapping each other's hair. The family trips. The sound of her father's off-tempo singing of The Temptations. She missed the happy days when she didn't care about a man's love because her father had showered her with so much. She didn't know why she kept falling for men who treated her with less respect than she deserved.

Dahlia didn't think she had daddy issues. Her father had always been in her life. He'd told her she was pretty and he loved her often. Dahlia thought of her father. It had been a little over a year since the last time she had spoken to or seen him. They'd gotten into a disagreement about how he'd chosen to deal with her mother's death. It bothered Dahlia that he never mentioned her mother. It was like she was nothing to him, like he'd never loved her.

The young girl in her blamed him for her mother's death because the men who'd come into their home was looking for her father and had killed her mother when she wouldn't give them what they wanted. Dahlia and Desman had watched the whole thing from the panic room installed in their home. Daniel was in his playpen napping just a few feet away from their mother when it happened. The grown woman she was knew it wasn't her father's fault. Her mother was a ride-or-die chick all around and played her part in the dangerous life her husband lived without a complaint. Dahlia needed to place the blame on someone. Since her father was present—yet absent at the same time and it was the life he'd led—she blamed him for her mother's death and him being out of their lives.

"Dahlia, baby, the people are here with the food," Mabel said, knocking on the bedroom door.

"Okay; here I come."

Dahlia wiped away the tears that lurked in her eyes. Pulling herself together, she made her way downstairs to pay for the food.

"Dahlia, why're you so slow? You don't even look like you attempted to start getting dressed."

"I got a call from a client," Dahlia lied.

"I'm ready for this party to start," Mabel spoke, looking around at how everything had come out.

"Everything looks so nice," Dahlia agreed, looking around the house.

They had the tables set up for everything her grandfather liked to do—chess, cards, and dominos. They had invited all of his chess club members, church members, family, and friends. They'd made sure to tell a lot of people last minute so they wouldn't mention anything to James, who didn't care for birthday parties and all the extra shenanigans.

"Well, this time, I'm really about to start getting dressed."

"Okay."

Dahlia decided not to get dressed in her old room. She gathered her bag, and went and dressed in her grandparents' bathroom.

❧•☙

As the guests began to trickle in, Dahlia played host and was praying everyone made it before her grandfather made it home or after he was already there. If someone was arriving at the same time as he was, it would be a giveaway.

"JAMES JUST PULLED UP!" Mabel yelled, letting everyone know to hush and be ready when he walked in.

"One of them-damn-kids must be about to have a-damn-party," James fussed, fumbling with his keys to get into the house. He'd noticed all the cars on the usually-empty street. "All in front of my-damn-house, coming with all that-damn-ruckus," he fussed.

"SURPRISE!" everyone yelled as James walked into the house.

"GODDAMMIT!" James yelled, dropping his lunch box. "Almost gave me a-damn-heart attack." James laughed as he scanned the many faces in the room welcoming him.

"HAPPY BIRTHDAY!" everyone shouted in union.

"Awww, this is really nice. This has my wife and granddaughter's names all over it. Thank you to everyone who came out." James smiled.

Mabel approached, grabbing his lunch box from the floor. "Your clothes are pressed and in the bathroom waiting for you. Hurry up, so we can get this party started," Mabel sang with a slight winding of her hips.

"Okay. I'll be back, everyone," James spoke before making his way up the stairs to change into his party clothes.

Once James returned with his Sunday's best on, looking shaper than a pencil on the first day of class, the party started. James' favorite songs played through the house as people played cards, danced, and even talked shit.

"Thank you for everything. If it wasn't for you, I wouldn't have been able to pull this off. We may not say it often, but we are truly grateful for you and appreciate all you do for us," Mabel spoke to Dahlia.

"Don't sweat it, Granny. Just make sure you have fun and enjoy. I know Granddaddy is."

Dahlia watched everyone having a good time, and was happy she was able to help her grandmother give her grandfather a gathering for his birthday. Not only did James help out his grandchildren, he helped every kid in the community and down at the church house.

"I see neither your daughter or grandson decided to show up for Granddaddy's surprise," Dahlia said, as she finally noticed she hadn't seen a sign of her auntie or brother amongst all the faces in the room.

"I expected that from Shamera," Mabel said, calling Sham by her full name. "You know how that child acts when she gets her a new piece of dick to screw. She gets all dick-crazy and shit, but I expected Desman to be here. Hell, the boy lives here; of all the days he isn't here. Usually, I have to beg him to get out the house for a few hours to do something besides sit on my-damn-phone all day."

"Granny!" Dahlia laughed at her grandmother's bluntness.

"Dahlia, yo' ass ain't a child. You know I'm telling the truth."

Dahlia didn't respond; she just shook her head. She was fed-up with her auntie and her brother. Their father/grandfather did any and everything they asked, and they couldn't spare an hour of their time to stop by his birthday party?

"As long as Grandpa's enjoying himself, then I'm happy. It's his party and making him happy is my only concern. I can't worry about who decided not to show up. You don't worry either. Enjoy your husband's day," Dahlia told her grandmother.

"Oh I am, but I'm still going to let both of their asses know how I feel. And if they don't show their faces here tonight, they'd better not fix their mouths to ask my man to do shit for them either," Mabel said.

"I hear you, Granny. Look who's calling."

Dahlia smiled as she waited for the FaceTime call to connect from her little brother Daniel. She knew seeing his face would bring a smile back to her grandmother's face.

"Hey, big head," Dahlia said into the screen.

"Hey, sis, where's Granny and Grandpa?"

"I'm right here," Mabel spoke, taking the phone from Dahlia. "I need to get me one of these so I can see you, grandson. Let me go find your granddaddy.

He's gonna be so happy to hear from you," Mabel said as she made her way through the people in search of James.

Dahlia stood laughing at her grandmother cussing out everyone in her way. When Mabel finally made it to James, his face lit up like a child on Christmas. Dahlia just shook her head. They acted like they hadn't seen or talked to Daniel in years.

"This food is the bomb, Dahlia," Traci said.

"I haven't even tried it. I've been making rounds, making sure everyone is good and enjoying themselves."

"It looks like everyone is having a ball to me."

"Which makes me happy, because that makes my grandparents happy. It would've been nice if Sham and Desman had decided to show their faces around here."

"Give them some time," Traci suggested.

"They should have been here before anybody else. They should have been here seeing if my grandmother needed any help getting everything together. She's getting old now."

"Why? They knew you were gonna make sure everything was all right."

"They shouldn't always depend on me. Then they want to say I'm her favorite. Hell, I'm the only one she can depend on."

"There Sham goes right there, getting out that car," Traci said.

"GMB?" Dahlia questioned, noticing the custom license plate on the car Sham was standing next to by the driver's door.

"Those fools are still around real heavy. They control all kinds of shit on the west side," Traci informed.

"I didn't know that."

"It's a bunch of young dudes. I don't think there are any older dudes who get down with them."

"So you're saying Sham's fuckin' a young dude?"

"Don't act like that's so farfetched for Sham."

"You're right." Dahlia laughed, making a mental note to ask her auntie who was her new man and what were his ties to GMB.

"Looks like Desman's on his way in, too," Traci said, seeing Desman headed up the driveway.

"It's about-damn-time," Dahlia said. "I'll be right back."

"Okay."

Dahlia continuing making her rounds around the house to make sure everyone was good and having a good time.

Chapter 9

"Dahlia, don't be all nervous. You were protecting yourself and your property. They'll probably just drop the case anyway."

"I'm not nervous, Granny," Dahlia lied.

She was beyond nervous. She had never been arrested before, let alone had to go before a judge. She had been in courtrooms plenty of times and witnessed the wrath of judges ripping people apart and taking their lives away. Dahlia didn't know her fate. She knew Antonio and Jasmine were petty. Jasmine could go before the judge and make all kinds of things up. She was the one who'd been taken to the hospital for injuries sustained in the fight. Could she stretch the truth and make Dahlia look like a vicious, violent attacker? The questions swarmed Dahlia's head as she waited with her grandmother alongside her to be let in the courtroom.

"Dahlia, you can tell that to someone who doesn't know you. I know you. I also know you've never been arrested or had to deal with the court system, but I have already prayed about it. Everything will be good."

"Thanks, Granny," Dahlia said.

It was a quarter past eight when the bailiff started to let everyone in the courtroom. Dahlia looked around and she didn't see Antonio or

Jasmine in the courtroom. She knew, if they didn't show up to court, chances of her case being dropped were looking good.

The hours passed slowly as Dahlia waited for her name to be called.

"You good, Granny? I didn't expect it to take this long."

"I'm fine. How are you though?"

"I'm just ready for all of this to be over with."

"It will be shortly," Mabel spoke.

Dahlia wanted to believe what her grandmother was saying, but there was a nagging feeling in the pit of her gut telling her something different.

"I'm going to go use the restroom," Dahlia spoke, crossing over her grandmother.

"Okay."

Dahlia found the bathroom and locked herself in the stall. She closed the toilet seat and loaded the cover with tons of toilet seat covers and sat down. She took a deep breath and said a small prayer. Once she was finished, she trashed the seat covers, washed her hands, and made her way back toward the courtroom to join her grandmother.

Just as she neared the courtroom, she saw Antonio and Jasmine entering the courtroom.

Jasmine was walking on crutches and had her arm in a sling. Dahlia was baffled. She knew they were going to try to pull something.

"Their petty-asses," Dahlia said to herself.

Dahlia stalled for a little bit before she went back into the courtroom. When Dahlia made eye contact with her grandmother, she knew her grandmother was pissed.

"What-the-fuck's wrong with her?" Mabel laughed. "Didn't we just see her and she didn't have none of that shit on?"

"I knew they were going to be up to some petty mess." Dahlia shook her head. "I should have gotten me a lawyer."

An older white woman, dressed in a pants suit with a stack of folders in her hand, scanned through a sheet of paper in her other hand. "Dahlia Willowbrook?" she called out, scanning the room.

"Right here," Dahlia said, her hand raised, making her way through the aisle.

"Hello, I'm Attorney Karen White. I'll be your public defender for this case. The case against . . ." She shuffled through the papers. "Against Jasmine James."

"Yeah?"

"Let's go outside and go over what we're up against."

Dahlia followed the court-appointed public offender outside as she prepared to hear the bullshit Antonio and Jasmine had come up with.

"Well, Ms. Willowbrook, you were originally charged with assault on the victim, Ms. James. I spoke to the victim's attorney, and they are seeking second-degree assault. It appears they're saying, during the altercation between Ms. James and yourself, she sustained fractures to her nose, leg, and arm. I have requested those medical documents to support what she's saying. In the police report from the night you two ladies were arrested, it did mention she was taken and treated at the hospital, but it doesn't list her injuries. Would you please give me your side of the story?"

Dahlia sat and filled Karen in on what had occurred, and she wrote down what Dahlia was telling her.

"So that we're clear: You and Ms. James' boyfriend, Antonio, recently broke up. You two had been dating for the last year. You just found out about her the night of the incident. She has been playing on your phone, admitted she slashed your car tires the morning of this incident, then she later returned and damaged your car. At that point was when you two came into physical contact," Karen stated, reading over the notes she had taken down.

"That is correct. I don't know where she got the crutches and sling from. I happened to see her and her child's father just a few days ago at the local police station and she didn't have either of those things. I'm not a violent person and have never been arrested or even had a simple moving violation. The only thing I did was defend myself and my property."

"I understand. I'm going to request another court date. I need to give the defendant time to submit those medical documents. I'm going to argue she's a scorned woman who caught her boyfriend cheating and is lashing out trying to hurt you because she believes he's still in love with you."

"I'm no home wrecker."

"I never implied you were. I have been on this job for a little over twenty years. I know what a home wrecker, as you put it, looks like. I also know what a woman scorned looks like. I have defended both. I've also been both. Trust me, I've got this." Karen smiled. "We should be going before the judge in a few."

"Okay," Dahlia replied, getting up and heading back into the courtroom as Karen headed down the hall.

"What did she say?" Mabel questioned Dahlia as soon as she sat down, noticing the somber look on Dahlia's face.

"They're trying to charge me with second-degree assault. She claims that, during the altercation, I fractured her nose, arm, and leg, which is why she has on that sling and the crutches."

"That's some bullshit. She didn't have any of that shit on the other night when we saw her."

"I told the public defender that. She said she's requesting the medical documents. I thought this would be over today. They are trying to drag out this mess."

"The judge has the last word once everything has been presented to them. Keep the faith. The judge can review the case and still drop the charges," Mabel informed Dahlia. She knew her granddaughter was stressing.

"I hope so, Granny, I really do," Dahlia replied.

The wait to be called dragged out for another hour before the judge called Dahlia and Jasmine's names. The judge talked so fast, Dahlia didn't know what was going on around her. She was somewhere lost in a daze. She was still stuck on the fact she was even standing before a judge, facing felony charges.

"Dahlia," Karen had called out twice.

"Yes."

"Are you okay?"

"Yes; this is just . . . just a little overwhelming for me; that's all."

"I know. I'll try to get this process over and done for you as soon as I can. Here's my card. I'll see you back here in two weeks. If she contacts you, threatens you, or touches your car, document it then call me."

"Okay, and thank you," Dahlia replied, walking toward her grandmother with a long face. She was pissed that this was going to be dragged out.

"Pick yourself up, girl. Don't let that bitch think she's won. You walk out this courtroom with your head held high. You have been through worse than this," Mabel reprimanded Dahlia. "Keep it high. Just like anything else you've been through, you're going to get through this. You have a praying grandmother."

Dahlia looked at her grandmother without saying a word. She could feel eyes on her. She turned and Jasmine was staring dead at her. Dahlia noticed the grin plastered on her face. Dahlia bowed her head to search in her purse for something. She pulled her head up with a small compact mirror and a stick of matte, bright-red lipstick. She pushed her lips out and smeared the lipstick over her lips. Dahlia checked herself in the mirror once more. She turned to face Jasmine with the biggest smile on her face. The smile Jasmine had worn was now replaced with a frown.

"Bitch!" she mouthed.

Dahlia laughed as she walked out the courtroom into the hall with her grandmother beside her.

"That's my girl. Don't ever let them see you sweat." Mabel smiled.

Dahlia was thankful for her grandmother. She was a tall bottle of wisdom that was indeed marked with a firecracker label across it.

"When they see you panic, they think they're in control. A lady never lets a bitch control her emotions or feelings. Hold this; I gotta go pay my water bill," Mabel said, handing Dahlia her coat and purse so she could go use the restroom.

Dahlia took a seat on the bench in the hall as she waited for her grandmother to return from the restroom. She took the time to reply to a few text messages she had received.

"Just know, I will have the last laugh, bitch!" Jasmine spat, standing in front of Dahlia.

Dahlia inhaled deeply. She didn't want to make a scene, but something about Jasmine struck a nerve in Dahlia that made her want to beat-the-shit out of her again.

"I'm glad you're getting a kick out of this, but I am telling you now, leave me alone." Dahlia stood. "Just bow out of this gracefully. You got the man;

he's all yours," Dahlia informed her with a smile on her face.

The last thing she needed was to cause a scene at the courthouse. She knew it was what Jasmine wanted. She refused to feed into her bullshit.

"I don't know what you saw in this fake-bitch. Bow out gracefully," Jasmine mimicked. "Nah, I come to destroy lives. Bitch!"

"Jasmine, I'm really trying to be very nice to you. I understand you're miserable because you have to live with the fact you picked a man who ain't shit. I would be mad if I was you, too. Hell, I've been there. Well, not actually, but keep fuckin'-with-me and that ass-whupping I gave you will not top what can come. Now you two have a good-fuckin'-day," Dahlia said, grabbing her grandmother's stuff and walking away.

"Let's go, Jasmine. Just let the courts handle it from here," Antonio pleaded.

"I know you ain't trying to defend her fat-ass? It's because you can't keep your dick in your pants that we're in this bullshit. That-bitch thinks she's slick. I'm gon show her I'm not the one to be fucked-with," Jasmine spoke, sending daggers Dahlia's way. "Her and that Barbie-ass-bitch you call wife," Jasmine mumbled, full of rage.

"You aren't helping the case approaching her in a crowded courtroom that has cameras. That-shit isn't smart at all," Antonio ranted. "You gonna fuck-around and lose the case."

"Just shut-the-fuck-up. Let me handle this-shit. You need to worry about finding a-fuckin'-job. Or I'm going to gladly ship you back to one of those-bitches," Jasmine snapped back as they waited to exit the building.

"That-damn-bathroom was crowded," Mabel said, finding Dahlia in the hall. The look on Dahlia's face let her know something was wrong. "What happened now?"

"She's really trying to get me to hurt her. She approached me, talking about she destroys lives and she will get the last laugh."

"You have to stay two steps ahead of her. You have to outsmart that woman. She knows she can get under your skin, so she'll keep trying to get there. You must remain unbothered by her bullshit. Next time that bitch comes in your face, let her know you've already got the last laugh. Every time you see her, smile," Mabel spoke. "Let's get-the-hell out of here."

Dahlia approached her car to find a sheet of paper stuffed under the driver's-side windshield wiper.

"What is that?"

"I don't know," Dahlia said as she grabbed it and got in the car.

Inside the paper was a makeshift card with the 'laugh now, cry later' clown faces printed on it. Dahlia handed the paper to her grandmother.

"What-the-fuck does this-shit mean?"

"I don't know her meaning behind it, but it means laugh now, cry later."

"So she's threating you? You know I'm never the one to call the police and shit, but this-bitch is deranged. You need to get a police report and report this-shit to that attorney lady, everything that has happened to you. This dizzy-bitch might try to harm you. I don't understand these women who do all this-shit over these no-good-ass-men," Mabel rambled. "How-in-the-hell did she know what you're driving?"

"She has to be watching me."

Dahlia pulled her car into traffic. She didn't know Jasmine's frame of mind or why she was so obsessed with messing over her life. It wasn't like she'd known she and Antonio were together.

"Dahlia," Mabel called out.

Dahlia was lost in her thoughts. "Yes?"

"Where-in-the-hell you going, girl?" Mabel questioned.

Dahlia looked up and noticed she had passed the exit to her grandparents' house three exits ago.

"I'm sorry; I was lost in my thoughts," Dahlia admitted, pulling off at the next exit so she could turn around. "I just have so many thoughts running through my head. I'm not focused. I need a vacation or something."

"You deserve one."

"Traci wants me to go with her to a birthday party with her this weekend. I told her no, but maybe I'll go to get out the house."

"You should. Get out and mingle amongst people. Don't let this-bullshit consume you. This is what that-bitch wants: You to be moping around the house, all stressed out. You're young; you have time to bounce back. Go have fun, live life. You're a beautiful girl with so much going for yourself. I wish your mother could see you. She would be so proud." Mabel smiled, missing her daughter-in-law herself.

"Granny, I miss my mother so much," Dahlia cried.

She could no longer control the tears. She pulled her car over and let the tears she had been holding in escape her eyes. Mabel unbuckled her seatbelt and just held her; she didn't speak. She knew Dahlia was still having a hard time without her mother being there. No matter how much she showered her with love, she couldn't replace the love a girl has for her mother or a mother has for her daughter. It was just an unspoken bond, created by God.

Dahlia cried until she felt she'd released all the built-up tears. "Thank you, Granny."

"Anytime." Mabel smiled, wiping the wetness away from her face.

Dahlia gathered herself together and pulled back into traffic. She was truly blessed to have her grandmother. There was a bond between them that never had to be spoken. Dahlia and Sham's daughter Shana were Mabel's only granddaughters. Desman's daughter Kai was the only great-granddaughter. All the other grandchildren and great-grandchildren were boys. Shana was always doing her and never really made time for Mabel. In her opinion, Mabel fussed too much. When Dahlia's mother was killed, Mabel had helped her son with the kids. When he was arrested, Mabel and James had taken sole responsibility for Dahlia and her brothers.

"Go home and get you a hot bath; relax your mind. Check in with me later," Mabel said as Dahlia pulled into the driveway.

"Thank you for going to court with me, Granny."

"It's never a problem. Now let me get in here and tend to this old man."

"Tell Granddaddy I said hello. I'm going to head home and lie down. I have a headache."

"Okay; call me later."

"Okay."

Dahlia watched her grandmother go into the house before she drove off.

Dahlia made it home, stripped from the two-piece suit she was wearing, and flopped on her usual spot—her couch in front of the TV. She flipped through the channels in search of something to watch and found nothing. She turned the TV off and scanned through the books on her Kindle and nothing seemed to spark her interest. Dahlia lay on the couch staring at the white walls. She needed to get out the house. With no destination in mind, Dahlia slid into a track suit and jumped in her car. She didn't care where she went. She just couldn't spend another moment sitting in the house.

Dahlia was passing the local strip mall not too far from her house when she felt the gripe in her stomach. She hadn't eaten since early that morning. Pulling into the shopping center parking lot, Dahlia scanned the food places trying to decide what she would eat.

'Buffalo Wild Wings, drinks and wings,' Dahlia thought as she pulled into the parking space.

For a Monday during happy hour, the place wasn't too crowded, which was perfect for Dahlia. She didn't want to be around too many people. Dahlia found a seat at the bar and took a seat.

"Is there anything I can get you started with today?" the waitress asked with a wide smile.

"Yes, I'll start with a mango margarita with a sugar rim." Dahlia smiled as she looked over the different flavors of wings.

"I'll put that in for you."

"Thanks," Dahlia replied as she went back to looking at the menu. Settling on a ten-piece wing meal, Dahlia sat the menu down to wait for the waitress to return. Dahlia was scanning the many faces in the place when she came eye-to-eye with a familiar face.

"Out of all the days to run into someone I know when I want to be left alone," Dahlia spoke to herself, seeing a dude she knew from high school headed her way.

"Dahlia Willowbrook," Jerome called out.

"It's me." She half-smiled.

"How've you been, girl? You're looking good."

"Thank you; I'm good. How about yourself?"

"I'm good. It's been a long time since the last time I saw you. It has to have been about seven or eight years."

"It has been some time."

"Are you here with someone?" he questioned, looking around.

"No; I came out alone to enjoy a few drinks and some wings. How about you? You here with the wife?" Dahlia questioned.

It was rumor he'd married Kimberly Tate, the most-popular girl in the school, who hated Dahlia with a passion because she'd had a thing for Dahlia's high school sweetheart.

"I came to meet my brother, but something came up and he bailed on me."

"How is your brother? I know he was injured last season."

"He's doing much better. His knee's good. He's still going to sit this season out though," Jerome spoke. His younger brother was a wide receiver for the 49ers.

"Tell him I said hello."

"I will. How is Traci's crazy-ass doing?"

"She's the same—crazy." Dahlia laughed.

"Here's your drink. Are you ready to order?" the waitress asked.

"Yes; I will take a ten-piece Thai wings, bone in, cooked crispy, please."

"Sir, is there anything I can get for you?"

"Yeah; let me get a twenty-piece blazin'-flavor wings and two double-shots of 1800 Silver," Jerome ordered. "So what's been up, Ms. Dahlia, or is it Mrs. Shad Harvard?" Jerome smirked.

"It's still Miss Willowbrook," Dahlia informed.

Back in high school, it was a known rumor that Jerome had the biggest crush on Dahlia. It had never been confirmed to Dahlia.

"What about you? I heard you changed Kimberly Tate's last name to Mrs. Morehouse?"

"Yes, I did. Two kids and six years later, we're now divorced."

"Ouch."

"You live and learn. I still love her; we just weren't meant to spend the rest of our lives together. We are better as friends and co-parents to our kids."

"That's good. You have to do whatever is best for the kids."

"So what happened to you and your boy?" Jerome questioned, referencing Dahlia's high school sweetheart Shad.

"Sometimes things don't work out the way we planned."

"If anybody I expected to still be together, it would have been you and him. Y'all were so madly in love with each other."

"I was, but what do they call it: puppy love? The woman I am today is much different than the young girl who thought she was in love with the bad boy," Dahlia said, reflecting on the young love she had for her ex.

She couldn't deny it. If they'd asked her back in high school where she saw herself today, she would have said as Shad's wife, mother of his kids, and the owner of her own salon.

"Sometimes life has a funny way of surprising you and showing you another plan."

"That's very true, because I never thought I would run into you and you weren't someone's wife. Correction, you weren't *his* wife."

Dahlia and Jerome sat at the bar and chatted over rounds of drinks and wings. They talked about the old days and how much so many people had changed. Dahlia had always heard the rumor of Jerome having a crush on her, but they were in high school, which was filled with catty chatter. Because she was so head-over-heels for Shad, she'd never paid any attention to any other boy or anything that didn't deal with Shad or her family, outside of her school work.

"Did you really have a crush on me in high school?" Dahlia questioned out of curiosity.

She was on her fifth drink and the liquor was beginning to help her relax. Dahlia was actually enjoying the company of someone to talk to rather than sitting by herself.

"I did have a crush on you in high school. Shit, I'm crushing on the woman sitting before me now." Jerome smiled.

"Oh boy. What time is it?" Dahlia chuckled, searching for her phone.

"I'm serious. You have always been the girl who stood out. You've never had to do a lot; you just shined." Jerome was laying it on thick and had Dahlia feeling some kind of way.

"Well, thank you."

Dahlia didn't know what to say. She was kicking her-own-ass in the butt for even asking the question. A small part of her was only curious because of her current self-doubts about her beauty.

"So why didn't you ever say anything?"

"I never had the courage to tell you, until now. I did tell a few people, which is how it got back to your boyfriend."

"I heard something about it, but I didn't really believe it. We were in high school where every day there was another rumor."

"The rumor got the attention of your boyfriend and his crew. One day after football practice, I was in the locker room when he and his boys approached me. He asked me if I thought you were beautiful. I told him yes. He told me to stay away from you and to never talk to you. I told him he would have to beat my ass because I was going to continue to speak to you. He gave me another chance to agree that I wouldn't talk to you. I said no. It wasn't the only fact that I had a crush on you—you were a cool girl—I also saw you as my friend. So I got my ass beat because I refused to back down and not speak to you."

Dahlia was speechless. She had heard they'd gotten into a fight, but when she'd questioned her then-boyfriend, he'd said he hadn't gotten into it with Jerome; that everyone wanted to make him out to be a bully.

"Jerome, I'm so sorry. I never knew it had actually happened. I did hear it from Traci, but he said it wasn't true. I feel so bad. I never asked you if it happened. Why didn't you ever say something?"

"I never expected you to ask me. That was your man and you have to respect a woman who stays loyal to her man. I couldn't see myself running to a man's woman telling her: He beat my ass because I have a crush on you." Jerome laughed. "You would have thought I was a punk."

"Yeah, but it's also a woman's duty to let her man know when he's wrong. I would have let him know he was wrong. I wasn't checking for you or any other boy. Hell, my world only consisted of him and my family."

"We can't change the hands of time. We have to live in the present day and enjoy it to the fullest."

"Jerome, is that why you missed a semester of school and stopped playing football?" Dahlia questioned.

"Yes," Jerome spoke.

The hurt that could be heard in his voice tugged at Dahlia. She knew that could have been the reason he never was able to go pro. In high school, Jerome had been a beast on the football field.

"He made a promise that I wouldn't play football again. My mother was scared, so she put me on home studies for a while and told everyone I was hit by a car."

"Wow! I am so speechless. I can't believe all of this happened right around me and I didn't know it. I don't put anything past him. I have seen many sides of him, trust me."

"You had no control over the situation. I knew when I wouldn't agree he would beat my ass. He was in front of all of his friends. It's all a code; I understood it. Had it been the other way around, I can't sit here and say I would have handled it differently."

"I truly apologize from the bottom of my heart. I know how much football meant to you. I'm sorry you had to go through all that trying to be my friend. It does say a lot about your character." Dahlia offered a weak smile.

"Look how life works. I'm in your presence now. He can't control that and it seems to me he obviously took you for granted."

"That he sure did," Dahlia replied. She had witnessed the good, the bad, and the ugly of her ex.

"Do you still keep in contact with him?" Jerome questioned. "I'm just being nosy. Some people are better off friends than they are in a relationship."

"That is very true, but Shad and I have nothing to talk about," Dahlia spoke with a raised eyebrow.

"What, after all these years, you want to come back and kick his ass?" Dahlia laughed.

"Nah, I just wanted to see what he's up to. Truth be told, I didn't think he would live to see the age of twenty-one. He lived a pretty thugged-out life, so to be pushing thirty, shit, he should feel blessed."

"Well, I don't know anything about him. I don't care to know anything about him either. Can we talk about something else? Hell, what time is it? I'm hanging out like I don't have anything else to do."

"It's a little after midnight," Jerome said, looking at the watch on his wrist that shined brightly and caught Dahlia's attention. She had seen one before. It was a presidential Rolex that had to be custom designed.

"Well, it was a pleasure seeing you. Thanks for keeping me company," Dahlia said as she pulled some cash out of her purse to pay for her drinks and food.

"Don't sweat it; I got it," Jerome said, pulling a wad of cash out of his pocket and leaving a crispy hundred-dollar bill on the bar. "I was hoping we could keep in touch, friend."

"Sure; here's my number." Dahlia wrote her number down on the napkin his drink was sitting on. "Get home safe. You've had a few drinks."

"I'm good. Let me walk you to your car," Jerome said, gulping down the last of his drink.

"I'm good; you don't have to," Dahlia said, starting to walk toward the exit.

Jerome caught up to her right before she exited the building.

"Damn, you move fast. Where are you parked?"

"I told you I was good. I could've walked to my car by myself."

"A gentleman never lets a woman walk to her car alone."

"Well, thank you. My car is right over there," Dahlia pointed.

"The Nissan with the flat?" Jerome questioned.

"What?" Dahlia questioned, moving closer to the car. Both of her back tires were flat. "FUCK!" she yelled.

"Do you have a spare tire?"

"I don't think so. It's a rental car; my car is in the shop."

"Okay. Do you live far from here? We can call a tow truck and I can drop you off at home."

"No, I don't. It's fine Jerome. I have roadside assistance. I'll just call them and have them tow my car home and have the rental place come switch out the car."

"You sure? I don't mind giving you a ride home."

"I'm good. I don't want to inconvenience anyone."

"It isn't an inconvenience."

"It's okay; I'm good," Dahlia repeated.

"Here comes the tow truck now," Jerome spoke, noticing the truck pulling into the shopping center lot.

"Thank goodness. I'm ready to get in my bed."

"Dahlia Willowbrook?" the driver questioned, stepping out the truck with a clipboard in hand.

"That's me. It seems I have two flat tires, the back ones," Dahlia spoke, showing the man her flat tires.

The driver bent to expect the tires. "Looks like someone intentionally put the tires on flats."

"Figures." Dahlia shook her head. The message left on her car popped in her head. "Can I get you to tow it to my home? I'll have it fixed in the morning."

"Sure; let me just get you to confirm your address and sign this for me," the driver said, handing Dahlia the clipboard. Dahlia signed the papers.

"Is that offer still available? Can you take me home?" Dahlia asked Jerome.

"Yeah."

"Cool," Dahlia said. "Are we done here?" she asked the driver.

"Yes; you'll be meeting me at this address, correct?" the driver asked, pointing to the paper on the clipboard.

"Yes, it's my home."

"Then we're done here."

Dahlia followed Jerome to his car.

"So what's good, D? Who's fuckin' with you?" Jerome questioned. "I know Shad isn't doing no chump-shit like this because you don't want to be with him?" Jerome chuckled.

"I told you I don't want to talk about fuckin'-Shad!" Dahlia snapped.

"Okay; I'm just trying to make sure you're good. You good?"

"Yeah. It's this last dude I was dealing with baby's mother doing this shit."

"You messing with chick's baby-daddies, D?"

Dahlia crooked her head to the side to look at Jerome, who was looking at her.

"Don't look at me like that. I'm not that kind of woman. I didn't know about her. Shit, his ass lied about damn-near everything. This-bitch is fuckin' crazy. This is the third time she's done some shit to a car I am driving. I am in a rental because she fucked-up my car."

"And you haven't laid hands on her? I know you ain't a fighter, but you ain't never let anyone bully you."

"And I didn't let her either. I beat her ass and got arrested. Today, I went to court for it. My public defender rescheduled the court appearance because the-bitch showed up in court on crutches and a sling. That's how I ended up here having drinks," Dahlia confessed. "It's been so much bullshit."

"Damn, you fucked her up!" Jerome laughed.

"I beat her ass, but I didn't fracture her nose, knee, and arm like she's claiming. She's being fuckin'-extra. Today, when we crossed paths, she told me she would be the last one laughing," Dahlia said as she filled Jerome in on what had transpired in her life in the last week.

"Don't let her scare you."

"I'm not scared. I just don't have time for this bullshit. I have other things to do in my life. I don't have time to be running back and forth to court, paying court fees, looking over my shoulder to see what-shit this scorned woman is going to do because the man she's with cheated and he ain't shit."

"That's how that-shit goes. Let me ask you something."

"What?"

"Do you have a restraining order in place?"

"No."

"She know where you live?"

"You know she does; I told you," Dahlia said with an attitude.

"Do you know where she lays her head?"

"No."

"Do you see the problem? She knows where you live, but you don't know where she lays her head. So why don't you have a restraining order on her? Back yourself up. That's all I am saying, D."

Dahlia thought over what Jerome was saying. It had never registered to her that she didn't know where Jasmine and Antonio lived, or even to get a restraining order against Jasmine.

"I never thought about it," Dahlia admitted.

"Look into it."

"I will; thanks for the ride," Dahlia said as she climbed out of Jerome's car and instructed the tow truck driver to back the car into her driveway.

It was well after midnight and Dahlia was worn out. She quickly showered and slid under the covers. She was out the minute her head touched the pillow.

Chapter 10

"Hello?" Dahlia answered groggily.

"Are you still sleep, Dahlia?" Traci questioned.

"Yes, I am."

"You don't have to work today?"

"Not until later. What is it, Traci?" Dahlia questioned.

She hadn't realized how many drinks she'd had. Her head was pounding and the sound of Traci's voice wasn't helping; she was loud.

"Your ass never called me yesterday to tell me how court went."

"I'm sorry. I was so pissed-off yesterday I just wanted to be alone for a few hours."

"Dahlia, were you drinking?"

"Yeah."

"How many drinks did you have? You sound like your-ass is over there with a hangover." Traci laughed.

"Shit! I don't know how many drinks me and Jerome had, but damn, my head is pounding. And you're being way too loud."

"Jerome?" Traci questioned.

"Yeah. I ran into him when I was at Buffalo Wild Wings."

"Him, as in Jerome?"

"Didn't I just say that?"

"Just so we're clear, we are speaking of Jerome Morehouse?"

"Yes, Traci. Shit how many times are you going to ask me? Yes, Jerome Morehouse who went to high school with us."

"I just wanted to make sure." Traci laughed. "Oh, we have to talk. I go on my lunch break in an hour-and-a-half. Meet me at the Beverly Center."

"Okay," Dahlia replied, hanging the phone up before Traci could say anything else.

Dahlia lay in bed, scanning through the messages on her phone. There were a few missed calls from her grandmother, a message from Jerome, and one from one of her clients, canceling for the day. After Dahlia replied to all her calls and messages, she went to look for something to wear.

Dahlia slid into jeans, a tank top, and sandals. She pulled her hair back into a ponytail. She hadn't called the insurance company or the rental car place to report the damages to the tires yet, so Dahlia booked an Uber to take her to the mall. Traci would have to drop her back off at home.

Dahlia traveled the distance to the Beverly Center to meet Traci. As she neared the entrance, she saw Traci pulling up.

"Look who I beat here," Dahlia said when Traci walked up to her.

Whatever," Traci said. "I had to submit my annual report. It took longer than I expected."

"Why'd you have me meet you at the mall?"

"I need you to help me find something to wear to the party tomorrow. You're still going with me, right?"

"I never told you I was going with you, Traci, but I need to get out, so I guess it won't hurt. So you only brought me here to help you pick out something to wear?"

"That's what best friends are for, but I actually wanted to see you and see how you were doing after going to court yesterday."

"Yeah, okay, but as far as court, it was so extra. I am so over this-bullshit. Do you know she showed up in court on crutches and in a sling?"

"You're kidding me?"

"No; she said I fractured her arm, nose, and leg."

"So she's being extra-petty?"

"She told me yesterday she would be the last-bitch laughing. I get to my car—mind you, I had my grandmother with me—and I find a note on my car with the 'laugh now, cry later' card in it."

"What-the-fuck? She's threatening you?"

"Yes; so last night, after being in Buffalo Wild Wings for a few hours, I go outside to leave for the night to find my rental back tires flat."

"Dahlia, it's time for you to get a restraining order. This-shit is getting out of hand. This-bitch is crazy. If she's doing all this, why-the-fuck is she still with his cheating-ass?"

"I have no clue. I just want them to leave me the-fuck-alone. I don't want any parts of his-ass any more."

"And what's this about you having drinks with Jerome?" Traci questioned. The question had been burning a hole in her tongue waiting to be asked.

"I was getting something to drink after all this-shit and he happened to be there."

"That man had the biggest crush on you in high school." Traci laughed as she recalled plenty of times Jerome had talked her ear off about Dahlia.

"According to him and his little actions, he still does."

"Did you exchange numbers?"

"Yeah; he waited for the tow truck to get there then dropped me off at home."

Traci didn't say anything; she just smiled. She wanted to see her best friend happy and in love. She hoped she would give Jerome a chance.

"Traci, did you know Shad beat Jerome up when we were in high school?"

"Yes, I knew," Traci admitted.

"And you never told me?"

"I didn't. I wanted to, but when I reached out to Jerome to see how he was, he didn't want me to tell you for fear Shad would do something irrational to him again, or worse, to you."

"Damn!"

"You two talked about that last night?"

"Yeah."

"Do you two have plans to see each other again?" Traci questioned.

"No."

"Why not?"

"Why not what, Traci? And what type of party is this?"

"Why don't you have plans to see him again? This man has been crushing on you since high school and even took an ass-beating over you. Just don't shut him out. Let it flow and just see where it goes."

"Traci, I am not trying to date no Jerome. He's cool and all, but not my type. Big-face Rolex watches, pinky rings, and a wad of cash in his pocket."

"Dope dealer?"

"All the signs are there. He drives a Benz on rims, tinted rims, and when I hugged him, I could feel he was packing heat."

"Well, okay, I understand that, but before you just write him off as a drug dealer, ask him what he does. Maybe he's a music mogul or some shit."

"I actually don't care what he is. I'm not interested in a relationship with him. Now what are we in here looking for? What type of party is it?" Dahlia questioned, changing the subject.

"It's a birthday party."

"I know that, Traci. Is it a theme party is what I'm asking?"

"I think she said it was a black-and-white affair."

"Okay. Do you have anything in mind you'd like to wear?"

"Now you know I'm a jeans-and-T-shirt kind of girl. I don't have the slightest clue. This is why I brought your ass along to help me figure it out."

"Do you want to do pants, a skirt, or a dress? Let's start there."

"No pants. My-ass is always in pants. I don't do a skirt often because of my little, chicken legs, so let's try a skirt this time."

"Okay," Dahlia replied as she scoped out stores that would have the perfect items to fit Traci's small frame.

Traci, unlike her full-figured best friend, was a dark-mocha-chocolate girl, who stood five-two, with wide hips, a small waist, and ample breasts. She couldn't weigh over one-twenty-five. She was down-to-earth, which made her get along with just about everyone—until you pissed her off. Being she was a super-big fan of sports, she was cool with the guys because she always entered a room talking the most-shit. She fit in with the women because, just like a typical woman with a small frame, she was slick with the mouth, and she had natural beauty.

After hours in and out of tons of stores, Dahlia found Traci the perfect sexy outfit to wear for the night.

"I love it," Traci replied, admiring her frame in the outfit Dahlia had picked out for her.

Dahlia had found a black, A-line skirt that snugged Traci hips and plump, round ass. To be a small woman, Traci had a big, ghetto booty. The skirt fit perfectly to say she was flaunting her goods but wasn't checking for anyone, which was the case. Traci only had eyes for her husband Charles. Dahlia paired the skirt with a form-fitting, low-cut on the sides, body suit that showed just enough breast to be sexy but not trashy. She picked out some gold, wraparound-the-ankle, strappy peep-toe heels to adorn Traci's feet, with matching accessories. She already knew the perfect hairstyle to give Traci.

"Charles' gonna have a fit."

"Girl, he is. He gon be like, 'Can your mom watch the kids? I want to go. I need to make sure nobody's trying to take my wife!'" Traci chuckled, mimicking her husband.

"He's gon be waiting for you at the door." Dahlia laughed.

"He always does that shit. Talking about, 'Baby, wake me up when you get in if I'm sleep,' knowing his ass gon be sleep. If I want it, I'll wake his ass up. If not, I'll see his ass in the morning." Traci laughed.

"You two are a mess."

Dahlia laughed as she walked off to wait for Traci to change back into her clothes. She was ready to head home. She didn't feel like going into the shop, so she rescheduled her appointments for the day.

"What else do you have planned for the weekend?" Traci asked once she came out the dressing room and they were headed to the register.

"Besides going to this party you're dragging me to, a nice cold bottle of wine and some rocky road ice cream, and I have a date with my sofa to watch—"

"*Love Jones*," they said in unison.

"Don't be acting like you know everything about me." Dahlia laughed.

"Oh, but I do. I know you have watched that movie more times than I can count since you discovered it. You need to find a new movie to watch."

"I love that movie. I will watch it as many times as I please. I'm not bothering anyone."

"You need a-damn-social life outside of your house and that shop with all them messy-ass-bitches."

"I'm fine. I like staying in the house and watching TV."

"It's boring-as-shit."

"Well, I like boring; it suits me very well, thank you," Dahlia replied.

She didn't want to admit to her best friend that she wanted to stay in because she was over running into Antonio and his bitch until her case was over.

"I know it has something to do with Antonio. It seems for the last few days, a lot of places you go, you run into him or it reminds you of him," Traci spoke, hitting the nail right on the head.

Dahlia just stood and looked at Traci. She had read her like she was one of her favorite books.

"Whatever!"

"That's why going to the party will be fun. I know you won't run into them there." Traci smiled. "But there may be some other nice-looking men in the room who can help take your mind off Antonio."

"That's one thing that isn't on my mind. I'm not interested in dating anyone but myself. It's time I sit back and reflect on why I keep falling for the same type of man with just a different face."

"I feel you, but you can't let your fear of running into another man like your past lock you in your house. You can't let them control you. If you do, you're gonna miss the man who's out there for you. I understand you want time to yourself—and everybody needs it—I just want to make sure you're good and don't miss the chance of finding real and true love. Once you find that true love, you aren't gonna remember any of them-damn-fools."

"They aren't controlling me."

"That's all you heard out of everything I said? Are you afraid of finding real love?"

"Traci, I hear you. I want to find love again, one that is deeper than anything I have experienced before. I'm just not ready to date right away. Just a month ago, I thought I was in love and now I'm here: fighting a criminal charge and having to watch my back because there's a crazy-bitch determined to, as she says, destroy my life because she's still in love with her cheating-ass-man," Dahlia spoke, slowly drifting off into her own thoughts.

"Just know that I support you and I'll always have your back. I don't want to seem like I'm rushing you to find love and another relationship. I just want to make sure you don't give up on it. Take the time you need, and when the time is right, your time, you will find someone." Traci smiled. She only wanted the best for Dahlia.

"Thank you," Dahlia replied.

She understood where Traci was coming from. When she had no one else, Traci was there with open arms and listening ears for all of her problems.

"Oh, can you squeeze me in tomorrow to do my hair? I can't go anywhere with my hair looking like this." Traci pointed to the ponytail on top of her head.

"That sounds like a personal problem. I'm booked, Traci." Dahlia laughed, trying to put on her most-serious face.

"C'mon, Dahlia. You're really going to allow your best friend to go to a party looking all-tacky about the head?" Traci questioned.

"Correction: My best friend is going to let herself go to a party looking tacky about the head since she seems to always forget to make hair appointments in a timely manner," Dahlia informed.

"D, now you know that's how I've always done it. I can't even recall the last time I called in the same week for an appointment."

"My point exactly."

"You know I'm always busy; I forget. Why don't you just make me appointments, then call and let me know when they are. I'm just use to calling and saying, 'Dahlia, I need my hair done tomorrow,' and you saying, 'Come at seven, Traci.'"

"I understand, Traci; I've spoiled you. But look, I am running a business. If I want to get my own shop, I need to run my business like a business. Hell, I don't even take walk-ins like that," Dahlia stressed.

"Okay; I promise to start treating you like the professional you are and your business like a business, not my best friend's business, and make appointments in a timely fashion. Can you hook a sistah up in the morning though, please?"

"Thank you," Dahlia replied, scrolling through her phone to see if she could fit Traci in. "You know I've got you." Dahlia burst into laughter.

"You are a bitch!" Traci laughed.

"I just love fuckin'-with-you." Dahlia smiled. "Now let's get out of here because you and I have to be up early-as-shit. If you're getting you hair done, you need to be at the shop at eight a.m."

"Damn, that's early!"

"That's what happens when you make last-minute appointments." Dahlia chuckled as they headed out the mall.

The ride back to Dahlia's was filled with laughter as they reminisced about when Dahlia first started doing hair. Traci had always been her trial person. She'd learned to press, color, and dye right on Traci's head.

"Traci, make sure you're on time. If you aren't, I won't be doing your hair," Dahlia informed her.

"I know, eight a.m. sharp."

"You got it."

"So uptight."

"Whatever, bitch. Just make sure your-ass is on time."

"I will be. Call you when I get home."

"Okay," Dahlia replied, getting out the car and making her way up her driveway. When she got to her front door, a vase of black roses sat on her porch. "What-the-fuck?" Dahlia said out loud.

"Who-in-the-hell sends someone ugly-ass black roses?" Traci questioned, walking up behind Dahlia. She'd seen from the end of the driveway Dahlia pick something up off her porch. With all that had been going on, she had to make sure her best friend was okay.

"I don't know," Dahlia spoke as she took the flowers and trashed them.

"It's probably that-bitch of Antonio's with her simple-ass."

"I know it is. That's the only person who has an issue with me."

"You really need to get that restraining order and some-damn-security cameras around here."

"Yeah, I'm going to look into getting both of them done. I'm good. Get home to your husband and children. Call me when you get in."

"Okay," Traci said as she headed back to her car.

Dahlia stood in the doorway and watched her until she drove off.

Dahlia flopped on the couch and pulled out her laptop to make a reservation for another rental car. Once she was done, she dialed her grandmother.

"Hey, Granny, how are you?" Dahlia questioned when her grandmother answered the phone.

"Hey, baby; I'm good. Just sitting outside on the front porch. All day someone has been calling my house phone then hanging up once I answer. Now there's a car sitting outside in front of my house. So since they want to watch me, I am going to sit here and watch them."

"How long has the car been there?"

"For a few hours now."

"Granny, you've been sitting on the porch watching them for hours?" Dahlia questioned.

"Nah; I only been out here for a little bit."

"You don't need to be sitting out there, period. Go inside, Granny," Dahlia pleaded. "You don't know who's sitting in that car or what frame of mind they're in."

"They not gonna run me in my house. I want to know who-the-hell is sitting in front of my house. I'm about two seconds from going to the car and asking them what-the-hell they want."

"Do not approach that car, Granny. Just call the police if you want them gone."

"Fuck the police! You know I'm not gonna call them-damn-people. Shit, their asses are liable to get here and shoot my-ass. I'm okay; I got this-shit here."

"Where is my grandfather?"

"He hasn't gotten home yet. He did a little job today."

"Where is your grandson?"

"Shit, I don't know where he is. I haven't seen much of him lately."

"Damn," Dahlia mumbled low.

"I heard that," Mabel informed.

"I'm on my way, Granny. You don't need to be there by yourself."

"I don't need you, Dahlia; trust me, I've got this."

"Granny, you are seventy-five years old. You are home alone and telling me someone has been sitting in front of your house. I am coming to your house. My Uber will be here in five minutes."

"What's wrong with your car?"

"We will talk about that when I get there," Dahlia informed.

She didn't want to tell her grandmother she was afraid Jasmine's crazy-ass had been following her or Desman's baby's mother's boyfriend could be waiting for Desman to get home. So many things ran through Dahlia's mind. She didn't want her grandmother to be harmed for her or Desman's bullshit. Dahlia slipped back on her shoes, grabbed her purse, and waited by the curb for the Uber to arrive.

Once she got into the Uber, she tried calling Desman several times to see if he could get home before she could make it there.

"Fuck," she mumbled as she heard the automatic voicemail message again. "This muthafucka is never around when you need his ass," Dahlia said to herself, dropping her phone on her lap. She prayed her grandmother was okay and no one had hurt her, or she did the hurting.

It took Dahlia forty-five minutes to arrive at her grandparents' house due to traffic and the Uber driver's slow driving. Dahlia rushed up the pathway to see her grandmother still sitting on the front porch. She sat with her legs crossed, a cigarette dangling from her mouth, and a book sitting on her lap.

"I got here as fast as I could. The driver was so slow."

"I told you, you didn't need to come. Now what is wrong with your rental car?"

"Someone flattened the tires last night while I was out eating."

"I bet it was that-damn-crazy girl Antonio's sleeping with."

"I'm sure it was."

"That girl is bat-shit-crazy over that nothing-ass-man."

"She is. I just want her to leave me alone. I don't want any parts of him."

"She keeps fuckin'-with-you for a reason. You may not want any parts of him, but he probably wants you and she knows that. She's probably doing all this shit to torture not only you, but him, too."

"That's crazy. He told me to my face he didn't want me. She was always his choice. He disrespected me something crazy in front of her that night."

"He told you a-damn-lie. Why else would a woman keep-fuckin'-with a woman when she has the man? Because she knows that man still cares for that other woman. She wants to break you down so bad so he won't think about you," Mabel schooled Dahlia.

Dahlia sat and pondered what her grandmother had said. She didn't understand why Jasmine was continuing to mess with her. She had won; she'd gotten her man back.

"Enough of that bullcrap. Now what car has been sitting out here, and how do you know there's even someone in the car?"

"That black Lexus, and I know because I saw them park down the street, then across the street. No one ever got out the car. They just move the car every once in a while."

"How do you know they're watching your house? They could be watching anybody's house? Granny, what have you been doing? Why're you paranoid?" Dahlia laughed.

"I'm not paranoid. I haven't done shit! My grandchildren are into it with folks, and before they think they're gonna harm any of my family, I will lay-them-the-fuck down," Mabel spoke. "I may be old, but I am far from dumb. Half-the-shit you youngsters are doing has already been done."

"That girl don't know where you live, Granny, and Antonio is not that stupid to tell her. Hell, well at least I hope not. He knows you'll hurt her." Dahlia laughed. "And Sarah knows you're no joke either. I'm glad you aren't sitting out here with that-damn-gun on your lap."

"You're a-damn-lie," Mabel spoke as she flipped the book open, showing Dahlia the gun concealed inside. The pages were cut so the gun could fit inside the book with ease.

"Whoa, you are full of tricks and schemes."

"What they say? If you stay ready . . . you don't have to get ready? Well, I'm gon stay ready."

"Granny, you are way too much for me. At your age, you shouldn't be doing anything but going to church and enjoying life at bingo or something."

"I go to church and the God I serve knows my heart. And I don't like no-damn-bingo; that-damn-place's filled with old men and women, looking to hook-up with each other."

"Old people still out here trying to catch?" Dahlia questioned as she stared at the car. The windows were tinted, preventing her from seeing who was sitting in the car. The window was half-cracked. She could see someone moving.

"Because they're old don't mean they're dead. They still have needs just like anybody else."

"Oh no, Granny, spare my ears the details. I don't want to hear it."

"I'm just saying."

Dahlia listened to her grandmother as she continued to stare at the car. She wanted them to know they had seen them. After five minutes of Dahlia staring at the car, it pulled off.

"Dang, they have paper plates."

"They'll be back. I have a feeling they're looking for someone or something," Mabel spoke.

"Well, they're gone for right now. You should seriously call the police and at least let them know what's going on."

"I'm not calling them."

"You're just stubborn."

"Call me whatever you want. I saw on the news the lady called the police because someone in her building was fighting. They went to her door and now that woman's dead. I'm not fooling with the-damn-LAPD."

"The LAPD didn't have anything to do with that shooting."

"They did beat that woman on the freeway."

"Okay, Granny," Dahlia said.

No matter what she said, her grandmother wasn't going to call the police. If the car came back, she was calling the police.

"Here comes Granddaddy," Dahlia said, seeing her grandfather's truck coming down the street.

"Hey, baby. How did you get here? I don't see the car?" James said when he got out the car and embraced Dahlia for a hug.

"The tires on the rental were put on flat last night."

"That silly-girl that boy Antonio's messing with?" James questioned Dahlia.

"Yeah, I think so."

"Damn-shame. Where's the car now? And when is your car going to be ready? Have they called you?"

"I had it towed to my house last night. I haven't called the insurance and rental car place just yet. I talked to the repair shop. He said it should take two weeks to get my car back.

"Okay. How're you getting home tonight?"

"The same way I got here."

"How was that, child? I wasn't here."

"I got here in an Uber."

"I'll take you home. I don't trust that Uber-shit," James huffed.

"I am good, Granddaddy. You just got home from working. Go take a shower, get some food, and relax. You know the reruns of *Walker* are about to come on."

"I didn't ask your smart-ass any of that, did I?" James scolded. "Now like I said, I'm taking you home."

"Okay, Granddaddy," Dahlia replied. She knew she wouldn't win the argument with her grandfather. He, too, like his wife, was stubborn and set in his ways.

"Just let me go in here and use the restroom."

"Okay."

"You knew that man wasn't about to let you get into the car with some strange person by yourself."

"It's just like a taxi."

"I'd rather catch a bus then ride in a car with someone I've never seen before and don't know shit about."

"They send you a picture of the person. They also send you the license plate and the make and model of the car."

"Okay; I still don't trust it. Who's to say that person didn't make that shit up? I watch Lifetime."

"Let's go," James said, coming out the house, wiping his wet hands on the towel he kept in his back pocket.

The ride to Dahlia's house was filled with bickering between her grandparents. James was upset that Mabel hadn't told him right away someone had been sitting outside their home all day. Mabel argued she didn't want to make him paranoid while on the job. Dahlia agreed with both of them, but didn't say a word. She let them deal with it. She knew better than to get in what they called 'grown-folks' business'.

"Thank you for the ride, Granddaddy," Dahlia spoke, giving her grandfather a kiss on his cheek as she climbed out his truck.

"You're welcome. Dahlia, please get a-damn-restraining order or something in place. I can see it now you gon have to Ali her-ass again. We can't have you sitting in jail again for protecting yourself."

"I told her that," Mabel chimed in.

"I will, I promise," Dahlia informed.

"Good; now get in the house. We'll see you later. I love you."

"I love you, too, Granny," Dahlia smiled, kissing her grandmother's cheek. "Thanks again, Granddaddy. I love you."

"Any time, any time. I love you," James replied, cranking the engine on the old truck.

Dahlia was beyond over the day. She jumped in the shower and climbed into bed to finish reading the book she had started the other day. She read until her eyes no longer could hold themselves open.

Chapter 11

Dahlia was up bright and early. She had to be at the shop by eight a.m. to meet Traci and she had a ten a.m. with her client Keisha Kane. She was happy her team had reached back out to her to style her hair. Doing Keisha's hair was a major key in Dahlia building up her clientele. Enterprise had already sent someone out to exchange the rental car and document the damages.

Dahlia arrived at the shop two minutes after eight and was surprised to see Traci sitting in her chair waiting.

"Look what the cat dragged in. Traci, don't be late," she mimicked. "I got here ten minutes ago. It looks like my hair stylist is late." Traci laughed.

"Bitch, shut up. It took longer than I thought with the rental car people."

"I was going to call you and see if you needed a ride, then Charles sidetracked me." Traci giggled.

"You're nasty," Dahlia said and laughed.

"I'm married and keeping my husband satisfied is my job."

"I feel you on that," Dahlia said as she applied shampoo to Traci's hair. "Go to bowl three and I'll be right over."

"Okay."

Dahlia made her way to the back of the shop where Chandra's office was.

"Hey, D; come in. How is everything? You okay?" Chandra asked.

"I'm good. I just needed a few days to myself. Thanks for handling my clients for me. Here is my booth rent and a little something extra."

"Thank you." Chandra smiled as she flipped through the bills.

"I have a client, so let me get back out there." Dahlia stood to leave.

Although Chandra was good people, Dahlia didn't trust telling her what was going on in her life. Chandra was messy; she couldn't hold water. Whatever she knew about someone, the whole shop was going to know, and Dahlia had already learned her lesson with sharing her business, thinking she was a friend.

Dahlia made her way back to the front to start on Traci's hair.

"My bad. I had to speak to Chandra real quick."

"You didn't tell any of these messy-hoes your business, did you?" Traci questioned, looking around the shop. She knew they loved to gossip in the shop.

"Girl, you know I've already learned my lesson. I just told her I needed some time to myself."

"Good."

Dahlia and Traci made idle talk as Dahlia washed and blow-dried her hair. People began to trickle into the shop.

"Do you know how you want your hair? Or do I have to figure that out, too?" Dahlia laughed.

"Shut up. I actually saw a style on this girl on a show I watched last night," Traci said as she scrolled through the pictures in her phone.

"Welcome back, Dahlia. How are you?" Jessie asked as she approached them.

"Hey, girl; I'm good. I just needed a little break. How are you?" Dahlia asked, not caring one bit.

She could see it a mile away. Jessie was about to be on some bullshit.

"I'm good. I thought we were gon have to come drag you out that house. That man giving you problems?" Jessie questioned.

"I'm good," Dahlia repeated.

"If you say so. I saw that man who use to come in here for you with another girl this weekend at my cousin Crystal's baby shower," Jessie informed. "I told her that was my friend's man. She told me that he's her baby-daddy and you know all about her. She said she beat yo' ass and you had her arrested."

"That's real good for him. I would love to chat, but as you can see, I'm busy."

"D, you sure you good?"

"Isn't that what she said five minutes ago? She's good!" Traci spoke up.

She knew Jessie was being messy, trying to meddle in Dahlia's business and confirm that Dahlia was some side-chick. Traci wasn't having it.

"I'm good; I'm also busy," Dahlia said as she turned Traci's chair to face the mirror.

Although her back was to Jessie, she could see through the mirror the funky look on her face as she walked off.

"These-bitches be doing the-fuckin'-most," Traci huffed, pissed off.

"Girl, I'm not worried about Jessie's ass. She's messy and that's why her-ass never has any clients, because she's too busy being in everybody else's business, instead of tending to her own shit."

"I was real close to fuckin'-her-ass-up."

"Calm down, pit bull." Dahlia laughed because she knew Traci was serious. "This is my place of business for the moment, so I handle them with a long-handle spoon. I try my best not to let these catty women get to me in here. I'm here to build my clientele and get my money until I can get my own shop."

"I feel you; plus, I know you don't need help whupping ass." Traci Laughed.

"Shut up. Where-the-hell is this picture?"

"Awww shit; I forgot when that bald-headed-bitch started questioning you. I like this look. It's something different for me. I've never done bangs."

"I like it. I think it will be cute with your outfit."

"Okay; well, hook-a-sistah-up."

Dahlia slicked Traci's hair in a neat ponytail that hung down to the center of her back with a faux Chinese bang.

"I love it; thanks, D. You're always hooking-me-up. It's real nice to have my own personal stylist." Traci smiled, admiring herself in the mirror.

"Get yo' ass out my chair so I can get ready for my next client."

"Damn, you're kicking me out and shit?"

"You don't have to leave, but you gotta get that-ass out of this chair. I have other clients coming and I need all my coins."

"I feel you. I need to be going anyway. I have to go stack-up on snacks for the boys. They're having movie night. Here's your money with a little extra tip for being the-shit." Traci smiled, handing Dahlia some money.

"Bye, Traci. I'll see you later on tonight."

"I'm glad you're still going. I thought you were going to flake on me."

"I am not gonna flake. I need to go out and get some drinks and be around people other than these messy-hoes and your crazy-ass."

"I only turned crazy after bring your best friend and hangin' with your gun-toting-grandmother."

"Fuck you." Dahlia smiled. "Speaking of her, I had to take an Uber to her house last night because she said someone had been sitting in front of her house for hours. She was sitting on her porch with her gun discreetly tucked inside a book."

"See! She's straight gangsta. My granny would've turned off all the lights, locked herself in her room, and called the police." Traci laughed.

"She could have gotten herself hurt. She is fuckin'-crazy."

"She's bout it-bout it."

"Get out of here."

"See you tonight."

"Eight?" Dahlia questioned.

"Yes, eight o'clock."

When Traci left, Dahlia began to get ready for her next client. As she cleaned the hair from the floor by her station, she could see a clientless-Jessie hawking her. Dahlia paid her no mind. She really wasn't trying to gain any more enemies, but Jessie had brought the shit on herself. When she was finished, Dahlia took a seat in her chair as she waited for her next client to arrive. She scrolled through her Instagram hair page to see if there were any potential clients who wanted to book appointments.

"Where can I find Dahlia?" a raspy voice questioned, entering the shop.

"Over there," Jessie said with an attitude as she pointed the woman with the baseball cap and oversized shades in Dahlia's direction.

Dahlia looked up from her phone, not recognizing the woman under the cap and shades. On her defense, she stood up as the woman approached.

"Keisha Kane?" Dahlia questioned as the woman got closer.

"Yes, it's me," she spoke, removing her glasses. Her voice was much raspier than it sounded in her music.

"Hello; you look different from the pictures on social media."

"I know. Sometimes you have to take a break from all that extra-shit."

"You're still gorgeous. Welcome to Team D." Dahlia laughed at her corny statement. "I did some research on your previous looks and spoke to your team. I was told you wanted to try something new."

"I need a change. I'm growing as a woman and in my music, so I kinda want to change-up my look," Keisha informed.

"I feel you. I work with a hair distributor by the name of Roni with Oh So Posh Hair and she provided me with some hair. The hair is a natural body wave, so it gives that natural flow-wave pattern, but also straightens very straight. It's a natural dark brown with a tint of toffee coloring. I was thinking of a deep, feather side-part, with long, luscious curls. You would just have to pin the bang and apply some flexi-rods at night to maintain the curl pattern. You'll be going on a five-city club appearance, right?"

"I am. I love that you be on your shit. I don't know a lick about hair; I rap." She laughed. "So I need something I can maintain myself. I have a makeup artist who goes with me, but she doesn't really fuck-with-hair like that. Shit, her-ass is bald."

"Don't trip. Let me work my magic and I promise you'll love it," Dahlia said.

She'd taken the time to go over Keisha's pictures since she'd surfaced on the scene. She had rocked braids, bad weaves, and ponytails. She was on her way to becoming the queen of L.A.'s female rap game. She needed a look to say she'd invested in herself and she was "that-bitch".

Dahlia and Keisha made small talk as Dahlia braided and installed her hair. They exchanged stories on how each other had gotten started in their fields. She was surprised to hear about the tragic life events that had fueled Keisha to mentally escape through her lyrics. It took Dahlia a little over two hours to braid and install Keisha's new do. It was totally different than what she'd ever seen Keisha rock.

"Tell me what you think," Dahlia said, turning Keisha toward the full-length mirror at her booth.

Keisha stood and turned her head from one side to the next, inspecting the new look. Dahlia watched on pins-and-needles, hoping she liked it.

"I love it." Keisha smiled, pulling out her phone and snapping pictures of herself. "Thank you so much for putting up with all the back-and-forth and late cancellations. I really love this new look on me. I never do color because I never know what colors are going to look good on me."

"You are more than welcome."

"I most-def will be back to see you for more styles. I'm really feeling this," Keisha said as she slipped Dahlia four crispy, hundred-dollar bills. "Keep the change as a tip. You deserve it."

"Thank you. Enjoy the tour."

"Thanks," Keisha said as she headed out the door.

Dahlia was excited to now have Keisha on-board. She needed an up-and-coming star to take her online presence and clientele to another level. Dahlia cleaned the hair from around her station. Her last client for the day was due any minute. Just as she finished cleaning her area up, she saw Shoney walking through the door, but she headed to Jessie's station.

"Hey, Shoney," Dahlia spoke, curious.

"Hey, D; I forgot to cancel with you. I hope you don't mind. I like the way Jessie braided my hair the last time."

"Shoney, you're good. Dahlia doesn't mind. She has a long client list. She won't even miss you," Jessie spoke. The envy in her words let Dahlia know she was on some shady-shit that had started way before today.

"Jessie's right; I don't mind. Keeping my clients happy is my only goal. If you ever want to come back home, you know my number. Jessie, make sure you don't pull her edges too tight. Shoney, you still using the oil twice a week?"

"Yes, I am. That-shit keeps my hair moist and I can see it growing," Shoney replied.

"Good, keep it up. You ladies have a wonderful day." Dahlia smiled at Shoney and Jessie.

Dahlia wasn't bothered by Jessie stealing Shoney from her. She knew it was part of working in a shop and missing days, or clients coming in for walk-ins without calling and getting a new stylist who was cheaper. You lose one client and gain another; plus, Dahlia knew Shoney would be back. Jessie was always late and extremely messy. Dahlia packed her bag so she could hit the mall to look for something to wear for the night. She had a closet full of clothes, but nothing came to mind to wear.

After two whole hours, several stores, and trying on way-too-many dresses, Dahlia left the mall empty-handed. She couldn't find anything that fit her well or looked good on her. She came to the conclusion she would have to settle for something in her closet to wear.

Dahlia made it home with enough time to take a long bubble bath and relax. Dahlia checked her mailbox, which was stuffed with mail since she had been forgetting to grab it when she came in. Struggling to open the door with all the mail in her hand, Dahlia dropped some. Finally, getting the door open, Dahlia bent over to pick up the mail that fell.

"WHAT-THE-FUCK?" Dahlia yelled.

Right before her eyes on her front porch was a dead cat. She was so disgusted she could have barfed. Dahlia almost trampled on the mail trying to rush to get in her house, leaving her shoes at the doorstep.

"I'M SICK OF THIS BITCH!" Dahlia yelled, flopping on the sofa to call the City pound to have the cat removed from her front door.

Dahlia was on hold for ten minutes before the automated system told her the office was closed for the day and to call back. She was on the verge of tears; she was just that pissed off. Dahlia was terrified of cats; leaving one slaughtered on her porch had her furious.

BUZZZZZ! Her phone bounced on the end table. She saw Jerome's name flash across the screen. She wasn't in the mood to talk. She picked up the phone to send him to voicemail.

"Hello? Dahlia?" Jerome called out.

"Fuck!" Dahlia mumbled. She realized she had answered the call, instead of sending him to voicemail. "Hey, Jerome," she replied dryly.

"How are you?" he questioned.

"I'm good."

"It doesn't sound like it. You sure you good. How's the car?"

"Enterprise came and replaced it with another one."

"Have you gone and put that restraining order in place?"

"Not yet, but after today, I will first thing Monday morning."

"What happened today?" Jerome questioned, genuinely concerned.

"I just got home and found a slaughtered cat on my front porch."

"What kind of crazy-shit are you into?" Jerome joked.

"Do you hear me laughing?" Dahlia questioned with an attitude.

"I'm sorry. I was just trying to make you laugh. Do you have someone to come clean it up?"

"I called the City pound. They're closed for the day and don't reopen until Monday morning. I was just about to call my granddaddy before you called."

"I am not too far from your house. If you don't mind, I can swing by and clean it up for you. There's no sense in calling your grandfather to come across the freeway when I'm not that far away."

"No, it's okay. My grandfather isn't going to mind coming to my rescue. He's my Superman," Dahlia informed.

She didn't want to seem like some damsel-in-distress who always needed help. She knew he was feeling her way more than she liked.

"I understand, but let's look at the reality of things. In the time it would take your grandfather to get to your house, I could have the porch cleaned up," Jerome said.

Dahlia sat and pondered the thought for a moment. The mere thought of the cat dead on her porch made her stomach turn and she wanted it gone fast, or she wasn't leaving the house.

"Okay; I'll leave the door open." Dahlia gave in.

"I will be there within five minutes."

"Okay," Dahlia replied, ending the call.

She began to call security companies to get quotes and see who could get out to her house the fastest. She wanted to catch Jasmine in the act of being on her property. First thing in the morning, she was going to get a restraining order.

Dahlia heard a car pull into her driveway and peeked outside to see Jerome stepping out his car looking like he was on his way to a video shoot, not to clean a dead cat off a porch. Dahlia watched him as he made his way to the back of this car and retrieved a nice-size duffle bag.

'What-in-the-hell is he doing with that?' Dahlia thought, seeing him heading in her direction.

Dahlia didn't want to make it seem as if she had been waiting on his arrival by the door, so she took a seat on the couch and scrolled through her phone.

"It's Jerome," he spoke, knocking on the door before opening it.

"I'm in here," Dahlia replied.

"Yo, somebody wanted to really fuck-with-you; that's a big-ass-cat," Jerome stated, coming through the door.

"Did you really have to come in here and remind me there's a fat-ass-cat on my porch that's dead?"

"My bad. Is there somewhere I can change to take care of that for you?"

"The bathroom is the second door to the right." Dahlia pointed in that direction.

"Okay; do you have any big trash bags and maybe some gloves?"

"Yeah; while you change out of your expensive clothes, I will grab those items for you."

"Thank you." Jerome chuckled at her statement.

Dahlia got up to retrieve the items Jerome had requested. She sat them close to the front door.

"Where can I sit this bag until I'm done?" Jerome questioned, coming into the living room dressed down in all-black.

"You can leave it on the couch."

"Cool; I know it may be farfetched, but do you have a shovel or rake?"

"I think my granddaddy left his rake in my garage. I can open it for you, but I'm not stepping foot out of this house until you've removed that-damn-cat," Dahlia informed him.

Jerome wanted to laugh at the serious look on Dahlia's face, but he knew she would chew him out again for laughing at her because she saw nothing funny.

"I'll go look," he said, heading out the door, grabbing the trash bags and gloves.

Dahlia watched as he took a further look at the cat that had gnats and maggots coming from the open wounds. Dahlia couldn't look; she took a seat on the couch and flicked through the TV to her recorded shows. She had missed last week's episode of *Blue Bloods*. It took Jerome close to twenty minutes just to remove and dispose of the cat, then get the porch washed down. He'd found some cleaning products in the garage and used them.

"All done. I used some stuff from the garage to clean off the porch. I hope you don't mind."

"That's fine as long as you got that nasty-shit off the porch," Dahlia spoke, pressing pause on the TV remote.

"I did. I'm just curious to why someone would leave a dead cat on your porch? Like what's the purpose?"

"I am terrified of cats," Dahlia admitted.

"Do you think it's ol' girl who put your tires on flat?"

"Yeah; I don't have beef with anyone else."

"I'm still not understanding the whole dead cat, like killing a cat and leaving it on someone's porch. What kind-of-shit are they into?"

"Antonio, the last dude I messed with—I told him. When Shad was pissed and didn't want me to leave the house, he would sit cat food on the porch so the stray cats would gravitate to our porch. He knew I absolutely would not go outside. One day, he left before any cats came, so I replaced the cat food with bleach, which kept the cats away, then I left the house. I would do this as much as I could when I wanted to leave the house. "

"Damn, that's deep."

"Who you telling? I had to live it. The only people who knew about this were Traci, Shad, Antonio, and now, you."

"I'm sorry you had to go through that. Any real man wouldn't put his woman—hell, anyone— through some shit-like-that. That-nigga must really have some-damn-screws missing in his head!" Jerome spat, furious that Shad had put Dahlia through so much. Dahlia was a woman who needed to be cherished and treated like a queen, yet Shad had treated her like she was some hoodrat he'd found down at the strip club.

"I'm not sure. I'm just glad I no longer have to deal with him and his-shit."

"Good for you. You deserve much more than what those two fools were offering. What do you have planned for the night? You want to go grab something to eat?"

"That would be nice, but I already have plans. I'm going out with Traci."

"Okay. Where are you ladies going, if you don't mind sharing?"

"To a party for her co-worker's birthday. I'm not sure where it is though."

"Well, I hope you enjoy yourself tonight. Do you mind if I use your shower?"

"My shower?" Dahlia questioned.

"Yes; I was sweating removing that big-ass-thing from the porch. A nigga needs to freshen up."

"Sure, you can use the shower. You know where the bathroom is. Do you need any towels?"

"Nah, I'm good. I have my own."

"So, is that your overnight hoe-bag?" Dahlia laughed.

"Damn, like that? Hoe bag? Why I gotta be all that because I like to keep extra stuff in my car? You never know what might happen or where you'll be stuck." Jerome laughed, grabbing his bag and making his way to the bathroom.

Dahlia grabbed the remote and continued watching TV as she heard the shower turn on.

Twenty minutes later, Jerome emerged from the bathroom, dressed in a Nike track suit with matching Airmax 95's on his feet. His eyes were occupied on his phone as his fingers moved rapidly, so he didn't see Dahlia staring at him.

"You smell good. What is that you have on? You going to see someone special?" Dahlia questioned.

She had never smelled the fragrance before, but the aura of it was enough to make any woman moist between her legs.

"I thought I was already in the presence of someone special," Jerome spoke, staring Dahlia right in the eyes.

Dahlia blushed, looking away. Jerome was putting it on thick.

"The fragrance I'm wearing is Bois 1920, the Come La Luna fragrance selection," Jerome spoke, pulling the small gold bottle of cologne from his bag.

Dahlia inspected the fancy bottle. "Smell's good. Never heard of the fragrance. I might have to look it up. Where did you get it?" Dahlia was curious. She was interested in buying her grandfather something for all he'd done for her in the last few days.

"Barneys." He smiled.

"Check you out, baller." Dahlia laughed.

"Far from a baller. I just like to look and smell good. I work hard; I deserve to splurge a little on myself every once in a while." He smiled.

"I feel you on that one."

"I'm gon get myself out of here. Again, I hope you enjoy yourself tonight."

"Thanks, and thank you again for coming to get that-shit off my porch. I owe you one for that."

"It wasn't a problem. Glad I could be of service. I would like to cash in my IOU for lunch or dinner tomorrow."

Dahlia really wanted to decline, but he'd had come to her rescue twice this week. He at least deserved a dinner date.

"I won't make any promises, but hit me tomorrow to see where I am and what I'm doing," Dahlia said, standing at the door waiting for Jerome to leave.

"Okay, and don't forget to just relax and enjoy yourself tonight," Jerome said, placing his arm around Dahlia and pulling her in for a hug.

"I will," Dahlia replied.

She could feel his semi-erect penis against her thigh, slightly arousing the horny woman inside her, which hadn't received any attention in a while. Dahlia pulled away quickly.

"Drive safely now," she spoke.

Jerome turned and smiled as he threw his duffle bag on his back seat and slid into the driver's seat.

Dahlia exhaled deeply, throwing herself on the couch to finish watching *Blue Bloods* until it was time to start getting ready to go out with Traci.

Chapter 12

Dahlia turned to get comfortable. Noticing the room was dark, she looked at the cable box to check the time. It was almost seven p.m. "Shit!" Dahlia groaned, pulling herself up from the sofa. She hadn't even realized she'd fallen asleep. She jumped in the shower to wake herself up.

Dahlia stood in front of her closet trying to figure out what she would wear to the party Traci was forcing her to go to. Everything she tried on, she found a flaw in how it looked on her. She went through pants, dresses, and skirts, and nothing was appealing to her eye.

Dahlia looked over to the clock and knew Traci was due any minute at her house. She was hoping Traci would be typical-Traci and be late, to give her some extra time. Dahlia searched her closet one more time and settled on an eggshell-colored strapless dress that stopped at her knees and clung to her every curve of her plush frame. She paired it with multi-colored, sling-back pumps. She let her curly mane hang free.

Just as she'd thought, Traci pranced through the door at nine o'clock, an hour after she was due to arrive. Dahlia was finishing up the final touches of her makeup.

"Now that's the Dahlia I know. Push through, bitch, push through." Traci laughed, looking her best friend over. When they said big women were sloppy and couldn't dress, they weren't talking about Dahlia. A solid size twenty, she always made sure she was laid and slayed from her hair and clothes to her makeup.

"You know when I dress, it's always to impress," Dahlia said seductively, doing her best catwalk.

"That's right. Now would you do my makeup, please?" Traci begged.

"I knew your late-ass was gonna ask that."

"Well, then, you should have been ready for me, shit."

"Just sit your-ass down. We're already late because you don't know how to get anywhere on time."

"We'll get there when everyone else gets there. You know black people are always late. Nobody wants to be the first one at a party."

Traci always had an excuse for why she was late; she never admitted she was just slow and always late. Dahlia shook her head as she applied the makeup to Traci's face.

"Sounds like a bunch of excuses to me, but that's just me."

"You act like you're always on time."

"This isn't about me," Dahlia spoke.

Traci just sat there and let Dahlia do her talking.

"Go check out your makeup so we can go."

"As always, I look good, thanks to my dearest best friend in the whole, wide world." Traci smiled, checking herself out.

"You sound like a little kid. Let's go before I decide to stay my-ass here."

"That's what isn't going to happen. Let's go so we can get our party on." Traci popped her butt.

"Don't be popping that all around my house. Keep that-shit at your house for your man; that's the only nigga trying to see that-shit."

"Whatever," Traci said.

They made their way out the house just as the Uber was arriving. Since they both wanted to drink, they'd decided to take an Uber so no one would be drinking and driving. Traci's husband had agreed to come pick them up.

Dahlia and Traci talked about the past week's events until the Uber turned into an exclusive neighborhood.

"Wow! Are you sure you have the right address?" Dahlia questioned, looking at all the ritzy homes the Uber was passing.

"That's what's on the invitation that was sent to me," Traci said, handing Dahlia the invitation.

Dahlia looked over the invitation then back to the house they were in front of; they were in the right place.

"Hello; welcome to the Beverly Hills Estate. Are you here for the Black-and-White Affair?" the woman on the intercom asked.

"Yes," Traci replied.

"Can you provide me with your names?"

"Traci Davis and Dahlia Willowbrook."

"Just one moment."

There was a brief moment of silence before the large gate opened up. "Have a wonderful time, ladies, and enjoy The Beverly Hills Estate."

"Thank you," Traci replied as the driver pulled through the gate.

The car traveled down a long pathway then around the long, wraparound driveway that led to the most-beautiful home Dahlia and Traci had ever seen. Men waited on each side of the car.

"Welcome to The Beverly Hills Estate; I am Jose. Do you need valet service?" he questioned, reaching out his hand for Traci's hand.

"No, we're being dropped off, but thank you." Traci smiled, accepting his hand.

The man led Traci over to the side of the car where another man waited for her with Dahlia. The man led Dahlia and Traci into the home that was breathtaking.

"This is beautiful," Dahlia said, looking around.

It looked like a home she would have only imagined she would ever step foot in, something she use to see on MTV's *Cribs*.

"It is," Traci replied, caught up in looking at all the breathtaking art covering the entrance way.

"I'm glad you could make it," Jennifer, Traci's co-worker, said from the top of the staircase. "I'll be down in a second," she said.

"She works with you?" Dahlia whispered to Traci.

"Yes; I don't see how she can afford this. I make more than she does. Hell, it isn't my business. The less I know the better if her-ass is doing some illegal-shit," Traci whispered back.

"Here she comes," Dahlia whispered as she watched the woman approach them.

Jennifer took her time coming down the left side of the staircase. She was dressed to perfection in a long, black, beaded evening gown.

"You look gorgeous, Traci. I'm so happy you were able to make it," she spoke, embracing Traci in a hug.

"I told you I would. This is Dahlia, my best friend," Traci said.

"Hello, Dahlia; I am Jennifer. I work with Traci. I'm glad you were able to make it out to my party." She smiled at Dahlia.

"Nice to meet you, and it's my pleasure. This is a beautiful place."

"Isn't it? It was a treat from my husband," Jennifer said and beamed.

"Does he have a brother? Dahlia's single," Traci uttered.

"Shut your mouth." Dahlia eyed Traci. "I'm not looking for anyone. Don't pay her any attention. She's just talking."

"No-the-hell I'm not. She needs a man. We'd prefer one with some money, too."

"There will be a lot of single men here, don't worry." Jennifer smiled. "Come this way, ladies; let me show you around," Jennifer said as she led the way around the house and showed them every detail of the mansion.

The house was filled with marble floors and granite countertops; crystal chandeliers hung from the ceilings and large paintings decorated the walls. The foyer alone was larger than Dahlia's whole house. Many party-goers hung out and chatted in the foyer, which was next to a room that served as a bar. It was stocked with every liquor you could think of.

"Jennifer, you outdid yourself for this party," Traci remarked.

"Right; your husband truly loves you. I know this ran his pockets deep." Dahlia laughed.

"After nearly thirty years of being married and four kids, supporting all his dreams, goals, and aspirations, this isn't hardly enough. For all-the-shit I've put up with, I deserve my own private island," Jennifer whispered.

"Now, on that, I feel you. Marriage is work," Traci added, having survived her own marriage highs and lows.

"Like I tell my daughters, let a man be a man, but never play the fool. Get all you can for a rainy day. Make him treat you like a-damn-queen if he wants to be the king," Jennifer schooled. "Now c'mon, ladies; let's have a wonderful time at my party. I plan on getting drunk-as-shit so I can sleep the whole plane ride to Bora Bora in the morning."

"He's taking you on a trip, too?" Dahlia questioned.

"Girl, yes; for two whole weeks. I can't wait to relax away from kids, grandkids, and work."

"Where is his brother, cousin? Hell, I'll take an uncle!" Dahlia laughed.

"There are a few of them-fools around here. When I come back from that, I'm going on my annual trip with two of my girlfriends to Jamaica. You ladies should join us. It will be fun and it's super-cheap."

"I'll give it some thought and run it past my husband."

"If Traci goes, I'm down. I need a vacation."

"Well, once I get back in town, I'll let you know all the details. Let me go mingle with everyone and make my rounds. Ladies, it's an open bar that's full of all kinds of liquor. Enjoy yourself," Jennifer said. Then she danced to the music over to the next group of people to mingle.

"I'm going home and telling Charles, next year for my thirtieth birthday, he'd better step it up." Traci laughed as they made their way to the bar.

"Traci, hush. Charles always goes out for you. You heard her say she's had to put up with a lot of bullshit to get this place rented for the party. Hell, this-shit is lovely, but I'd rather have the money."

"I know that. Charles and I have had our ups-and-downs in marriage. The highs outweigh the lows, and that's for sure. I just want to be able to go on a trip with just me and my man, without my bad-ass kids," Traci admitted.

"In due time, you and Charles will be able to do all of that and more. I just don't want you to be going hard on my homeboy because of what someone else's man is doing for them. We don't know how much-shit they're putting up with," Dahlia spoke.

She admired Charles and Traci's marriage. They had been through the fire and made it out, and she was a living witness. They had God in their marriage, and as her grandmother had told her, "God is the glue that holds marriages together and keeps the foundation solid." Traci and Charles had been high school sweethearts. They had been together since they were fifteen years old and shared two young boys together.

"You don't have to tell me that. I know that. I just want to know if you're listening to what you're telling me?" Traci questioned.

"Yes, and I'll apply everything I just told you. I've learned from my past relationships," Dahlia replied as they made their way to the bar.

"Can I get a pineapple Ciroc with a splash of cranberry juice?" Dahlia ordered.

"You can make that two," Traci added.

"I have two pineapple Cirocs with a splash of cranberry juice coming up," the bartender repeated as he made his way to the other side of the bar to make their drinks. The bartender returned in no time with their drinks.

"Thank you," Dahlia and Traci said in unison as they grabbed their drinks and made their way to the dance floor.

Song after song, Dahlia and Traci danced and partied like old times. After the fifth song, Dahlia was tired. The shoes she'd worn were meant to be cute in, not to become the dancehall queen in.

Dahlia excused herself from the dance floor to let her feet rest.

"I think the beautiful woman needs a glass of water," a male's voice spoke from the side of Dahlia.

"Thanks; I could've ordered it myself." Dahlia smiled, trying to catch her breath.

"It isn't a problem. Are you okay? You look a little flustered. Here, take my seat," the man insisted, getting up from the stool.

"Thank you, but you don't have to give up your seat." Dahlia smiled.

"It's my pleasure."

"Well, thank you. That was really nice of you to do that."

"You're welcome. You look familiar," the man spoke.

Dahlia hadn't paid him much attention until then.

"I don't get out much and you don't look familiar," Dahlia spoke.

"I can't place where I have seen you before, but I have. I can always remember a beautiful face. You enjoy the rest of your night," he spoke. His voice was smooth and charming.

"You do the same," Dahlia blushed, just hearing him tell her she was beautiful. She hadn't heard those words in a while.

Dahlia turned and faced the crowd of people getting their groove on. The DJ was good. He had played music for every age range in the building.

"This DJ is the-shit." Traci danced in front of Dahlia to Uncle Luke's hit jam, *Me So Horny*.

"I think you've had way-too-many drinks tonight." Dahlia laughed at Traci's offbeat dance moves.

"I don't think you've had enough. You're sitting down. We came to a party, so let's party."

"My feet are hurting, and you still don't have a lick of rhythm."

"Don't be hating on me; but, what I want to know is, who was that man you were over here talking to?"

"What man are you talking about?"

"Dahlia, the one who gave up his seat for you. I was dancing, but I was watching, so what was he saying? I saw the both of you smiling."

"Just some man who gave up his seat for me because I was out of breath."

"I saw how he was looking at you, even when he was walking off."

"You've had way-too-many drinks. *That-man* ordered me some water and gave me his seat because he thought my fat-ass was about to pass out," Dahlia replied, laughing.

"Yeah, okay. Bartender, can I get a glass of ice water with a lemon, please?" Traci ordered.

"Sure; coming right up." The bartender smiled.

"Are you ladies having a great time?" Jennifer questioned.

"Yes; where did you find that DJ? He's jammin'; that's how you turn-a-party-up."

"The DJ is my son; he's my youngest."

"He's good with the DJ-stuff," Dahlia commented, rocking her head to the latest Chris Brown song coming through the speakers.

"It's what he wants to do. As his mother, I support him, so I told him he could DJ my party. I'm glad you ladies are loving his skills," Jennifer said, her eyes focused somewhere else. "I'll be right back, ladies."

"Okay," Traci said.

"OH, THIS IS MY JAM!" Dahlia yelled, jumping up from the bar stool and dancing in front of her seat.

"Hmmm . . . Watch where you move that thang; you might hurt somebody," a deep voice spoke, causing Dahlia to stop dancing.

Dahlia and Traci looked at the man up and down who had approached with a wide grin on his face.

Dahlia stared for a moment without speaking; his face was familiar.

"I'm sorry," Dahlia spoke, moving the bar stool over a little and sitting back down.

"I'm not. I might like to be hurt." His eyes roamed Dahlia's frame. "You are beautiful."

"Thank you." Dahlia faked a smile. She was creeped-out by the tall man with the salt-and-pepper hair. He was much older than any man she would ever date—well, again, at least. He reeked of money. From his custom suit, diamond cufflinks, Cartier watch, to his Gucci loafers. Dahlia knew his face, but she didn't know from where.

"There you are. I was looking around for you," Jennifer spoke, putting her hand on the man's back.

"I came to tell the bartender to have his help start pouring the champagne for my toast." The man smiled, then placed a gentle kiss on Jennifer's lips. "Are you enjoying your night, honey?" he questioned.

Dahlia and Traci sat with their mouths wide open.

"I am. I have a nice reward waiting once this is over," Jennifer whispered, but not low enough because Dahlia and Traci heard every word.

"I'll be anticipating the ride." He winked, smacking her on her butt as their lips locked in a passionate kiss.

"Hey, ladies, I'm sorry about that. We were lost in our own little world. This is my husband, Wesley. No, correction: the Honorable Judge Wesley Weston." Jennifer beamed. "This is my co-worker Traci and her best friend. I'm sorry I forgot your name."

"Dahlia, Dahlia Willowbrook. It's nice to meet you, Judge." Dahlia smiled.

Wesley's eyes bulged at the mention of her last name. Traci nudged Dahlia, catching the look the judge gave.

"Likewise; are you ladies enjoying the party?"

"We are," Traci replied.

"Yes; this place is lovely. I told Jennifer earlier, she is very lucky," Dahlia added.

"I like to think I'm the lucky one. This one came and saved my life. My wife is a real gem," Wesley spoke.

"Oh, stop it." Jennifer blushed.

The man who had given his seat to Dahlia approached and wrapped his arm around Jennifer's husband Wesley's shoulder and whispered something to him.

"It was nice meeting you, ladies. I hope you continue to enjoy the party." He smiled as he was about to walk away with the man who had approached.

"Wait," Jennifer called out. "Dahlia, this is my nephew Gavyn. Gavyn, this is a mutual friend of mine," Jennifer spoke, pointing to Dahlia.

"Nice to meet you." He smiled and reached his hand out to shake Dahlia's.

"Likewise." Dahlia half-smiled, not liking being put-on-blast.

"Wesley, would you let the driver know Sharon needs to be taken home? She's had way-too-much to drink," Jennifer informed.

"I will."

"Thank you."

"Jennifer, would you point me in the direction of the ladies' room?" Dahlia questioned.

"It's down the hall to your right." Jennifer pointed in the direction of the bathroom.

"Thank you. Traci, I'll be right back."

"Okay."

As Dahlia made her way out of the restroom, she bumped into Gavyn.

"I don't mean to bug; I didn't catch your name."

"It's Dahlia."

"Yes, Dahlia, I think I know where I know you from. Do you happen to do hair?" he questioned.

"Yes, I do," Dahlia replied.

"You did my grandmother's hair."

"Who is your grandmother?"

"Janice."

"Oh, yeah; she's one of my new clients. How is she?"

"She's fine. Crazy-as-hell, but she's good."

"That's good. I'm sorry I didn't remember meeting you. There's been a lot going on. I'll have to let her know I ran into you again." Dahlia smiled.

"You can leave it out. Next thing you know, she'll try to get you to hook me up with someone. She insists, since I'm nearly thirty-years-old, I should be married with the kids by now." Gavyn smiled, showcasing his white teeth.

"Yeah, I know the feeling; sounds just like my grandmother." Dahlia laughed, thinking how much Ms. Janice reminded her of her own grandmother.

"I'M NOT GOING NO-FUCKIN'-WHERE!" a woman yelled coming down the hall. "TELL THAT-BITCH TO PUT ME OUT IF SHE WANTS ME OUT!"

Wesley rushed behind her, stroking her shoulders.

"This is her night. You're doing too much," he spoke in a hush tone.

When he looked up and noticed Dahlia and Gavyn in the hall, he backed up a little from the woman.

"Gavyn, can you see that Sharon gets a car to take her home. She's drunk," Wesley spoke, looking dead at Dahlia.

"I got you, Unc. Just go make sure Jennifer's enjoying her night," Gavyn spoke, shaking his head.

"Enjoy the rest of your night, Dahlia," he spoke as he made his way to the drunken woman leaning against the wall for balance.

"You do the same, Gavyn," Dahlia replied, proceeding back down the hall.

"What kind of peeing did you do? You've been gone forever," Traci said once Dahlia finally made it back to her seat at the bar.

"I think we should leave. This party is going to get a whole lot more interesting. I can feel it," Dahlia told Traci, filling her in on what had occurred in the hall.

"That's a-damn-shame, and why did you have to give his-ass your full name? Do you know that man? Is he the one who convicted your father?" Traci questioned.

"No; I gave his cheating-ass my last name because I wanted him to know I was someone who's related to Sham."

"Sham? As in your auntie?"

"Yes. You remember last year when she ended up in the hospital and she wouldn't tell us what happened?"

"Yeah; we just left it alone and thought she was covering for a nothin'-ass-dude she was fuckin'-with, or someone's wife had beat her ass."

"Well, one day she wanted to borrow money. I made her tell me what happened. Sham had been messing with this judge, and when he was done and said he'd moved on to something else, Sham said she would tell his wife. He beat her so she wouldn't tell and threatened to say they'd made a mistake in some cases he'd had dropped for her."

"What-in-the-hell?" Traci asked, flabbergasted.

"How long have you been working with her?"

"For the last two years. I had no clue that was her husband. I'd heard from other people that Judge Weston is a trick. Jennifer only showed me pictures of her kids," Traci informed.

Judge Weston was known around the Los Angeles area for tricking his money on women. Most of them were young girls who came through his courtroom for small things or dumb things, looking for a quick way to not pay for tickets or serve jail time.

"Sham got into a fight and was arrested and ended up in Judge Weston's courtroom. Using her gift of gab after court, she ended up in bed with the judge. For months, they had a fling. He had all of her cases dropped and was giving her money, but like all men, he fucked Sham when he wanted and how he wanted. She had put a price tag on herself and he had bought her.

"When he was done, he dropped her like a bad habit. Addicted to the money he was giving her, Sham threatened to call his wife and let her know he was creeping with her and a few other women. Like he always did, he rented a penthouse suite and called Sham over for their weekly freak-fest. When Sham got there, he laid out his demands. When Sham didn't agree, he laid hands on her and dropped her off at the hospital with a fracture rib."

"Wow! I'm at a loss for words. This is a small-fuckin'-world," Traci spoke, replaying what Dahlia had just told her over in her head.

"Then, he has the nerve to flirt with me at his wife's party and doesn't even know who I am to her. I could work with her," Dahlia blurted. She felt bad for Jennifer. Wesley was a serial cheater.

"Can we get everyone to head outside to the front?" the DJ said through the speakers.

"Let's go see what's going on?" Traci said, sliding off the bar stool.

"All right," Dahlia agreed, and followed closely behind Traci as a herd of people rushed out the door.

When Dahlia and Traci made it outside, a crowd of people stood around Jennifer and her husband.

"Thank you to everyone who came out tonight to help this beautiful woman, who also happens to be my wife of a very long time, celebrate another year.

"Baby, I hope you enjoyed your night and that the party turned out to be everything you imagined it would be," Wesley spoke, grabbing Jennifer by the hand. "I know you've been asking for this gift for the last few months. I heard all the hints you dropped." He chuckled. "This is just another small token of my appreciation for always standing by my side all of these years, for giving me four beautiful children, and simply for being you," he added as a shiny, white Porsche truck with a big red bow wrapped around it was pulled in front of the crowd.

A man stepped out the car and walked around to where Jennifer was standing. "I'm looking for Jennifer Weston."

"That would be me," Jennifer spoke, raising her hand.

"Well then, these keys are for you. Enjoy your new car." The man smiled, handing her the keys to her new car.

"HAPPY BIRTHDAY, BABY!" Wesley yelled, embracing Jennifer and planting a kiss on her forehead.

The crowd erupted in ooohs and ahhhs, and few grunts, followed by people walking off, complaining.

"There sure is a bunch of bitter-bitches in here tonight." Traci laughed.

"There sure is and a lot of lustful eyes," Dahlia replied.

She had lost count of how many times Wesley had eye-fucked her since she'd first encountered him. Dahlia turned to face Jennifer, inspecting her new ride.

"I think you have a crush lurking at this party."
Traci nudged Dahlia.

"Fuck-a-crush; that man is a-fuckin'-creep,"
Dahlia lashed out.

"Who? The man I saw you talking to several
times tonight with a smile on your face?"

"What are you talking about? I'm talking about
Wesley's creepy-ass."

"I'm not talking about him. I'm talking about
him in the white suit."

Dahlia turned to see who Traci was talking about
and locked eyes with Gavyn.

"You talking about Gavyn?"

"You know his name and everything." Traci
grinned.

"Traci, stop it. I know his name because he told
me. I did his grandmother's hair."

"I think Mr. Chocolate has a crush on you. He
isn't looking at you like his grandmother's hair
dresser."

"Traci, you've had too many drinks; that-man
was only being nice."

"I haven't had *enough* to drink. I don't know if
you have forgotten the signs of when someone is

checking for you, but I haven't. Mr. Chocolate Gavyn is checking for you," Traci informed.

Dahlia just shook her head and laughed at Traci as she turned slightly. Sure enough, Gavyn was checking her out. Dahlia smiled coyly back at him before turning to go back into the house. Gavyn was handsome, a lot thinner than she liked. Standing at least six feet, Gavyn looked to be about two hundred pounds. His white suit fit him perfectly and complimented his dark-chocolate skin and perfect, bright-white teeth that sat between two deep dimples on his cheeks. Although he was handsome, Dahlia wasn't ready to put herself back out there like that for another man. She still needed time.

"Now, tell me I'm crazy?" Traci asked once they'd stepped back in the house and Dahlia was still wearing a smile.

"Whatever, Traci," Dahlia replied, not wanting to admit Traci was right.

The ladies ordered another round of drinks and continued to party for another few rounds of songs.

"My feet have had it for the night. I'm ready to go," Dahlia said as she wobbled to the bar area to take a seat.

"Yeah, I think it's time. My kids will be up in a few hours wanting breakfast. Bartender, can I get a cranberry juice on ice?" Traci ordered, standing next to Dahlia. "I'm going to step away and call Charles so he can be on his way. Get my drink for me."

"Okay."

The party was slowly dying down and clearing out. Many people had left right after Jennifer's lavish gift. Dahlia had her head down looking at her phone and didn't see Traci walk back up.

"D, remember what you told me earlier about that woman?"

"What?" Dahlia looked at Traci, confused.

"Some-shit is about to go down," Traci spoke, pointing at Jennifer.

The look on Jennifer's face said she was pissed as she pushed party-goers out of her way, marching across the room.

"Yeah, something's going on. She looks furious."

"I wanted at least to tell Jennifer bye, but shit, she looks pissed. I'll just have to text her tomorrow. I don't need to check-a-bitch for lashing out at me because she's going through something," Traci said, drinking the rest of the cranberry juice she'd ordered. "Charles is on his way. Let's wait outside."

Dahlia and Traci were making their way to the front entrance to leave when they heard a loud, crashing sound followed by a loud commotion. People began to surround around whatever was going on. Curiosity got the best of Dahlia and Traci, and they moved closer to the crowd of people to see what was going on.

Jennifer was dragging the woman Dahlia had seen Wesley talking to earlier by her hair.

"FUCK YOU, WESLEY!" she yelled. Tears coated her cheeks.

Wesley followed behind Jennifer, pleading for her to let the woman go as he was zipping up his pants.

"Jennifer, baby, just let her go. We can work this out in private, between just us."

"Save that bullshit! I'm tired of covering up bullshit, lies, and the-fuckin'-cheating! I've had enough of you, muthafucka. This shit ends here! Now! At my birthday party? Really? You just had to get your dick sucked *at my birthday party* by another woman? Hell, the bitch who's supposed to be my best friend? A woman I would have given the shirt off my back for?"

"It isn't like that, Jennifer!" the woman cried.

"SHUT-THE-FUCK-UP, SHARON, BEFORE I REALLY EMBARRASS YO' ASS IN FRONT OF EVERYONE IN HERE, YOU SNEAKY-BITCH!" Jennifer ranted, tugging on the woman's hair even more.

She dragged her like she was a five-year-old girl dragging a doll around the house.

"I am more pissed that you couldn't have picked a better-bitch. This-bitch doesn't look better than me. What is it she has that I don't for you to cheat on me with her?!" Jennifer questioned.

"Nothing, baby. I was tripping; it was mistake. I messed up," Wesley admitted.

"HE'S LYING!" The woman yelled, tears in her eyes. "HE SAID YOU FUCK LIKE AN OLD WOMAN THESE DAYS AND REFUSE TO SUCK HIS DICK!" the woman blurted out, leaving everyone's mouth wide open. "HE WANTS A DIVORCE!"

"Oh really? Well, I'm glad you let this-bitch do the job. I won't suck your dick because I don't know where-the-hell it's been. If it's been in this-bitch's pussy, never in a million years will it ever touch me again. Remember, I know everything about this-bitch, including the STD's she's had and all the men she's slept with. Let's not forget the countless abortions."

Wesley was getting agitated with Jennifer; the look on his face said so. "Can we just talk about this later, once everyone's gone? We don't need everyone in our business!"

"I don't give-a-damn about these people! I'm tired. Fuck what they think! That's why I stayed with you this long, because I cared what they thought. You don't; why should I? Thank you for always making everything about you. Bravo, bitch; I want a-fuckin'-divorce.

"Any other-bitch in here fuckin' him? You can have him. You won't have much because I'm gon take his ass for everything he has and that's a promise!" Jennifer yelled at the crowd.

She released the woman's hair, causing her head to hit the floor, as she ran out the room.

"Damn!" Dahlia released.

She felt so bad for Jennifer. She could only imagine how she was feeling. To find out your husband was cheating, and with a woman who was supposedly your best friend. Dahlia thought she had drama in her life—Jennifer's situation took the cake.

"His-ass should be ashamed," Traci added as they watched Wesley go to the woman's aid, instead of after his wife.

Dahlia and Traci went in search of Jennifer to check on her, but she had already left the party.

It was way after three in the morning when Charles, Traci's husband, pulled in front of Dahlia's house.

"Thank you, Charles.

"Traci, call me later when you think I'm up; not when you get up." Dahlia laughed.

"Okay; thanks for joining me tonight."

"You're welcome."

Dahlia climbed out the truck and made her way up her driveway. She could see a figure sitting on her porch. Dahlia stopped. There wasn't a car in her driveway besides the rental car. Dahlia began to back up.

From the car, Traci and Charles noticed Dahlia's actions and jumped out.

"You good, sis?" Charles questioned.

"It looks like someone's on my porch."

"Get back in the truck," Charles instructed the ladies.

"Hell nah! We're all going to see what-the-fuck is going on!" Traci barked.

Charles just shook his head as they approached the figure on the porch. Once Dahlia got closer, she recognized the sleeping man.

"Desman?" she called out. "Desman?!" she called out a little louder. "Is that you?"

The man moved. "Yeah," he replied. He had been out there waiting for Dahlia to get home.

"What's going on?"

"I was waiting for you to get home."

"Why didn't you call me?" she questioned.

"I thought I was gon have to whup yo' ass." Charles laughed, embracing Desman.

"My bad if I scared y'all," Desman replied.

"Make sure she gets in safe. We're out of here," Charles told Desman as he and Traci turned to walk back to the truck.

"She's good," Desman replied.

"What's going on? Is Granny okay? Is it Granddaddy?" Dahlia questioned in a panic.

She didn't know why Desman was sitting outside her house in the wee hours and hadn't once tried to call her.

"Calm down; they're fine. I just came by to give you this," Desman said, pulling a manila envelope out of his pocket.

"What's this?" she questioned.

"It's some money for Granny's house. Pay whatever she used to bail me out with it.

Whatever's left, you can keep it, or give it to them to fix something around the house or pay a bill."

"Desman, where did you get this money from?" Dahlia questioned, glancing at the bills in the thick envelope.

"Does it matter? Just do what I asked of you," Desman spoke, walking off and leaving Dahlia standing there.

Dahlia didn't have enough energy to fight with Desman. With the thick envelope in hand, she made her way inside her house, stripped, lay down, and was out.

Chapter 13

It was well after eleven a.m. and Dahlia was still nestled under the covers. She had tried her hardest to ignore the buzzing sound of her cellphone on her nightstand. It wouldn't stop. For the last hour, it seemed to beep every minute. Thinking maybe there was something wrong, Dahlia finally got up in search of her phone, knocking the envelope Desman had given her to the floor. The money scattered. Dahlia climbed out the bed and started to scoop the money up.

"Where-in-the-hell did he get all this money from?" Dahlia thought out loud. She'd counted at least sixty grand. "What-shit are you into now, Desman?"

The beeping sound of her cellphone caught her attention again. Dahlia stood up to retrieve her phone and the dozen messages she had, some from Facebook and Instagram, and some emails. She had a few texts from Jerome and one that caught her eye from Keisha Kane.

Thank you again for the slayage of my hair. You got me straight poppin in these LA streets. I was gon be selfish and keep you to myself as my secret weapon, but blessings don't come that way. I posted you on the gram. Good luck with all the new clients. You deserve it. I saw the hate from that bald-head-bitch in the shop. Don't let the haters stop your shine.

Dahlia was beyond-happy to see Keisha liked her hair. She scrolled through her Instagram DM and smiled at all the people requesting an appointment. Dahlia went to search for her planner and began to reply to messages and book appointments. After two hours of replying to messages on social media, Dahlia had booked twelve appointments over the next several days. Dahlia got up from the floor and headed to take a shower to get her day started.

It took Dahlia a little over an hour to get ready. She was headed out the door when she saw the money peeking out the envelope. She grabbed it and stuck it in her purse.

"Hello?" Dahlia said into her cellphone as she was getting in the car.

"Hello there, little lady. How are you this morning?"

"Hey, Jerome; I'm good. How are you?"

"Shit, I'm up and alive, so I'm good. What're you up to? We still on for lunch or dinner?"

"I'm not sure; I am just leaving my house for the day. I have some errands to run and I'm headed to L.A. right now to my grandparents'. I'll hit you up in a few hours and see where you are," Dahlia said.

"Okay; I'll be waiting on that call."

"Okay; give me a few."

"Have a good day, little lady."

"You, too."

Dahlia ended the call, slid on her shades, turned up her music, and headed to the crowded freeway. When Dahlia pulled onto her grandparents street, before she could even turn into her grandparents' driveway, a car whizzed past, nearly hitting her.

"WHAT-THE-FUCK?" Dahlia yelled, laying on the horn.

She glanced in her rearview mirror and saw the taillight of the same black Lexus that had been sitting outside her grandparents' house days before. Dahlia shook her head and proceeded to park her car in her grandparents' driveway.

"Hey, Granddaddy," Dahlia spoke, kneeling to give her grandfather a hug and kiss. As always he was sitting in his favorite chair, watching the rerun of some cowboy show.

"Hey, baby; how are you? I called down there to check on your car, but that boy Mario wasn't in. Have you heard anything?"

"I'm good. They told me they'd pulled all the dents out. They were just waiting on the paint to arrive. Where is that feisty wife of yours?" Dahlia questioned.

"She's upstairs, getting ready. We're going out to Sizzler for lunch."

"Okay; just the two of you?"

"Yup."

"Good; that's how it should be. Has Desman been here?" Dahlia questioned out of curiosity.

"I haven't seen that boy since all that foolishness happened over here."

"When I got home last night, he was waiting on my doorstep. I came over here to talk to you and Granny about something he gave me."

"What-the-hell is that boy up to now?" James questioned.

"That's what I want to know, Granddaddy."

"Who's up to something?" Mabel questioned, coming down the stairs in a long floral dress.

"You look gorgeous," Dahlia told her grandmother.

"Thank you. This is the dress you bought me."

"I know; I'm glad you're wearing it. I thought you would never wear it."

"It's not really my style, but it's perfect for this hot-ass-weather we're having today."

"I don't want to hold you two up. Like I was telling Granddaddy, when I made it home last night— well, this morning—Desman was sitting on my front porch; scared the holy-crap out of me. He gave me this." Dahlia paused as she reached in her purse to retrieve the envelope full of cash. "There's over sixty grand in this envelope, and when I pulled into the driveway just now, that same Lexus that was parked outside the other day, sped down the street, almost hitting me. I think Desman is up to no-good," Dahlia informed her grandparents.

"Oh, Lord, what has this child gotten himself into?" Mabel said, sitting down on the sofa.

"That, I'm not sure. I just thought you should know. I don't like the feeling. If he's going to do dirty stuff, he needs not to bring it to your doorstep," Dahlia spoke, getting pissed. Shit wasn't adding up.

"When we get back, I'm going to call him and make his-ass come over here and explain this-shit. I'm told old for this-shit," Mabel spoke.

"Well, I'll leave this here. He said it's to pay off the loan we took on the house to bail him out of jail. He said the extras are to fix whatever you want around here."

"HELL NO!" James blurted. "I don't want that blood money! That child don't have a-damn-job.

Where-in-the-hell did he get that type of money from? He can keep it. We don't need it."

"We gon talk to him and figure it out."

"Okay; well, you two enjoy lunch." Dahlia reached in her purse, pulled out some money, and handed it to her grandfather. "Lunch is on me."

"That's okay, baby; I got it. You help us enough."

"Granddaddy, I insist," Dahlia spoke, the money still in her hand.

"Okay, child." James took the money and laid it on the table.

"Have you guys spoke to my dad?"

"Yes, he called a few weeks ago. He asked about you, like always. You should go see him, Dahlia. Holding it inside won't fix it. Tell him how you feel. He is your father, and remember, you only get one," James spoke.

"I will, Granddaddy. Next time he calls, tell him I love him," Dahlia spoke. She loved her father, but the anger she felt inside wouldn't allow her to speak those words to him.

"He needs to hear those words from you, and you need to hear those words from him," Mabel added.

"I know, Granny," Dahlia spoke.

"I mean it, Dahlia Nicole Willowbrook."

"I hear you, Granny, and I understand what both of you are saying. I will write him a letter."

"Good."

"I'm gonna get out of here and let you two go enjoy lunch."

"See you later."

"Okay; I love y'all," Dahlia told her grandparents as she walked out the door.

"Love you, too," James and Mabel said in unison.

Dahlia left her grandparents' house to finish running her errands. Her first stop was to meet her hair distributor. Dahlia pulled up in front of a small business front. Although So Posh Hair was a small storefront, the owner, Ronni, was making a killing. She had every kind of hair you could think about and the quality was the best in L.A. Dahlia had been working with Ronni for the last two years, and she always hooked Dahlia up with the best prices. Dahlia made custom wigs for her clients, and since she'd booked a new list of clients, she wanted to have some on display.

"What's up, girly? How've you been?" Dahlia spoke as she walked in the shop.

"I'm good; working hard."

"I feel you on that one, which is why I'm here."

"That's always good." Ronni laughed. "I see you slayed Keisha Kane's hair. I love how you added those colors. What hair did you use?"

"Yes, I did, thank you. I used a mixture of the body wave and loose wave, so it gives different curls and a more-defined look when it's wet."

"Okay; so what do we need today? You should have called me. I would've had it ready for you."

"It was last-minute and it slipped my mind," Dahlia admitted. "I need three bundles of every length, in the body wave, loose curl, and deep wave hair. I also need six bundles of straight hair in twelve inches."

"I got you," Ronni said as she started to gather the hair Dahlia wanted.

Dahlia sat and scrolled through her phone. The friend requests and appointment requests were still coming in.

"Here you go," Ronni said, handing Dahlia a box full of hair. "As always, I added some extra hair in there, some new hair I'm trying. Let me know how you like it."

"Okay; I also need a few of the cleansing creams. Give me about ten of them."

"Gotcha; anything else?"

"I think that's all for now. What's my tab?"

"The usual."

"That's why I keep coming back." Dahlia smiled as she slid her normal two grand for the hair to Ronni.

"You know I got you."

"Thanks; have a good day. Hopefully, I'll be seeing you sooner than later."

"Get that money. You always know where to find me."

Dahlia left the hair shop and headed to the only beauty supply in all of Los Angeles County to get her money. It was owned by two of Dahlia's childhood friends.

Dahlia pulled up to the light. She glanced over to the car to her right to see who was driving the car with the loud music that was making her windows rattle.

"SHAMERA!" Dahlia yelled, trying to gain her auntie's attention.

Sham's music was way-too-loud for her to hear anything. Dahlia shook her head and blew the car horn, causing everyone around her to look around to see why she was laying on her horn.

"SHAMERA!" she yelled again.

Sham turned her head to look at the driver blowing the horn and noticed it was Dahlia.

"Hey, niece; pull over." Sham smiled.

"Meet me in the shopping center," Dahlia spoke, driving off once the light changed.

Sham followed behind Dahlia into the shopping center parking lot where the beauty supply was located. She stepped out the car and approached Sham in the truck she was driving.

"This you?" Dahlia questioned, checking the custom Range Rover out. She knew like-hell it was Sham's car.

"Somethin' like that. It's my man's, so it's just like my shit."

"Nice. How've you been? I haven't seen you around. I just asked Granny had she talked to you."

"I'm good. I know; I've been busy. My man has a lot of business dealings and I've been helping him run them. I know I need to check on my parents and show my face. I'm surprised my mother hasn't called me, going off."

"You delivering packages, Auntie?" Dahlia blurted out.

"What?" Sham asked, shocked by Dahlia's question.

"Auntie Sham, don't try to play me. I'm not my granny. The plates on this truck say GMB. I already know what that is and how they get down. You fuckin' with one of them?"

"Yeah, but he don't sell drugs. That ain't all they do."

"Tell me anything. They are known for drugs. You're grown, so I can't tell you what to do. All I can say is be careful. Did you hook Desman up with one of them?" Dahlia questioned.

"Nah; why you ask me that?"

"Because he came to my house and dropped off a large amount of money. I'm trying to find out how he got the-shit."

"Large like what?"

"Like over sixty grand."

"Damn! Where-the-hell that-nigga get that money from. I hope his-ass ain't out here robbing anybody."

"You think it's that?" Dahlia questioned.

"Shit, I don't know; I'm just talking. Let me get out of here. I got an errand to run," Sham said, starting the car up.

Dahlia knew her auntie knew more than she was letting on by the way she'd hurried up and left when she mentioned Desman and the money. Dahlia pushed it to the back of her mind and made her way in the beauty supply store.

"What's good, Ken? Where's Moonie?" Dahlia asked, walking in the beauty supply store.

"She just ran to Louisiana's to get some chicken. How've you been?"

"I'm good; how about you?" Dahlia asked as she embraced Ken.

He was part owner of the beauty supply with his twin sister Moonie. They'd grew up on her grandmother's block.

"I'm good; business is good. I just saw Sham the other day. She came in here looking for a discount, but looking like new money pushing a Range Rover," Ken said, smacking his lips.

"Yeah, I saw her and the new truck she's pushing just now. You know Sham; it's all a façade. She's got herself a new man."

"I know. She's fuckin' one of them niggas from GMB," Ken informed.

Dahlia loved Ken, but he was as messy as they came. He knew all the gossip.

"I know. You know they label everything they own so people know who they are."

"A bunch of flossers," Ken added. "I hear Desman is connected to them, too."

"Oh really?" Dahlia questioned.

If anybody knew the word on the street, Ken knew. "Yeah."

"Where'd you hear that?" Dahlia questioned. She knew Ken wouldn't hold back and would tell her everything he knew.

"You know I do my shit. I was creepin' and the-nigga I creep with from time-to-time is connected to GMB. He needed some-shit picked up and called someone to do it. When the person got to the motel room, he went downstairs to meet him. You know me, being nosy, I went to look and saw Desman."

"That-shit explains a lot."

"I was surprised, but of course I couldn't ask any questions."

"When was this?"

"The other night."

"Thanks for that information," Dahlia said.

She wouldn't mention it to Desman, Sham, or her grandparents until she had concrete information. She trusted Ken and his information, she just needed more.

"What're you two in here gossiping about now?" Moonie laughed, coming through the door, seeing Ken and Dahlia.

"Bitch, we're talking about you. What you gon do about it?" Ken questioned with a roll of his neck.

"Hey, girl. You know Ken knows all the scoop on everything," Dahlia said, giving Moonie a hug.

"That's why his ass is always into some shit."

"And I always handle my shit. These niggas and bitches know Ken Doll don't give a damn. I beat asses and fuck-over names when I come through. They know 'bout me."

Dahlia and Moonie laughed at him. Ken was a full-mess. He was telling the truth. People didn't fool with him.

"You are a fool. I came to get some items."

"Get what you need. I know this gossiping-fool already told you Sham is messing with one of them young dudes."

"Yeah, he told me. That's her business; Sham's grown. I just told her that today."

"Well, get what you need. I'm about to sit here and feed my fat-ass-face."

"Bitch, that's all you do," Ken sniped.

"Fuck you!"

"I would, but you aren't my type."

"You two are a whole mess-and-a-half." Dahlia laughed as she made her way around the store to get the items she needed.

"Thank you for that information," Dahlia said as she piled her items on the counter.

Ken and Moonie made sure they kept their shelves fully-stocked with every hair product you could think of.

"You know I got you; you my girl. How're your grandparents?"

"They're good; I just left their house. They're still crazy."

"Tell them I said hello."

"I will, and thanks again. I have some new clients and I wanted to make sure I had everything I need."

"Hey now. I can't wait for you to get your own-shit. That-bitch Chandra is so-damn-messy." Ken frowned. "We banned that bald-headed-bitch from coming in here, too."

"Jessie?"

"Yeah. Bitch thought her ol' bald-headed, ugly-ass was going to come in here with that slick-ass-mouth and make foul comments about you. That-bitch knows that isn't tolerated in these walls. She tried it twice; now she's out."

"You know I love your crazy-ass. She stole one of my clients, too. In due time, I will have my own." Dahlia smiled as she walked out the store.

Since she was still local and by the shop, Dahlia decided she would stop by the shop and drop everything off. When Dahlia entered the shop, as always, Jessie was the first one she saw twirling in her empty chair.

"Hey, Jessie?" Dahlia said, being petty.

"Hey," she replied dryly.

Dahlia wanted to laugh in her face, but instead, she left well enough alone and brought her stuff in to arrange everything for when she arrived the next day. Dahlia left whatever she wouldn't need for the night at the shop. When she was finished, she made her way to the back of the shop to let Chandra know she had brought some stuff in. She didn't trust Jessie.

"Hey, Chandra," Dahlia knocked on the door. "I just came back to say hey. I was in the area and dropped off some new supplies I bought."

"Hey, D; how's everything?"

"Everything's good. How's everything with you?"

"I'm good; waiting on my next client to arrive. I'm ready to go. My baby has a cold."

"Awww, I hope he feels better."

"After this client, I'm done for the day. If he's still running a fever in the morning, I'm going to take him to urgent care. I'll leave keys with whoever is still at the shop when I leave, or send my husband to open in the morning."

"Well, I hope everything is okay with your little man; just let me know. I'm gon get in this traffic and head-my-ass home to work on some of these wigs."

"Okay; be safe."

"Thanks," Dahlia said.

As she made her way out the shop, she didn't say anything to Jessie. There wasn't any use.

Chapter 14

After being stuck in traffic for close to two hours, Dahlia was happy to finally be home and ready to work. Dahlia stripped out of the dress she had on and changed into some old basketball shorts and a tank top to be more comfortable while she worked on the wigs. She prepared the five dolls she would use for the night, turned on the music, and grabbed a glass of wine.

Dahlia started with the hair she was dying, so once she was finished with the other dolls, the hair would be ready to install. Dahlia was so tuned-in to what she was doing and the *Best of Whitney Houston,* she hadn't heard her phone. Reaching over to get another needle, she saw her phone flashing. There were several missed calls, text messages, and social media hits. Most of the calls and texts were from Jerome and an unknown caller.

Dahlia decided to text Jerome back instead of calling.

Dahlia: I'm sorry. Can I get a raincheck? I'm tied up with something for work tomorrow.

Jerome: Okay. Since you said it was work related, I'll give you a pass. You still in LA?

Dahlia: No; I'm at home.

Jerome: Have you ate?

Dahlia: No; not hungry at the moment. Having me some wine though. If I get hungry, I can always run and get something or whip something up in the kitchen."

Dahlia held her phone in her hand for a few moments to see if Jerome would text back. When he didn't reply, she threw it back on the sofa and finished working on her third head of the night. Once she was done with all of them, she would post them to her hair page, for sale starting tomorrow.

After several hours and numb legs, she was finally finished with all of the wigs. Dahlia was cleaning up her living room when she heard a knock at the door. It was nearing midnight and Dahlia wasn't expecting any visitors. Dahlia grabbed a knife from the kitchen and peeked out the window to see who was at her door.

"What are you doing here?" she asked after she'd checked through the peephole and opened the door.

"I was out eating with a friend and thought you might want something to eat."

"Oh really? And did your phone happened to break, preventing you from calling me before showing up at my house?"

"I wanted to surprise you. With all you're going through, you don't need to be out in these streets late, trying to get some food, so I brought food to you." Jerome smiled. "Are you going to let me in or you don't want the food?"

"Oh shit; I hadn't even realized I hadn't let you in." Dahlia laughed, moving to the side to let Jerome in.

"Damn, you had a knife ready and all." Jerome laughed. "Where can I sit these?" he questioned, holding the bags up in his hand.

"Shit, I didn't know who was at my door! You can sit them on the counter in the kitchen," Dahlia spoke, her voice drifting off as she got lost in reading the text she had just received from Ken.

"What do you know about the dudes from GMB?" Dahlia questioned.

"There're a bunch of dudes moving weight and shit. Why'd you ask that? What do you know about GMB?" Jerome questioned, opening the small bottle of Hennessey and taking a swig from it.

"Not much these days. I actually didn't even know they were still in operation. I hadn't heard anything about them in like, two years. I know my auntie is creepin' with someone who's in deep with them, but she won't tell me who. I ran into a childhood friend and they told me my brother's been kickin' it with them. I just want to know how deep in he is. He dropped off sixty grand to me last night when I got home."

"So you think your brother's working for GMB?"

"I don't know if he's selling drugs, but he's dropping off large sums of money. My source just texted me and told me they'd seen my brother again dropping off money and picking up something to deliver somewhere else."

"So you're trying to figure out what's going on?"

"Yeah. My brother stays at my grandparents, but he hasn't been there for a few days, and there's been this car sitting outside my grandparents' house. I don't know what kind-of-shit my brother is into, but I need to make sure my grandparents are safe. I would lose it if something happened to them," Dahlia spoke. "They won't come here and stay with me until we figure it out. They're too ornery for that."

"I will check with a few niggas I know who fuck-with-them, and I'll keep my ear to the street to see what's what. What's your brother name again?"

"Desman."

"I got you; don't trip."

"Thank you."

"Don't worry about it, but, ummm . . . What-in-the-hell is going on here?" Jerome questioned, noticing all the wigs. "Did I come when you were deciding what wig you were going to wear tomorrow?" Jerome laughed.

"Screw you!" Dahlia laughed. "I make these and sell them to my clients."

"How much do women pay for these?"

"My prices vary; depends on the type of hair and the style. I buy the hair and install the weave on the wigs and style it."

"So, what's like, your average price for one of these wigs?"

"I'll say two hundred dollars. I don't make wigs for under two hundred; most are two-to-three hundred."

"Damn. So you blew me off to make wigs?"

"I didn't blow you off. I had business to handle. It's always gonna be business over pleasure. Doing hair and these wigs are my business. It's how I keep a roof over my head, survive, and take care of my family."

"I see you. Women pay you to doll-their-asses-up and be up to some trickery. Niggas be trying to pull the baddest chick walking, not knowing once it's time to hit the sheets, she'll pull layers off, and you'll get another person." Jerome laughed.

"How is it trickery because we can remove a layer of our hair at nighttime? That isn't trickery; that's us protecting our natural hair," Dahlia replied. "Men be up to trickery with all their-damn-lies, games, and cheating," Dahlia added.

"Not every man is about lies and games. You just have to know when you're in the presence of a good man, not fuckin' with one of these lames."

"That's what they all say, until they start with their bullshit and lies. Then it gets flipped on you, and all the shit you don't do or didn't do. Or they aren't ready to commit. I've heard it all."

"Some men have grown up from that bullshit and are looking to find a woman who can complete the new man he has grown into. You just have to recognize when you're in the presence of that-man."

"What'd you bring to eat, since you're showing up at people's houses unannounced and shit?" Dahlia questioned, making her way toward the kitchen with Jerome following not too far behind her, drinking the Hennessey straight from the bottle. She didn't want to have that conversation with him, so she changed the subject.

"I brought shrimp fettuccine, ravioli, spaghetti, and soup and a salad."

"That's a lot of food. What you gon eat?"

"I already ate. That's for you."

"I'm not gonna eat all of this," Dahlia stated with a slight attitude. "Just because I'm big doesn't mean I eat a lot."

"I'm sorry if I offended you," Jerome spoke sincerely, his hands held in the air. "I didn't know what you wanted, so I got a few things for you to choose from. To be honest, I think you're fuckin'-beautiful. I've always thought you were one of the most-beautiful women I've ever laid eyes on," Jerome spoke.

"You've been with so many clown-ass-niggas, you can't tell when you're in the presence of a real-nigga," Jerome spoke, stepping in Dahlia's personal space. "One who appreciates your inner and outer beauty."

Dahlia stepped back with her hands folded across her chest, bouncing on one leg as she stared at Jerome. She was about to walk out the kitchen to put some distance between herself and Jerome. Jerome grabbed her arm just in the nick of time. He brought her in closer to his body. This time he cupped her chin.

"Look at me!" he demanded. "You are beautiful. When you look in the mirror, don't you see that?" he questioned. "Any nigga who told you different is a-fuckin'-lie and didn't deserve a woman like you. Let me be the man to tell you that every morning," Jerome said, pressing his lips against Dahlia's and using his tongue to force Dahlia's lips open.

'No . . . no . . . Dahlia, make him stop . . . but fuck, it feels good!' Dahlia thought as she embraced

Jerome's tongue in her mouth. She could taste the bitterness of the liquor he was consuming.

Jerome gripped the nape of her neck, forcing his tongue deeper in her mouth, backing her against the wall. He used his free hand to caress her vagina through the thin fabric of the shorts. Dahlia wasn't big on wearing underwear, and tonight was a night she didn't have any on.

Dahlia shrieked at the unfamiliar pleasure Jerome was showing her body. She wanted him to stop . . . but it felt too good. Dahlia almost lost it when she felt Jerome's fingers part her wet lips and let his fingers explore the depths of her vagina. He worked his fingers with persistence; he was aiming to please. Almost in an instant, Dahlia felt her vagina contracting and her juices coated his fingers.

Jerome released Dahlia's tongue from his mouth and made his way to her neck. "Let me make love to you?" he whispered in her ear.

"Nooooo," Dahlia replied low, pushing him off her. "We can't do this. We're crossing the line. We're friends," Dahlia let out.

"Dahlia, in case you haven't noticed, I want to be more than your friend. I want to be your man," Jerome admitted. "That is my intention."

"Jerome, you're a nice guy, but I'm not ready to date. I'm sorry if I led you on just now; I got caught-up. I'm not looking for anything more than a friendship right now."

"Okay; well, can I be the friend to help you release all that pent-up tension and tend to your needs?" Jerome questioned, trying to back Dahlia into the wall, but she moved. He tried to fondle her vagina again, but Dahlia smacked his hand.

"I can't do that. That would mess up the friendship we have. It would be me using you and you using my body when you felt like busting a nut. I'm not that-kind of woman," Dahlia informed him, putting some distance between Jerome and herself.

"I understand, but if you ever change your mind, give me a call." Jerome smiled as he grabbed his keys and bottle of liquor, and was out the door, leaving Dahlia with a wet vagina and mixed emotions.

Dahlia needed to speak to someone. She didn't know how to feel about what had just happened. Dahlia called the only person she could trust— Traci.

"Is everything okay?" Traci answered in a panic.

"Yes; I just need to talk."

"What's wrong?"

"Jerome just left here."

"Dahlia, did you do what I think you did?"

"No, I did not sleep with him."

"Did he rape you?" Traci questioned, just above a whisper.

"No," Dahlia informed her and began to explain what had occurred minutes ago in her kitchen.

"You did right by stopping it before it went any further. You cannot beat yourself up about it; you got weak. You're a woman with needs and you were vulnerable. Shit, he knew that. If you don't feel comfortable being alone with him, tell him that. He's being a little too pushy for me. Didn't you say you told him what you just went through?"

Yeah, I told him."

"I suggest putting a little distance between you two right now, especially since he has played in your juices. You know good-pussy can drive a man crazy." Traci laughed, causing Dahlia to laugh. "I'm glad I could make you laugh. Now go wash that nigga off you, eat that food he paid for, and get some rest. You have money to make. I saw all the new wigs on the Gram; they're cute. My-ass needs one of those so I can transform for my man. I'm gon walk in here like Becky with the good hair." Traci laughed again.

"I can't play with you." Dahlia laughed. "Thank you. I can always count on you to make me laugh and listen to all my drama."

"That's what friends are for."

"Thank you."

"No need. Just know, when you make it big, bitch, you owe me a vacation to somewhere tropical, where I can go without my nagging husband and bad-ass-kids." Traci laughed.

"I got you." Dahlia laughed also.

"Good. Have a good night. Call me tomorrow."

"Okay," Dahlia replied and ended the call.

Dahlia was still upset she'd allowed the situation to get as far as it had, but talking to Traci had made her feel a little better about what had happened. Dahlia turned on the shower and let the bathroom steam up. She peeled herself out of the clothes she had on that reeked of Jerome's cologne and stepped in the shower. Dahlia scrubbed her body, wanting any reminder of what took place to be erased.

When Dahlia was finished showering, she threw on an oversized T-shirt, warmed up some of the food Jerome had brought, and climbed in the bed to eat.

Chapter 15

Dahlia was the first one at the shop, which almost never happened, but she knew she would have a long day and wanted to make sure she was ready. She had six clients booked for the day and was willing to take any walk-ins she could. Dahlia sat in her car texting Chandra to see what time she would get there to open up the shop, or if she could send someone to open it. Dahlia had a client coming within an hour and still needed to prep.

Chandra: *My baby is still sick. Jessie is en route.*

Dahlia: *Okay.*

Dahlia had already grabbed her morning dose of coffee, so she sat in her car, replying to messages and emails. She had seen the message from Jerome when she woke up. She didn't even click on it to see what it said. She agreed with Traci there needed to be some distance between the two of them. She couldn't bear looking at him, knowing what had happened between the two of them. She didn't see Jerome in the image of being her boyfriend—just a friend. She knew she would have to keep her distance because his approach was extremely strong and Dahlia's hormones were on fire.

Dahlia hadn't realized how long she'd been waiting in her car until she got a text from her client saying she was in front of the shop and it was closed. Dahlia got out of the car and made her way to the front of the shop.

"Krystal?" Dahlia asked, seeing the woman standing in front of the shop.

"Yes," the woman looked up, recognizing Dahlia from a picture she had posted on her social media handles.

"Hello. I'm sorry; the shop is usually open. The owner is sick and sent someone else to open up Let me see what's going on," Dahlia spoke, pissed that Jessie hadn't shown up.

Dahlia walked to the side of the building and dialed Chandra to let her know it had been more than an hour and Jessie hadn't shown up, and she had a client waiting. Chandra assured her Jessie would be there within minutes. Dahlia was pissed but had to remain professional in front of her new client. Dahlia made her way back to the front of the shop.

"I'm so sorry. Someone should be here in a few minutes. This isn't something that happens all the time," Dahlia said, letting the client know this wouldn't be something she would normally have to deal with.

"It's okay; I know how it is when you're in someone else's space," Krystal spoke, offering the stressed-Dahlia a soft smile.

Just as Dahlia was about to say something, Jessie came walking around the corner with a Starbucks cup in hand and a smirk on her face, which pissed Dahlia off even more.

"Good morning," she sang.

"Good morning," Krystal spoke with a smile. "I'm Krystal, a new client of Dahlia's."

"Morning, Jessie," Dahlia spoke as calmly as she could, despite how she felt.

"Welcome, Krystal. I'm sure Dahlia is going to give you some slayage to brag about."

"Slayage?" Krystal questioned, clueless to what Jessie was talking about.

"Don't worry, I'll explain later." Dahlia smiled.

Krystal looked like she was under twenty-five years old, and stayed so far in the books, she didn't know what her generation was doing.

"Okay," Krystal said.

Dahlia turned the music up a little and made small-talk with Krystal to find out a little more about her. She found out Krystal was twenty-six years old, was from the valley, and in her last year of law school. She had no kids and was engaged to be married right after she finished school; her fiancé was already working as an intern at a big criminal law firm. Since Krystal was willing to try something different with her waist-length hair, Dahlia cut long layers throughout her hair before finishing it with a silk press.

"How do you like it?" Dahlia asked, turning the chair for Krystal to see her hair.

"Oh my gosh, it's so shiny. I love it," she beamed, running her hands through her newly-layered mane. "It has so much volume. I am so used to seeing it flat and just blah," Krystal said. "Lance is going to love this. He has been begging me to get a new style," Krystal said, reaching in her bag. She pulled out her compact mirror and applied her lipstick.

Dahlia watched in amazement. Krystal had become another person.

"Thank you so much, Dahlia. You are so awesome."

"You're welcome; I'm glad you like it." Dahlia smiled. This was the joy of being a hairstylist, being able to make women feel good.

"How much do I owe you?"

"Because you had to wait, I'll give you a discount. The cut was on me, so fifty dollars."

"You're a blessing. I use to pay my old hairstylist seventy-five dollars just for a wash and flat iron, and it was flat and never shiny like this."

"Thank you," Dahlia said, taking the money from Krystal.

"Can I book my next appointment now?"

"Sure; let me get my book." Dahlia reached in her bag to get her appointment book. "When did you want to come back?"

"In two weeks."

"What works for you, morning or afternoon?" Dahlia questioned.

"Do you have any midday appointments?"

"I have one on the twenty-second at three p.m."

"That works for me."

"I have you down. I have your number and I'll call to confirm your appointment sometime in that week. It was a pleasure meeting you."

"No; thank you. My hair is so awesome. I can't wait to go show this off," Krystal bragged, grabbing her bag.

Like always in the beginning of the month, the shop was packed and busy with customers flowing in and out all day. Dahlia had knocked out her six appointments, a few walk-ins, and had managed to sell five of the six wigs she'd made. Although she was tired, it had been a good day. Dahlia was the last one in the shop. Everyone had gone home for the day and Jessie, as always, had disappeared early. Dahlia was packing her bag to leave for the day when she heard the chime of the shop's door open. Dahlia glanced up and noticed it wasn't Jessie or anyone she recognized.

"I'm sorry, but we're closed for the day," Dahlia informed the woman.

"I know. I've been outside waiting for the last hour for Jessie to come back to do my hair," the woman blurted out. The sound of frustration could be heard with every word she spoke.

"I'm sorry about that. I can give her a call for you to see where she is," Dahlia offered.

"I've called her three times," the woman replied. "I have to be in court early Monday morning, and I have to be up-to-par to get my children back." The woman broke down, crying. "I have called her for two days, confirming this appointment. I need to get my kids back. I can't live my life without my kids," the woman cried.

Dahlia didn't know what to say. She hadn't expected the woman to break down like she had. Dahlia looked around to make sure this wasn't some kind of scam to rob the place since she was the last one inside. With the luck she'd been having, she didn't know what was what. Dahlia walked closer to the woman, saying a silent prayer that the woman was really in need and not running some scam.

"I am sorry." Dahlia embraced the woman in a hug. "God will make everything okay for you. Just keep your faith and keep praying," Dahlia spoke, not knowing where the words were even coming from. "If you'd like, I can do your hair for you. I want you to walk in that courtroom looking and feeling your very best."

"It would mean so much to me. You look so tired."

"It's okay. How do you want your hair?"

"Anything you're willing to do for me that won't take too much of your time. I'm already washed," the woman spoke.

"Sure; I'm Dahlia. How do you normally wear your hair?"

"Nice to meet you, Dahlia; I am Shantel. I normally wear it in a ponytail. I work so much I don't have time to get my hair done. I have four kids who need my time. What time I have left, I spend it studying."

"Nice to meet you as well, Shantel. What are you in school studying for?"

"I am a nurse assistant and studying to become an LVN. I only have a few more classes left. My ex-husband's new girlfriend wanted to be petty and called Child Protective Services on me because I said I didn't want her around my kids. That-man has changed his women like he changes his clothes. I have daughters. I don't want them to see all of these women, and I don't want my son to think it's okay. She told them I leave my kids at home alone while I work my night job and I starve my kids.

"My kids know not to let anyone in. I feed them, make sure their homework is done, and they bathe before I go work my night shift. Between what I make and the little money my ex-husband gives, after rent, school tuition, food, and household items, I'm not left with much to take my children anywhere, let alone pay for childcare, and my children aren't going to a public school."

Dahlia just listened to the woman rant as she pressed her hair. The passion and devotion in her voice about her children and their education warmed Dahlia's heart.

"Have you done everything they've asked of you?" Dahlia questioned, trying to see if there was anything else she could do to help Shante.

"I have done everything they've asked of me and then some. I just want my kids back. This last month without them almost drove me crazy."

Dahlia didn't know how Shantel was feeling to be away from her kids because she didn't have any. It made her think of her father. She couldn't imagine how he felt being stripped away from his family and forced to live in a cage like an animal.

"All done." Dahlia smiled, turning Shantel toward the mirror so she could see herself.

Shantel stared at herself in the mirror. There was something about the way she looked at herself in the mirror that Dahlia connected with.

"I love it!" she cried.

"I'm glad you like it."

"How much do I owe you?"

"Nothing."

"*Nothing?*" Shantel questioned.

"Yes, nothing; keep your money. When you get your kids back, do something special for them with that money."

"Are you sure? I can pay you."

"I'm positive; keep it. When you get your girls back, bring them by and I'll do their hair also."

"You are a true blessing. At first, I wasn't even going to come inside. I was just going to leave and never, ever book with Jessie again, but something led me in this shop. I can't thank you enough."

"You're welcome. Here's my card. Call me when you want to bring the girls by to get their hair done. I also cut hair, so feel free to bring your son, too."

mmIItahSh

"I will."

Shantel walked out the shop with a smile on her face, which caused Dahlia to smile as she walked her out and locked up the shop for the night. Jessie had yet to return.

"DAHLIA!" a woman's voice called out as she knocked on the shop's window.

Dahlia grabbed the hot flat iron as she turned to see who was yelling her name. Dahlia move a little closer and noticed it was Gabby, one of her regular clients.

"Gabby, what-in-the-hell? You scared the living-hell out of me," Dahlia admitted, letting the woman in. "You do know I'm closed and going home. It has been a long day."

"I know. I was trying to catch you, but this nigga was playing with giving me this money to get my hair donc. Do you have any of those wigs left?"

"I only have this one," Dahlia said, showing Gabby the last wig she had, which was a lace-front, sharp-angled bob.

"That's cute. I'll take it," Gabby said, handing Dahlia three, crispy, hundred-dollar bills.

"Thanks," Dahlia said, taking two of the hundreds and giving Gabby one back.

"How much is it?" Gabby questioned, looking at the money Dahlia had given back to her.

"It's two-twenty-five, but I gave it to you for two hundred. Now, get out of here so I can finish getting myself together so I can go." Dahlia laughed.

"This one just like the other one I got?"

"Yes."

"Good. Thank you, Dahlia. I'll see you next week for my regular appointment."

"Okay."

Dahlia made sure her station was clean, grabbed her bags, and locked the shop up as best she could. Jessie still hadn't shown her face or called. Once Dahlia made it to her car, she called Chandra to let her know what had happened. Chandra thanked Dahlia and said she was on her way there to lock up. Jessie's boyfriend had called and said she had been arrested.

Dahlia ended the call and made her way to check on her grandparents, which was only a short drive from the shop.

"GRANNY?" Dahlia yelled as she walked in her grandparents' house. It was dark, which was kind of odd.

"Girl, be quiet," Mabel spoke, just above a whisper.

"Granny, where are you and why is it dark in here?" Dahlia questioned, clueless.

"That-damn-car was back out there today. So, since I hadn't left out the house all day—I wasn't feeling too well this morning—I pretended like I wasn't here, to see if the bastard would get out the car so I could see who the fuck it is, but that bastard didn't. I see the car's gone now."

"Have you talked to Desman?"

"No, not yet. I called him, but he didn't answer, which isn't like him. I don't know what that boy's up to."

"I think Desman's in trouble. Think about it: This car starts sitting outside your home, and Desman hasn't been home; then he brings sixty thousand dollars to my house. We both know he doesn't have a job, and a friend of mine saw Desman hanging with some bad people."

"I understand your concern, and I'll talk to him; trust me, I will. I'm just not gung ho on believing hearsay. If he's up to no-good, it's going to catch up with him."

"Okay; where's Granddaddy?" Dahlia asked. She knew her grandfather would make more of a fuss.

Her grandmother always protected Desman—no matter what he did.

"He went to a meeting down at the church."

"Is the church having some special program?" Dahlia questioned as she shuffled through the sack of mail, looking for mail with her name on it.

She came across a letter addressed to her. It was from her father. Dahlia put the letter in her other hand and looked through the rest.

"Can you pull all the bills out I need to pay? I'll pick them up after court."

"Okay."

"When will Granddaddy be back?"

"He should be on his way."

"Are you okay being here alone?"

"I was here alone before you brought your tail over here. I'm fine. I have Jesus . . . and a whole lot of ammunition." Mabel laughed.

"You're too much for me, old lady. I'm going to get out of here. It's getting late and I've been on my feet all day."

"Call me when you get in the house."

"Okay; see you later," Dahlia said, walking out the house.

As she neared her car, she saw Desman getting out of a car. Dahlia got in her car and watched through the rearview mirror as the car drove off. Just like the car Sham was driving, it was marked with GMB plastered on the license plate. Dahlia wanted to confront Desman, but she didn't feel like arguing at the moment, so she started her car and drove home.

When she got home, Dahlia followed her regular routine. She showered, tucked under the covers, and turned on the TV.

Chapter 16

Monday had fast approached. Dahlia made her way inside the court building with Traci and her grandparents beside her. She couldn't help but be nervous. Her palms sweated. Although the case was minor to some, it was major to Dahlia. Jasmine was determined to destroy her character and paint her to be some crazy, bitter woman who wanted her man.

Dahlia, her grandparents, and Traci were waiting in the hall for the case to be called when Jasmine and Antonio passed by. Like the true fraud she was, Jasmine was still on crutches. She walked past, making sure to give Dahlia a smirk.

"So that's his woman?" James questioned, staring at Antonio, who didn't have the dignity to even look back at James. "I'm not impressed."

"Yeah."

"The girl must have no life to keep this court-shit going on," Mabel spoke.

"Let's say a prayer. Dahlia, baby, I know you're okay and any judge with eyes can see that. You don't come to someone's house, then be mad when you get what you deserve," James said as they joined hands and bowed their heads.

James led them in prayer. When they were done, Dahlia had her head down, looking at something on her phone. Traci glanced up and recognized the face of the man headed their way. She nudged Dahlia to get her attention.

"Isn't that Jerome?" she questioned.

Dahlia looked up to see Jerome headed down the hall in search of a courtroom.

"That's him."

"What's he doing here?"

"Shit! I forgot I told him I had court today."

"Well, here he comes," Traci whispered.

"Good morning, Dahlia. Traci?"

"Yes, it's me. How are you, Jerome?"

"I'm good. How are you?"

"I'm good, married with two kids."

"To Charles?"

"Well, of course. I heard who you married. I can't say I saw that coming."

"Some things happen when the woman you want is taken," Jerome said, eyeing Dahlia.

"So you settled for a whore?" Traci spoke.

"Traci!" Dahlia nudged her.

"I'm sorry, but you know I never liked that-bitch," Traci mumbled, hoping James and Mabel didn't hear her.

"Trust, you aren't the only one." Jerome laughed at Traci's bluntness. "I see not much has changed about you."

"Sure hasn't."

"Who is this fella?" Mabel questioned. She'd noticed Jerome the minute he walked up and how he looked at Dahlia.

"Granny, this is Jerome. He's a friend of ours from high school. This is my grandmother, Mabel, and my granddaddy, James," Dahlia said, introducing everyone.

"Hello, Mr. and Mrs. Willowbrook," Jerome spoke in a pleasant tone, shaking her grandparents' hands.

"Nice meeting you as well, youngster," James spoke.

Mabel just stared at him. There was something about Jerome she just didn't like already.

"How is everything going this morning?" Jerome asked Dahlia.

"Waiting; we've been here for like, an hour. I haven't spoke to the attorney today. When she called me on Friday, she said Jasmine hadn't submitted documents from the hospital to support her injuries, which is a good sign. She also said she was going to put in a good word with the judge."

"That's good. Hopefully, the case will be dropped today."

"Hopefully,' Dahlia replied. The tension between the two was so thick everyone felt it.

"Dahlia, can I speak to you in private?" Jerome asked. "No disrespect to anyone."

"None taken, young man," Mabel spoke, looking at Dahlia to make sure she was okay with walking off with Jerome.

"Sure. I'll be right back," Dahlia said, looking at Traci.

"Who-the-hell is that and what was that look all about, Traci?" Mabel questioned as soon as Dahlia and Jerome stepped away.

"That's a dude who went to high school with us. And, Ms. Mabel, I don't know what you're talking about. What look?" Traci replied, playing dumb.

"Traci, you do know I'm smarter than I look, right? I saw how Dahlia looked at you. I know something's up. I don't like him. I hope he isn't trying to date my baby. He reeks drug dealer," Mabel said, looking at Dahlia and Jerome, not far away, in the corner talking.

Dahlia and Jerome made sure not to walk off too far, so just in case her name was called, she would be able to hear it.

"What's up?" Dahlia questioned.

"I don't know; you tell me. I called you and texted you a few times and didn't get a reply. You good?"

"I'm good. I've been busy at the shop, that's all."

"There's something else. You aren't acting the same," Jerome spoke, reaching for Dahlia's hand.

"I'm just going through a lot," Dahlia spoke, pulling her hand back.

"I apologize about the other night. Not about what I said, because I mean every word. It's the truth, but I could have handled my actions a little differently. I was drinking, and I let my feelings for you and my emotions take over. For that, I am sorry. I don't want things between us to be awkward."

"I accept your apology, Jerome. Right now, I'm working on me. I'm not looking to date. I'm still trying to wrap my head around the bullshit I just went through with the last dude. What happened between us never should have happened, but it did. I acknowledge my part in it. I was lonely and vulnerable at the time. I don't want to ruin our friendship because I can't control my hormones. I do appreciate your support by being here today. It means a lot to me."

"I understand your position, and in no way am I trying to rush you into anything. I do want you to know I'm here for you any time you want to talk, and I meant what I said: I want to be more than your friend. I'll settle for being your friend until you feel you're ready, but know my plan is to be your man—always has been," Jerome spoke with a look on his face Dahlia didn't quite like.

Before she could respond, she heard her grandmother calling her name.

"Dahlia," Mabel called out.

"I have to go."

Dahlia made her way back to where her family stood awaiting with the court-appointed-attorney Karen. Jerome followed behind.

"Good morning, Dahlia; how are you?"

"I'm good. I'll be better once all of this is over with."

"I understand. Like I told you a few days ago when I called you, Jasmine still hasn't provided those documents and has requested additional time to get them. I'm asking for the case to be dropped, based on the fact she cannot prove you caused her bodily harm, which is the charge against you. Do you still want to move forward with the charges against her?"

"No; I just want this to be over with."

"Okay," Karen spoke, jotting down some notes on the stack of files she had in her hand. "They should be calling you in a few. I will say this: This judge is a very good friend of mine and I'm confident we will have these charges dropped." Karen winked.

"Will this appear on my record?"

"This is your first brush with the law. I'm sure this won't come up."

"Okay," Dahlia replied.

"See you in a little bit. Cheer up; this is almost over with." The attorney smiled as she walked off, calling the next client on her roster.

"She seems confident the charges will be dropped. Let's just hope little, bitter Betty Jasmine doesn't have anything slick up her sleeves," Dahlia said, hopeful.

They sat around the court waiting area for another hour before being led into the courtroom. Dahlia, her grandparents, Traci, and Jerome sat on one side of the courtroom, and Jasmine and Antonio sat on the opposite side. Dahlia could see from the side of her eye that Antonio kept looking

over to where she sat next to Jerome. The curl of
Antonio's upper lip let Dahlia know he was pissed.
Dahlia didn't even want to talk to Jerome, but
seeing how it made Antonio mad, she laughed and
smiled like she was having the time of her life.

Traci looked over to Dahlia laughing and was
confused at her being so giggly with Jerome.

"I have to go to the restroom," Traci spoke.

"I'll come with you," Dahlia sad. That had always
been the routine for the ladies. They never went to
the restroom alone when something was going on."

"I'll be back," Dahlia told her grandparents and
Jerome.

"What's got you all-giggly with Jerome?" Traci
questioned as soon as they stepped foot out of the
courtroom.

"Pissing Antonio off. I don't care what Jerome is
talking about. I just saw how Antonio was looking
seeing another man showing me some attention. I
know he's trying to figure out who Jerome is and
how long I've known him. And I'm getting a kick
out of it," Dahlia laughed, "because Lord knows I
don't want to talk to Jerome. I actual feel some
kind-of-way knowing he was all finger-deep in my-
shit. He probably sniffed-the-shit out of his fingers
when he left my house because he sure-in-the-hell
didn't ask to wash his hands."

"The way that man's been looking at you, I wouldn't be surprised if you found out he'd sucked his fingers like he was two years old, trying to get a taste of that honey."

"You are so nasty." Dahlia laughed.

"I'm serious. You'd better watch him because I'm gonna make sure I keep my good eye on his-ass. He wants that nookie bad."

"I'm not worried about Jerome. I told him I'm not looking to date and we are better off just being friends."

"Okay; let's get back in here before he comes looking for you," Traci joked.

"Whatever," Dahlia said as they neared the entrance to the courtroom.

Dahlia reached to open the door. When it opened, she was met with Antonio staring right at her.

"I see you have a new boyfriend," he spoke with a smirk.

"Wouldn't you like to know who he is?" Dahlia chuckled. "He damn-sure isn't married or eligible for AARP."

"I was just about to come looking for y'all," Jerome spoke from behind Antonio.

Traci nudged Dahlia and they both laughed, making their way inside the courtroom.

"I told you, my good eye," Traci said.

"Whatever," Dahlia replied, taking her seat.

"Next case!" the judge called out, banging his gravel.

Dahlia looked up to see who was behind the strong voice. She nearly choked on her own spit when she looked up to see Wesley sitting there. Traci raised her head in shock as well.

"What-a-fuckin'-surprise!" Traci said low.

"Right," Dahlia replied, watching her public defender walk across the room, approaching the judge. She slid him a piece of paper and walked out the courtroom, returning moments later.

"Dahlia," she called out.

Dahlia got up from her seat and made her way toward the attorney.

"You're next. I have already requested that the case be dropped and the judge is agreeing. You don't have anything to worry about." She smiled.

"Okay; you know the judge?"

"Yes, he's a good friend of mine. Why? Do you know the judge?" Karen raised her brow.

"I don't know him personally. I know people who know him. I just met him recently at his wife's birthday party."

"Bitch!"

"Excuse me?"

"Never mind all that; just know the charges are going to be dropped," Karen informed her.

Dahlia glanced over to see Jasmine and Antonio talking to Jasmine's attorney.

"We're just waiting for him to finish talking to his client."

Just as the words left her mouth, Jasmine's attorney, an older man dressed in a suit that had seen better days, walked up and handed the judge a piece of paper, then walked back to where Jasmine stood.

"Let's get this over with," the attorney spoke as Karen and Dahlia took their seats.

Jasmine's attorney took the floor. Jasmine sat with a grin on her face as her lawyer tried to make the case against Dahlia. Just as Dahlia had thought: Jasmine wanted to make her out to be a side-chick who'd gone crazy after being cut off. When Jasmine's attorney finished with his lies and pictures of Jasmine after the fight, it was Dahlia's attorney's turn.

Dahlia watched as her attorney got straight to the point to prove Dahlia didn't know anything about Jasmine until the night the fight had taken place at Dahlia's house. She presented the judge with the insurance claim for all the damages that had happened to Dahlia's car as well as a statement from Sharon, Antonio's wife, stating that this wasn't Jasmine's first time doing this. Jasmine had had the last woman he'd cheated with arrested and tried to have Sharon arrested but couldn't because they were legally married. Police reports from domestic-related calls to their home were presented. When she was done, even Dahlia was left with her mouth open.

"Where did you get all that information from?" Dahlia asked.

"I told you: I've been doing this for over twenty years. I know a bitter woman when I see one and I can smell bullshit ten miles away. Now fix your face. You never let a woman who is trying to break you see you doing anything but smiling," she scolded.

"Okay," Dahlia said, putting a smile on her face. From the corner of her eye, she could see Jasmine talking to her attorney with a frown on her face.

Judge Wesley took a moment to look over all of the documents that had been presented to him before he cleared his voice to speak.

"In this case, I'm ruling that all charges be dropped for both parties. I suggest that you two ladies keep your distance from each other and move on with your lives. There is much more to life than arguing and fussing over a man," Judge Wesley said.

"I told you, you didn't have anything to worry about."

"Thank you," Dahlia said.

"You're welcome. Learn to play the game of chess and leave the checkers alone." She smiled before she walked off.

Dahlia stood for a moment processing her last comment before she walked over to where her family waited for her.

"Thank goodness." Dahlia smiled with her hands in the air. "Let's get-the-heck out of here."

"I'm glad you beat the charges. I know it had you stressing. When you have some time, hit me up so we can celebrate you putting this shit behind you," Jerome said.

"Okay, and again thank you for coming to support me."

"I wouldn't have it any other way. I'll let you get back to your family. I can sense my presence isn't wanted by your grandparents." Jerome chuckled.

"Have a good one," Dahlia replied with a slight chuckle at his statement. Her grandparents never hid it when they didn't like someone.

Dahlia had ridden to court with Traci. After they made sure Mabel and James were off, they headed to Traci's car.

"LET'S GO CELEBRATE PUTTING THIS ISH BEHIND YOU AND MOVING FORWARD!" Traci yelled.

"Hell yeah! I guess I got the last laugh." Dahlia smiled as they passed Jasmine and Antonio.

"Where do you want to get something to eat?" Traci questioned as she pulled her car out the parking lot.

"I don't care. All I know is they better have drinks because I'm in need of one, maybe two." Dahlia laughed.

"Jennifer texted me when we were in court about meeting her for lunch at the marina."

"I'm down with that. How has she been since the party?"

"I haven't seen her since then. She hasn't been at work."

"That shit was crazy," Dahlia said, scrolling through her phone, stopping at message that had just come through. "I think Desman's selling drugs for them GMB fools," Dahlia blurted.

"What?"

"Yeah; I ran into Ken Doll. You know he's always gonna give me the real," Dahlia said as she began to fill Traci on what she had found out about Desman and her running into Sham.

"Damn! They have really grown over the years; they started off as a little crew. Charles told me they have shit locked up all around Los Angeles and the I.E., but I hadn't heard anything about them in a while—until I saw Sham getting out of that car."

Dahlia sat and pondered what Traci had just said.

"Do you think Shad will come back around?"

"D, don't think like that. There are too many people out here who want his head. Last I heard, while eavesdropping, was he was in New York in prison on some drug charges."

"I haven't told anyone, but for the last couple of weeks, I've been having these weird dreams and they always involve him."

"What kind of weird dreams?"

"Most are flashbacks of the fights and beatings. The one that has tripped me out the most is the wedding one; I've had it a few times. I'm having a wedding. My daddy is walking me down the aisle and everyone in my family is there, even my mother. When I get down the aisle, the face of the man I'm marrying . . ." Dahlia paused. "It's Shad," she said low, trying not to cry.

Traci pushed her car to the max, pulled into the first empty spot she saw, and embraced her best friend.

"D, don't start that negative thinking. Remember, he's a thing of the past; he isn't coming back around here. Too many people want him dead. Positive vibes and thoughts. That's the devil just trying to fuck-with-you. Plus, I don't think Shad wants to go to war with Mabel Willowbrook. She's straight gangsta, and you know she loves you like a fat kid loves cake. You know her style; she'll pop a nigga and catch a case to see her baby girl smile," Traci joked, trying to get Dahlia to laugh.

"You are so corny." Dahlia chuckled.

"I'm glad I can make you smile. Now let's get in here and have us some-damn-drinks and think about moving forward—like, getting a shit-load of clients; you in the shop, working ten-hour days, six-to-seven days a week, pissing that bald-headed-bitch off; and finally, getting your own shop and telling that messy-bitch Chandra to kiss yo' black-ass," Traci sang.

"Exactly what I need," Dahlia agreed.

Dahlia and Traci made their way through the marina to Killer Shrimp, where they were meeting Jennifer for happy hour.

"She said she's at a table outside," Traci said as they entered the restaurant.

The crispy breeze from the water and the rays from the sun setting provided the perfect background for the ladies.

"Hey, Jen; how have you been?" Traci asked, embracing Jennifer, who'd stood to hug her. "You remember my best friend Dahlia?"

"I'm good. Yes, I remember her; it hasn't been that-damn-long." Jennifer laughed, embracing Dahlia.

Dahlia, who normally wasn't quick to let people in her inner space, hugged Jennifer back. There was something about her embrace that made Dahlia feel the warmth of a mother.

"Traci, didn't give me much background out of respect for you and your situation. How was court?"

"Thanks to your husband and the court-appointed attorney, I was able to get all the charges dropped."

"Correction: my cheating ex-husband. While he was at work, I was filing for a divorce from his-ass.

I had a meeting with my children and I explained it all."

"How are they taking it?"

"My oldest daughter asked me what had taken me so long. She said she'd known for a while he was cheating." Jennifer laughed. "I never knew why she'd moved out and hardly came around. I thought it was the white man she married. My son is questioning everything his father ever told him about being a man."

"Damn, it's hard on kids when their parents have been together so long and they've seen so much love, then it's over," Dahlia said.

"They're grown now and they understand life, which is why I didn't leave when they were younger. I didn't have a father growing up, but I wanted that for my children, so I took more than the average woman. My kids turned out all right though, and for that, I'm grateful. So now it's time I enjoy me; celebrate being fifty, single, and sexy-as-hell," Jennifer sang.

"I know that's right. I want to feel like you."

"What's stopping you? Please don't tell me *a man*! What I should have learned long ago was don't put up with a man's bullshit. He's feeding you bullshit, leave the table. When you know what you bring to the table, you will never settle for bullshit served hot like it's lobster," Jennifer schooled.

"Well, damn, on that note, I need a drink," Dahlia said.

"I'm telling the truth. I was fed so much bullshit over the years, I should leave shit everywhere I go."

The ladies sat and ordered drinks and talked for what seemed like hours. It was refreshing for Dahlia to hear all Jennifer had been through with Wesley and still managed to smile.

"I was going to cancel the trip I'd booked to the Bahamas with those sneaky-bitches, but y'all should come. It's already paid for. I would just need to call the booking agency and change the names."

"You want to go?" Traci questioned. She knew Dahlia could use a vacation with all that was going on; plus, it was free.

"You know, I could use some time away from all this crazy-shit." Dahlia laughed, starting to feel the effects of the shots she'd guzzled.

"I will run it by my husband when I get home and see what he says. If not, Dahlia, you'll have to talk to your boy." Traci laughed.

"You know I got you."

"Well, I have to get my married-ass home and get dinner on the stove for my husband and kids," Traci said as she pulled her wallet out of her purse to pay for the drinks and appetizers she and Dahlia ordered.

"I got it," Jennifer said as pulled out her black card.

"No, it's cool; I have it. You're about to go through a divorce."

"I got this. Shit, this isn't my money; it's Wesley's." Jennifer laughed.

"Well, in that case, go ahead." Traci laughed.

The ladies exchanged goodbyes and went their separate ways. Traci dropped Dahlia off and headed home to her family.

The emotions of the day and the liquor in her system had left Dahlia drained. She ran a hot bubble bath, stripped out of the suit she had on, grabbed a book, a glass of wine and settled in the bath.

Chapter 17

Dahlia woke up feeling better than she had in the last few weeks. She had been carrying the weight of the case on her. She hadn't known how it would go. She knew she was only off because of Wesley, even though she hadn't done the things Jasmine had claimed. She had beat her up badly and it was easy to say she deserved it after the-shit she'd done to Dahlia. She knew Wesley had let her off on the strength that she knew dirt on him. Had another judge walked in that courtroom, the outcome could have been different. It wasn't right, but Dahlia was grateful for Wesley's lustful, cheating ways.

Dahlia turned up the music and started to clean and rearrange her house. The security company was coming to install the camera system in her house. Although the case was over, she still didn't trust that Jasmine would leave her alone. Traci had called early that morning and given her confirmation they were going on the cruise, which left in a few days. Dahlia was ecstatic to be getting out of the city.

After cleaning and rearranging her living room, Dahlia pulled out her suitcase from the back of her closet and dragged it into the living room. She began to pack the things she would take with her, making a list of the items she would need to pick up. Dahlia was booked up for the week, and if she didn't start packing now and waited until the last minute, she was sure to forget something.

Dahlia was headed back to her room when she heard the doorbell. Without looking out the window first, she opened the door and was met with Jerome with a wide grin on his face.

"Is this your thing?"

"What?"

"Showing up to people's homes unannounced?"

"I was in the area and wanted to drop this off to you. I'm going to be out of town for a few days and wanted to make sure you got this before I left."

"Got what?" Dahlia questioned, confused.

"Is this your thing?" he questioned, mimicking Dahlia.

"What?" she asked with an attitude.

"Leaving people outside?"

"No, it isn't my thing. It isn't my thing to show up at people's homes without calling either."

"My apology. I just was in the area and saw your car parked and decided to bring this to you myself," Jerome said, handing Dahlia a bag.

"What is it?"

"Open up the bag and see for yourself. I hope you like it. I know the case was a lot on you and I wanted to just reward you with something."

Dahlia stepped aside and let Jerome in. She hoped he didn't try anything today because she was liable to hurt him and his feelings. She really wasn't up for it.

"It smells good in here. You planning to skip town?" Jerome questioned, noticing the suitcase on the floor.

"Thank you. It's the new candle I got from Bath & Body Works, and no, I'm not skipping town, nosy. I'm going on a vacation."

"Vacation? And I wasn't invited? Damn, you're cold."

"I was invited, and it's all girls," Dahlia said, taking a seat on the floor to open the bag Jerome had handed her.

Dahlia pulled out several gift cards to a wide range of stores for women.

"Did you go into the store and pick every gift card they had?" Dahlia questioned with a chuckle as she pulled out a small box of her favorite perfume, Flora by Gucci, and a pair of Gucci sandals she had been eyeing.

"How did you know this was my favorite perfume and that I had been eyeing these sandals?"

"Because I pay attention. As far as the gift cards, I couldn't decide which ones to get you, so I got all of them."

"Thank you, but I can't accept this stuff from you."

"Why not? There're gifts. People accept gifts every day from friends."

"Like I told you the other day, I'm not looking to date. Accepting lavish and expensive gifts can give the wrong message. I'm not trying to confuse you; I'm not interested."

"Dahlia, this is a simple gift from a friend. Don't trip. I get it you aren't interested in dating right now; I'll wait."

"What if I'm never ready to date you?"

"Only time can tell, but I have a few errands to run before I leave this afternoon. I'll let you get back to what you were doing," Jerome said, preparing to leave.

As he neared the door, he stopped, dug in his pocket, and pulled off several crispy bills from the wad of cash in his hand. "Here; make sure you have a good time." He smiled, handing her the money.

"I don't need your money," Dahlia said, looking at all the hundreds in his hand.

"I'm not asking you if you need it; I'm giving it to you."

"I am good, Jerome. I don't need the money. My account is looking good."

"You are so stubborn." Jerome laughed, laying the money down on the table close to the door. "Like I said, enjoy yourself on me. You deserve it."

"Please take your money with you."

"I'm not taking-shit with me. That's your money, not mine," Jerome said, walking out the door.

"What are you doing here?' Traci questioned, coming up the driveway.

"Hello, Traci; I just stopped by to check on our friend. You going on the ladies-only cruise?"

"Why?"

"I see why you two are best friends. I was just asking so I could say enjoy it."

"Oh; thank you." Traci smiled, bypassing him.

"What was he doing here?" Traci questioned, coming into the house.

"He just showed-the-hell-up again, this time with gifts and leaving money and shit," Dahlia huffed, slamming the front door.

"Damn, bitch, you have gift cards for damn-near every store in the mall. He gave you all of this?" Traci said as she flipped through the dozens of gift cards.

"Yes."

"That man is crushing real hard on you."

"Too-damn-hard! I told him I see him as a friend and I'm not interested in dating. He's gon say, in due time. What he doesn't know is, I'm never going to be interested in dating him. I don't fool with his kind."

"Just keeping telling his-ass that. You want me to tell him? Because you know I have no-damn-problem telling his-ass."

"No; I've got it."

"Okay; well let me know. He did hook you up with all this shit though."

"And he left money. I told him to take it back. I don't need it or want it."

"Damn, bitch, you sure you didn't give him a little taste of the nookie?" Traci questioned.

"Traci, I'm sure. The only thing we did was kiss and he fingered me, which sounds nasty, like I'm some young, high school girl with a hot-ass."

"You didn't even do that-shit when we were in high school."

"You're damn-right. My granny would kill me if she knew I was letting someone feel me up." Dahlia laughed. "Ladies don't do that shit; that's for them nasty girls with no-damn-home-training and class," Dahlia mimicked Mabel. "Why are you at my house anyway? Aren't you supposed to be at work?"

"It's my lunch break," Traci said, picking up the money Jerome had left on the end table. "Did he give you all of this?"

"Yes, and leave that-shit right there. I'm giving it back."

"Why?" Traci spoke, counting the bills.

"Because I don't need that-man's money. I have my own. I'm not rich, but I'm good."

"And your point is? This is twenty-five hundred dollars of someone-else's money for you to spend."

"That I will be returning back to its rightful owner. I don't want it."

"I don't see why. If he wants to just give his money away, let him. You have already made it clear you don't want him and he's still giving away shit. Take it. I know like-hell I would. As your best friend, I'm saying take the money. Use it, save it, just don't give-the-shit back. You want your own shop? Well, here's twenty-five hundred dollars toward it."

"He's going to want something back in return. They all do. I'm not falling for it, so he can take all of this-shit back. The days of putting a price tag on me are over. I've got my-own-shit."

"Shit, if you don't want the money, I do."

"Traci, put that-damn-money down."

"I'm serious. I need a new bathing suit and some other-shit. I don't have a man buying my-ass Gucci and giving me thousands of dollars just because. I have to work for what I get."

"Bitch, you're married."

"That's my point. When Charles gets a raise or bonus at work, he comes home talking about, send the kids to your mom's; I got a little extra cash. What new trick you gon show me?" Traci laughed. "Shit, you've got a man, who didn't even get to stick the tip in, throwing shit at you, and you're talking about giving it back."

"I don't want him to feel I need him or his money, because I don't. If I take his money, that's letting him know I'm gonna take it the next time, and eventually, no matter what he says, he's going to want something in return. That's like playing with the devil, knowing ya-ass is gon get burned."

"Okay, do what you want, Dahlia. He gave it to you and told you he wasn't taking it back."

"Are you ready to be in the Bahamas?" Dahlia questioned, switching the subject.

"Hell yeah! A weekend away with no husband asking me to make him something to eat and no kids arguing over a toy. Lord, I deserve it. Let me get my-ass back to work. I just came to see what you were up to, but as always, not a-damn-thing."

"Whatever, bitch! Like I told you before, I like my boring life. It works for me. You must like it, too, seeing you're my best friend. What the old folks say about birds of a feather flocking together?"

"Whatever," Traci replied, waving her hand in the air.

"Don't be waving me off because I'm telling the truth. You love me and my boring life." Dahlia laughed.

"I do, but I miss the fun one; like the time you called me like I'd already talked to Charles and he knew we were going to Palm Springs for the weekend. I love you regardless, but I want the old, fun chick mixed with the grown woman you are now, that's all."

"Once everything gets in order, we are gonna have them random, red-eye flights out the country just for the hell-of-it." Dahlia laughed, reflecting on the times Traci was talking about.

It was back when she was still heavily-in-love with her ex. Due to his lifestyle, money was never a problem. He'd given her wads of cash just like he'd given her busted lips and black eyes. She was able to live the lavish life of random trips out the country, foreign whips, Gucci, Cartier, and diamonds, some things some women only wished for. But, it all came with a price: dignity, self-esteem, and self-worth. Dahlia could no longer sacrifice her life for materialistic things and love that was controlled like a light switch.

"D, you good?" Traci questioned, noticing Dahlia had drifted off.

"Yeah, I'm good," Dahlia replied. Thinking of all the fun they use to have made her think of how unhappy she was. How afraid she was.

"Although I miss the fun we use to have, Traci, I don't miss the old days," Dahlia admitted. "Missing them would say I miss being unhappy, scared, and lonely, being beat on and controlled, and a whole bunch of other shit," Dahlia spoke, wiping away the few tears that had escaped her eyes.

"I understand and I'm sorry I even brought it up. I never want to put you in a bad head-space, where you even have to think of all that-shit you didn't deserve to go through. You're like a rose. You've been through a lot, yet every day, you seem to blossom more and more."

"Thanks, Traci, but let's talk about something else. You know I'm a crybaby. Let's talk about this trip. Have you got a new bathing suit? I got my big-ass this real cute one from a plus-size boutique shop off Melrose the other day."

"I found this real cute two-piece from Macy's. I have to make sure Charles doesn't see me packing it because he's gon be hot!" Traci laughed. "Let me get my-ass out of here and back to work."

"Right, before you have no job." Dahlia laughed.

"They need me around that-damn-place.

Just as Dahlia was walking Traci out, she saw the AT&T truck pulling in front of the house. After going over everything and signing the paperwork, the technician began installing the security system.

"Ms. Willowbrook," the agent called out in broken English.

"Yes," Dahlia said, coming from the kitchen.

"I'm all done here. Let me show you how to work your new system."

Dahlia wiped her hands and joined the technician in the living room, where he went over a pamphlet of all the features she could use on the new security system. He showed her how she could see who was at her door from the TV in her room and in the living room, how she could turn the lights on and off, and how to lock the doors right from her cellphone. She could also watch her house when she wasn't home.

Dahlia settled in the living room in front of the TV with the dinner she had just cooked, which consisted of grilled catfish with a lemon garlic butter she learned from watching The Cooking Channel. She'd paired it with wild rice and steamed broccoli with a sprinkle of cheese. Dahlia grabbed her champagne glass and the cold bottle of Moet from the freezer.

Dahlia had been so busy the last week, she'd missed all the shows she had become accustomed to watching. Dahlia flipped through her recordings, looking for something to watch. She settled on Oprah's new TV show *Greenleaf* since there wasn't that many episodes to watch so far.

Chapter 18

Dahlia was at the foot of her bed, struggling with her suitcase, waiting for Traci and Charles to arrive. Her week had been long with all the extra appointments. She was looking forward to the trip away from all the drama, being with the girls, and having drinks and enjoying life.

Dahlia checked everything around the house, making sure everything was unplugged or turned off in her absence. She had gone to check on her grandparents earlier in the day to make sure they had money while she was gone.

"LET'S GO, BITCH!" Traci yelled, banging on the door.

"Can you be any louder?"

"Whatever, Dahlia; just bring your bougie-ass on. I haven't been on a vacation in a very long time. I'm excited."

"I know; I can't wait to feel that breeze and smell that fresh water and put my feet in that clear water," Dahlia spoke, pulling her oversize luggage out the door.

"Damn, you two pack like you'll be gone for weeks instead of a few days." Charles laughed as he took Dahlia's luggage from her to put it in the truck.

"A lady has to always have options," Dahlia replied.

"Tell him again."

"I understand options, but shit, it feels like you tryna smuggle a-damn-human in this suitcase."

"Don't tell everyone my secret life," Dahlia joked.

"My bad; I forgot that was top-secret information."

"Right; we're top-flight security of the world, Charles." Dahlia laughed.

"Will you two get your silly-asses in this-damn-truck? We're gonna miss our-damn-flight," Traci fussed.

"We're gon make it," Charles replied, getting in the truck.

Just as Charles was turning and pulling away from Dahlia's house, they saw a car pull into Dahlia's driveway.

"Who's that?" Traci questioned.

"D, you want me to turn around?" Charles asked as they neared the end of the street.

"Nah, that's just Jerome. I told him to stop popping up at my-damn-house unannounced."

"Jerome?" Charles questioned.

"Yeah," Dahlia replied dryly. She was over the annoying pop-ups without him calling her.

"Are we talking about Jerome Morehouse?"

"Yeah, that one."

"D, you're fuckin' with Jerome?"

"No, we're just friends like it's always been. That's what it will always be, but he wants more. I've told him I'm not ready to date."

"Did you make it clear you don't want to date him, or just anyone at the time?"

"I said anyone, but I made it clear we were friends and I didn't want to mess that up."

"What'd he say?"

"Some shit about he'd wait until I'm ready— which is going to be never. I'm not interested in him," Dahlia spoke.

"D, you gon have to make it clear to him you're good. I'm not trying to be all in your business because you're grown, but you're my sister and that-nigga-Jerome is trouble. Try your best to stay away from the dude," Charles informed.

"You're good, Charles. You don't have to worry. Like I said, I'm not feeling him like that. We're good as friends; that's it. Plus, dude's still in the fast life. I want no part of that."

"Good; plus, you deserve someone better than that-nigga. I thought he married that one chick from high school, the chick who was smashing everything walking."

"He did marry her. They are now divorced."

"Figures," Charles replied.

The trio made small talk as Charles struggled through the hectic LAX traffic. After thirty minutes and the exchange of vulgar language, Charles was finally pulling in front of the Delta Airlines drop-off area. Charles hopped out the truck to let the ladies out and help them get their luggage.

"I hope you ladies have a good time. Don't get too drunk or too close to the edge of the-damn-boat," Charles joked as he gripped Traci in his arms and kissed her lips.

"That's enough, guys. Charles, she'll only be gone for a few days," Dahlia joked. "Make sure you don't burn down the house in that time."

"Screw you, D; I can cook. You just make sure you watch out for this fine thang, and make sure she's returned to her boys just as she left."

"I got you."

"And, baby, you do the same. Make sure my sis returns. I know you two are going with someone else, but shit, you two are all y'all got. Safe travels and have a shit-load of fun, but not too much since

y'all are leaving the real party animal at home."
Charles laughed.

"Bye, Charles," the ladies said in unison then
made their way into the terminal. Dahlia and Traci
made it through TSA screening and met Jennifer at
the bar.

"Hey, girl; you ready for this trip?" Traci
questioned as they approached Jennifer.

"You see I have already started on my first drink.
I am beyond ready. Today, I found out my husband
has two other kids with a girl I considered my-
damn-goddaughter. So, yes, I am ready to get the-
hell-out of California, even if it is only for a few
days," Jennifer spoke.

"You can count on it. We gon have a shit-load of
fun and leave all the unhappy-drama-shit right here
in L.A. Once we board this plane, only positive and
fun thoughts; everything else can wait," Traci said,
looking at Dahlia and Jennifer. "Do we all agree,
ladies?"

"Agreed," Dahlia and Jennifer responded.

"Good. Now, bartender, can we get a round of
apple martinis with an extra shot of vodka?" Traci
ordered.

The women had several drinks before boarding
the flight that would take them to Miami, where
they would get on the ship for the cruise.

Chapter 19

After a two-hour delay and a five-hour flight, the ladies had finally made it to Miami.

"About-fuckin'-time," Jennifer blurted out as the women fought to get off the plane.

It was the worst flight ever and they had missed the docking time for the cruise.

"What are we going to do if we've missed the cruise?" Dahlia asked, concerned.

"I'm calling Carnival Cruise Line right now. I know they'd better get me on another-damn-ship. It isn't my fault this-damn-airline is a piece-of-shit. This is the one they highly-recommended during my booking process," Jennifer spoke.

"Let's find our luggage and somewhere to sit. There's no telling what time we'll be leaving here," Traci added.

"I was looking forward to being on an island, but if we can't do that, we can stay right here in South Beach and have a ball." Dahlia laughed, trying to cheer everyone up.

"We can do that, but then I want my money back for the cruise. Miami is nice. I just want to have a-fuckin'-good time. This shit is starting out fuckin'-horrible," Jennifer spoke. "Move-the-hell out my-damn-way!" she cursed, getting annoyed with the lovebirds making out in front of them.

The girl released her man's hand and turned around with her nose flared. Dahlia, Traci, and Jennifer glared back, causing the woman to turn back around without saying anything.

After an hour of going back-and-forth with the cruise line, Jennifer was finally able to get them on another cruise ship, but it didn't leave until the next day.

"So, ladies, I was able to get us on another cruise, but it doesn't depart until tomorrow morning. I was able to get a chunk of my money back since we're losing a day. They also booked us rooms for the night here."

"That's fine with me," Traci said.

"I'm cool with it. I just want to relax and get-the-hell out of these clothes," Dahlia added as they sat in the small café in the airport.

"Me, too, and get some-damn-food. I have eaten enough peanuts; I need some food," Traci spoke.

The women went outside to catch the hotel shuttle that made periodic trips back-and-forth between the hotel and the airport. After showering and changing their clothes at the hotel, the women hit South Beach in search of fun and food.

'It so peaceful out here,' Dahlia thought, looking around at all the people surrounding the beach and bars. The sun was going down and there was a perfect breeze for the strapless romper Dahlia wore. She sat at the bar, awaiting her food and nursing a peach mango margarita. She watched Traci and Jennifer on the dance floor. They had already eaten and thrown back a few rounds of vodka.

Dahlia moved side-to-side to the music playing; she could feel someone approaching next to her.

"How can I help you?" the bartender asked, placing the order of hot wings in front of Dahlia.

Dahlia looked over to see who the bartender was talking to. Her eyes landed on an overdose of dark chocolate in the form of a man standing next to her. She didn't want to stare, but his body was amazing. He was skinnier than she liked her men, but he was good-looking from the side view.

"I'll take three Coronas, a mango margarita, and a virgin strawberry daiquiri. She doesn't need any liquor to add to her mouth or her behavior." The man laughed. "It's for my grandmother."

Dahlia, who had turned her attention back to the drink and food in front of her, quickly glanced back over. She had heard the voice before. It was the guy from Jennifer's party. Dahlia turned as she tried to remember his name. She glanced over again, still trying to remember his name to say hello, but her brain was drawing a blank. *'Ms. Janice's grandson,'* Dahlia thought.

"Gavyn! What-in-the-hell are you doing here?" Jennifer questioned, approaching.

'That's his-damn-name—Gavyn,' Dahlia thought, after hearing Jennifer say it.

"GiGi finished her first semester of college, so we decided to come down here as a family to spend some time with her," Gavyn explained.

"Is Wesley here?" Jennifer questioned, looking around.

"No; he decided not to come."

"Good. I sure couldn't stomach running into his ugly-ass," Jennifer spoke.

"Hello, Dahlia, and I'm sorry I can't remember your name; something with a T?" Gavyn spoke, looking at Traci.

"It's Traci," Traci spoke, nudging Dahlia.

"Got it. Hello, Traci." He smiled.

"Hello, Gavyn. How are you?" Dahlia questioned.

"I'm good; out here to celebrate my little sister finishing up her first semester of college," Gavyn smiled.

His words made Dahlia think of Daniel and how he was in Texas by himself, and that her family should surprise him with a trip to see him.

"Awww, that's sweet. I bet she loves it."

"She does," Gavyn spoke, grabbing the drinks he'd ordered from the bartender.

"How are you, Jen? You hanging in there?" Gavyn questioned. "I talked to Jr. He's taking it very hard."

"I'm doing better since I dropped that cheating-ass-uncle of yours. I hope-like-hell he doesn't try to drag-this-shit out. Just tell his ugly-ass to give me what I'm asking for, or I will suck him dry of everything he owns," Jennifer replied, glaring at Gavyn.

"With all due respect, I will not repeat that and I will stay out of your personal life with Unc. That's between you and him."

"Go fuck-off, Gavyn. I guess his cheating was between y'all, too. I bet you and all of your family knew he was fuckin'-around on me and just watched me looking all stupid and shit," Jennifer ranted, getting in Gavyn's face.

"You'd better back-the-hell-up, Jennifer," an older woman said as she approached. "Wesley's cheating has nothing to do with my child, so you'd better get-the-hell-out of his face with that-bullshit.

Wesley is a grown-ass man. You knew he was cheating before you two got married. I know the truth," the woman spoke, pushing Gavyn back.

"This-shit's about to get messy," Dahlia said low to Traci.

"I know," Traci replied as they watched the drama unfolding.

"Fuck you, Gwen; you and the rest of that-damn-family, sitting up there acting like y'all care about me and my children, knowing my husband is fuckin' everyone around town—hell, even people close to me!"

"That's my brother, and my loyalty is to him. As a woman, I feel your pain, I do, but I also know you accepted the cheating. You accepted it more than once. Did you think he would change? So, if you want to be angry with anyone because your marriage failed, look at your husband and the woman who's looking back at you in the mirror every morning and night. Don't lash out at us. We didn't do anything. If my memory serves me right, my mother asked you why you were taking him back. We can't control who's in our family, so please stay out my child's face. The next time won't be so pleasant, sister-in-law."

"What-in-the-hell is taking so long with these drinks?" Janice said, approaching Gavyn and Gwen.

"I was just over here having a conversation with your daughter-in-law," Gwen spoke.

"Jennifer, what are you doing here?" Janice questioned, giving Jennifer a dirty look as she looked around to see who she was with. "Dahlia, is that you?"

"Hello, Mrs. Janice, how are you?" Dahlia spoke.

"How do you know her?" Jennifer questioned.

"She does my hair. How do you know her?" Janice questioned with a roll of her neck.

"I know Jennifer through my best friend Traci," Dahlia spoke up. She could feel the tension between the family members.

"Oh," Janice said, looking over at Jennifer with her lip curled and her nose in the air. "Dahlia, I'll be calling you once I get back in L.A. to get my hair done."

"Okay," Dahlia replied.

"You, ladies, enjoy your night. Gavyn, where is my drink?"

"Here it is, Granny."

Gavyn handed Janice the drink he'd ordered for her. Janice took her drink from Gavyn and made her way back over to the rest of her family followed by Gwen.

"Despite everything that has gone on, I still consider you my auntie. That's what you've been my whole life. I wish nothing but the best for you," Gavyn told Jennifer.

"Whatever." Jennifer spoke, waving her hand, and turned around. "Bartender, can you bring me a-damn-drink, and make it strong-as-hell," Jennifer spoke.

"You, ladies, have a wonderful night," Gavyn spoke with a smile before he walked off.

"You do the same," Dahlia, followed by Traci, spoke.

"That man is feeling you," Traci said when Gavyn walked off.

"No, he isn't. Stop it."

"Save yourself some time and leave his-ass alone. Just like the rest of the men in that family, including my own son, they ain't shit. Fuck 'em and leave 'em; that's all they're good for. I wish I had known that so many years ago," Jennifer spoke as she guzzled the drink the bartender had sat in front of her.

"I'm good. I just want to enjoy life. After all the drama in my life with men, I'll leave it in God's hands to bless me when He's ready," Dahlia replied, finishing up her drink. "I'm about to take a walk," Dahlia spoke.

Getting off the stool, she straightened out her dress. She wanted to shake off some of the negative energy she felt circling.

"I'm coming with you. We're in another state and some of these people look strange," Traci spoke.

"I'm good; I have my cellphone on me," Dahlia spoke, walking off into the sand.

Dahlia had always had a thing for the beach. Something about the sound of the waves was like therapy to her soul. Dahlia took a seat on a nearby rock, turned on some music, and sang along to the smooth sounds of Sade. She reflected on life and everything she had been through in the last weeks. Something in the pit of her stomach told her more was coming. Dahlia sat on the rock listening to music until her phone was about to die. Dahlia made it back to the small villa where Traci and Jennifer were slumped at the bar.

"I was waiting for you to return. I knew you were with them," the bartender told Dahlia.

"Thank you." Dahlia smiled, looking at Traci and Jennifer.

"They've had a lot of drinks."

"Okay," Dahlia replied.

It was hard, but with the assistance of Gavyn—who just happened to be passing by at the same time—Dahlia was able to get Traci and Jennifer to their hotel rooms.

"Thanks for the help. I don't know how I would have gotten both of their drunk-asses up here."

"Don't worry about it. Have a good night, Dahlia." Gavyn smiled.

"Good night." Dahlia smiled back shyly as she made her way into the hotel room.

Chapter 20

The sun was blazing hot as the women stood in the long line waiting to board the ship for the cruise.

"I hope-like-hell they hurry. I have a-damn-hangover and this sun is draining all the little life I have," Traci complained.

"Shouldn't have been doing all that drinking. You know you're a lightweight," Dahlia laughed.

"Fuck you, Dahlia." Traci giggled. "I was trying to keep up with Jennifer, but I'm no match for her-ass. She was throwing them-damn-shots back so fast, I lost count of how many I'd actually had."

"You need to learn your limits."

"Shit, I'm ready to get some more liquor. I'm on vacation, which equals liquor and more liquor." Jennifer laughed.

"You need to get some rest and some-damn-food in your system before you drink another-damn-drink."

Dahlia laughed. Traci and Jennifer had sat downstairs at the party in the hotel bar until four in the morning, drinking.

"I'll rest once I get back home; I want to party," Jennifer sang, dancing down the line that had finally started to move.

It took over two hours for all the people to get on-board the ship. Dahlia and Traci headed straight to the room. Dahlia was drained from standing in the heat so long. Traci and Jennifer needed to rest to get rid of their hangover before they did any more drinking.

Dahlia had been to a lot of places, and on some of the most lavish planes and yachts, but to date, none were more beautiful than the ocean-view cabin she stood in. It was like a mini-suite in her room. The room had a king-size bed, plasma TV, and the bathroom was bigger than Dahlia's at home. She sat her bags down and went to wipe the room and bathroom down so she could shower.

Once Dahlia had changed her clothes, she went to look for Traci and Jennifer. All of their rooms were next to each other's. Dahlia started with Traci's room. She knocked on the door and got no answer. Something told her to just turn the knob, and like she expected, Traci had left the door unlocked and was slumped on the bed with her mouth wide open. Dahlia moved down to Jennifer's room and found the same result. She was laid out on the bed in a coma.

"These bitches." Dahlia laughed, making sure both ladies were locked in their rooms.

Since she didn't have anything else to do, Dahlia went to explore the ship by herself. Dahlia walked around in amazement at all the ship had to offer. It was like another community in there. Dahlia had actually forgotten she was in the middle of the ocean. She walked around for close to two hours before she stopped for drinks and food. After her meal, her feet were tired, so she made her way back to the cabin to take herself a nap.

Hours Later . . .

Dahlia, Traci, and Jennifer were well-rested as they stepped off the ship in the Bahamas. The women had slept the whole way there. They now had eight hours to enjoy the lovely island before re-boarding the ship.

"DAMN IT, I LOVE IT HERE!" Dahlia yelled, soaking up the fresh breeze.

"I can't wait to get my feet in that water," Traci said.

"I just need a-fuckin'-drink with lots of liquor." Jennifer laughed.

The women all went different ways, agreeing to meet back up for their appointment at the spa. Dahlia decided to go look for what stores the resort had to offer, and wandered into different stores, finding items for her grandparents. After going in almost every store the resort had, she was beat. She found a seat and was able to see the dolphins put on a show. By the time Dahlia made it back to where she was supposed to meet Traci and Jennifer, she was late.

"Even on vacation, she's late."

"Traci, hush. I lost track of time while I was shopping. We're still going to the spa, right?"

"Yes; we were waiting on you," Jennifer chimed in.

The women spent the rest of the time on the Bahamas in the spa. They were treated to full-body massages, facials, manicures, and pedicures. Bottles of champagne kept coming as the women enjoyed the day of relaxation before having to re-board the ship.

Chapter 21

Dahlia was happy to be home after a weekend away from everything and everyone who was stressing her. She felt relaxed. She was excited to take a nice long, hot bath and to be back in her own bed. Dahlia hadn't bothered to unpack her bag. She filled the bathtub with hot water, dropped a bath bomb into the water, and stripped out of her clothes. Just as she was about to step foot in the bathtub, she heard someone beating on her door. She hadn't been home more than an hour and someone was already at her door.

"Who-in-the-hell?" Dahlia mumbled, searching for her cellphone to see who was at her door. From the front camera, she could see Jerome standing at her door with a bag in his hand. "This man!" Dahlia huffed.

She thought about just getting into the tub and ignoring him. How did he even know she was back in town? She hadn't told Jerome how long she would be gone. Just as the thought popped into her head, her cellphone began to ring in her hand, Jerome's name popping up on the screen.

"Why are you at my door? Didn't I tell you about that popping-up-shit" Dahlia said into the phone. "How did you even know I was back? Are you some kind of stalker?" Dahlia half-joked.

"I came by because I have some information for you on what you asked me to look into. And I knew you were here because the mail was cleared out the box. I have been swinging by since you left to make sure nobody was over here fuckin'-with-your-shit," Jerome informed. "Come open the door. You got me out here waiting like I am some stalker." Jerome laughed.

"You're going to have to come back. I'm about to get in the tub. I'll call you when I get out, in about an hour," Dahlia said.

"Okay; I'll be waiting outside," Jerome spoke, before ending the call.

"This muthafucka's got his-damn-nerve hanging up on me," Dahlia said, stepping in the hot, waiting water and turning on the music to relax while she soaked.

An Hour Later . . .

Dahlia climbed out the bath, wrapped herself in her bathrobe, and made her way to her room. Grabbing the stack of mail from the dresser, Dahlia sat on her bed and started to sort through it. After going through a few pieces of mail, she remembered the letter she'd received a few days ago from her father. Dahlia made her way into the living room to pick up the letter from the mail slot in the kitchen, then made her way back into her room. Plopping back on her bed with her feet propped up, she opened the letter.

Dahlia,

How are you my beautiful daughter? It has been a long time since I last saw or talked to you. I said I would let you reach out to me when you were ready to talk, but as always, you and your brothers are always on my mind—you more than anyone because you are my only daughter. It hurts not to be able to see your face and hear your voice on the regular.

I know I'm the only reason I'm sitting behind these walls, but know everything I did was to ensure you and your brothers had a good life. I love my parents, and they both worked very hard to keep a roof over me and my siblings' heads growing up. We didn't have much and what we did have, I watched my parents struggled to get. I vowed that my kids would never see me struggle or know anything about the struggle.

When I first heard your little cry and held you in my arms, I knew I wanted to protect you from guys like me. I wanted to school you on guys and provide you with the finer things in life, so when a man approached you, you would never be impressed. You were my princess, and I wanted to mold you into a queen who only a king like your father could step to you.

Dahlia, I know I have failed you as the first man you were born to love, as a male figure in your life, because I spoiled you with so much. Due to my lifestyle, your mother was removed from your life, then me, too, maybe creating a void within you.

I know my parents love you and your brothers very dearly. I also know they will go to war for you and on the strength of you. Trust me, they raised me. My mama has always been a loose cannon. I don't know how it feels to have a gap without your parents because I've always had mine. I've always had my backbone. How ironic is it, I'm not being what my parents were to me to my own children? I thought my lifestyle was providing my family with the best so they wouldn't see the struggle. It wasn't until now that I realized that my lifestyle did the opposite, and took from my family and took me away from my family.

I just want to say I'm sorry I failed you at being your father. I know it may have left you with some self-doubt within yourself, baby girl. I would love to hear what is going on in your life from you. Just know, Dahlia, you are beautiful, baby girl, inside and out. If a man cannot value you and what you offer, he isn't the one for you. Never lower your expectations for a man. Set them so-damn-high a man must seek God before he can step to you.

Last, but never least, I have replayed our last conversation over and over in my head since we had it. Dahlia, it isn't that I don't think of your mother, I think of my wife every day, but being in here, caged like a fucking animal, fucks with me. I am without the only woman to have my heart outside of you and my mother. It has been years, but that is a pain that will never go away.

This was never our plan, but somehow this has become our reality. Life had other plans for us. I would love to see your face and hear your voice. I think we are both long overdue. What do you say? Do you have some spare time to spend with your old man?

Until my paper and pen meet again, you take care, remain focused on your goals, work hard, and pray even harder. No matter the situation, you will get through it. You are a Willowbrook. You were born with the blood of a beast.

Smile, love always
Your first love, Dad.

By the time Dahlia was finished reading her father's letter, her face was covered in tears. He'd said everything she needed him to say. She'd never told her grandparents, but at times she'd hated her father for leaving her. Dahlia curled up in her bed and wiped the tears from her face. She was going to make it her duty to see her dad within the next few weeks.

Dahlia was lying in bed, watching TV, when she heard banging on her front door again. Dahlia popped up. She had forgotten Jerome was outside waiting. Dahlia threw on some clothes and went to let Jerome in.

"Damn, what kind of bath were you taking?" Jerome questioned.

"A relaxing one."

"You've been crying. What's wrong with you?"

"I'm good."

"You sure?"

"I'm good. What information do you have for me?"

"You remember you asked me to look into the GMB dudes and your brother?" Jerome questioned, making himself comfortable on the couch.

Dahlia took a seat on the other couch, opposite Jerome. "Yeah."

"Well, I asked around, and a few dudes I know confirmed that Desman is, in fact, working with the GMB. He has become the new face of the team. He is in charge of the loading and unloading of their product and money. Word on the streets is they are moving major product daily and are feuding with this dude name Jay. The thing is, nobody really knows who Jay is. All of his people are pushing his work and making moves. He sends them orders through different ways, but nobody has ever seen dude. He has sent messages to the streets that he is going to wipe GMB out, starting with the head, who seems to be playing the background.

"D, like for real, you need to tell your brother to stay from around them GMB dudes. Some-shit is about to go down, and if you don't want to bury him, you'd better convince him to step back," Jerome informed.

"That man is grown. I can't tell him what to do; he doesn't listen to me. The only thing I can do is inform him and pray he takes heed to it."

"You'd better do some kind of enforcing. The streets are about to see a war with the GMB and Jay's crew. The-shit has been circling in the streets for weeks. There's about to be a lot of bloodshed in these streets."

"Thank you for the information," Dahlia replied.

She didn't know how to bring this to Desman since she knew he would deny his ties with GMB and tell her to get out of his business.

"You're welcome, but let's talk about you."

"There's nothing to talk about. Thanks again for the information," Dahlia said.

"So you aren't gon tell me why your eyes are red and puffy? Looks like you were in here crying."

"Jerome, I'm fine. Thanks for your concern though."

"The eyes are the windows to the soul. Your words say you're good, but your eyes say something else. The eyes never lie," Jerome spoke.

"Jerome, I'm good," Dahlia said again, this time more forceful.

"I'll leave it alone for the moment. How was your trip?"

"It was good. I enjoyed myself," Dahlia replied. "I don't mean to be rude, but I have to get ready. My brother is going to meet me at my grandparents in a little bit, and I have a few errands to run."

"You aren't being rude, I did just show up; plus, I have some shit I have to handle. I hope it works out with your brother. This isn't a game out here. Shit is real."

"I'm going to talk to him," Dahlia replied, annoyed.

"Okay, pit bull. Let me know how everything goes. You still owe me a dinner." Jerome smiled, trying to get Dahlia to smile.

"Yeah, okay."

Dahlia was caught up in her thoughts about what he'd just told her, and how could she convince Desman that the GMB were bad people and someone was out to wipe the whole squad out.

Once Jerome left, Dahlia slid into some clothes so she could meet Desman at their grandparents. She had texted him, and he was willing to meet to talk with her, which was a first. Usually, he just ignored her text messages and calls.

Dahlia pulled up to her grandparents' house and didn't see any other cars. She knew her grandparents would be gone to their weekly meeting at the church for game night. She proceeded into the house, hoping Desman really showed up. The house was dark. Her grandmother always left the light above the stove on. Dahlia was about to flip the light switch, when she saw someone sitting in the kitchen.

Dahlia reached for her mace as she began to back up toward the front door to leave. She could hear someone coming down the steps. Dahlia wanted to panic, but she knew she had to remain calm. She didn't understand how they hadn't heard her come in the house. She ducked in the corner where the coat rack hung, filled with jackets people had left.

"Desman, nigga, how much longer are we gon be here? I have some shit I have to do. My baby-mama's trippin'. I gotta get this money to her," a male's voice Dahlia didn't recognize spoke, coming from the kitchen.

"Nigga, I told you I have to meet my sister. She should be here," Desman spoke. "When I'm done here, we gon shake. It isn't gonna take that long."

"I'm here," Dahlia spoke, coming from behind the coat rack.

"What-the-fuck?" Desman jumped, startled. "Why are you hiding and shit?"

"Because I didn't see any cars outside and the house was dark. Who-in-the-hell sits in someone else's house in the dark? What kind-of-shit is that?" Dahlia questioned.

"I just ran inside. I wasn't worried about no-damn-light. What's good?"

"And who-in-the-hell did you bring into our grandparents' house?" Dahlia questioned, looking at the tall, chubby dude headed their way.

"That's my-nigga, Chubbs. He's cool people."

"So you say," Dahlia spoke, looking the man Desman had identified as Chubbs up and down. "Can I speak to you in private?"

"What's this all about, Dahlia?"

"I don't know him. I'm not speaking about anything in front of him, so would you send your company outside?"

"Chubbs, wait for me outside," Desman told the dude.

"A'ight," Chubbs said as he walked past them, staring at Dahlia.

Dahlia turned her nose up. She didn't know what Chubbs stare was about and she didn't care.

"Anything wrong?" she questioned.

"Nah, sweetheart, nothing at all," he spoke. "Des, I'll be waiting in the car."

"What was all that about? You know him or something?"

"No, I don't. He was the one staring at me. You shouldn't be bringing random fools in this house anyway. I see you didn't question him," Dahlia spoke, with a shake of her head. She didn't understand Desman at all.

"Whatever. What did you need to talk to me about?" Desman questioned, folding his arms together.

"I don't know what you're doing out in those streets and I know you aren't going to tell me, but the word on the street is the people you've been hanging with are into some serious shit that's about to escalate into some real deep ish that's going to leave people dead," Dahlia explained.

"Are you serious?" Desman spoke, staring at her for a moment before bursting into laughter. "Dahlia, I'm grown. I can do what I want and hang with whoever I want. I don't know where you're getting this false information from, but tell them to mind their business and stop reporting shit to you like I am your-damn-kid. If this was all you wanted, I'm out."

"That's real selfish of you, but what did I expect? Since you seem not to care about how your grandparents would feel if something happened to your trifling-ass, how do you feel knowing that since you've been hanging out in these streets doing God knows what, there's been a car sitting outside of your grandparents' house for days and hours at a time? Are you so concerned about only yourself that you don't see your bullshit could bring harm to your family? Since you don't give-a-fuck, neither will I. I will promise your black-ass this though: Anyone brings harm to James and Mabel Willowbrook, I'm coming for you. Nobody was coming around here, doing little weird-shit, until you got into it with Sarah and you start hanging in the streets," Dahlia barked, meaning every word she spoke to Desman.

"Dahlia, nobody's scared of you, and I can bet my life on it that nobody sitting outside this house is looking for me," Desman spoke, raising his shirt to show the butt of the gun tucked in his pants.

"I am not scared of no-damn-gun. I've had a gun up to my face daily before. Hell, my grandmother even owns a gun. I'm not impressed. You do know bullets don't have a name on them? I mean what I say. I will find out who keeps sitting outside this house, and if they're looking for you, we gon have a problem," Dahlia spoke.

"Like I said, I don't know who-the-hell's sitting outside this house, but it don't have shit to do with what I'm doing. I will find out, but what happens if the person is looking for you?" Desman questioned with a light chuckle.

"Nobody's looking for me. If they were, they would be sitting outside my house, not here."

"Whatever, Dahlia; I have other shit to tend to, rather than going back-and-forth with you about some shit you know nothing about. I'm out," Desman said, heading out the door.

"Like always!" Dahlia spat, slamming the door behind Desman.

Dahlia took a seat on the couch and fumbled through the stack of mail that was on the table. She picked out the bills she paid for her grandparents. Stuffing the mail in her bag, she headed out the door and headed to the shop. Chandra had texted

Dahlia and asked if she could come into the shop to knock out a few walk-ins. She had agreed since it was a few heads and she was always trying to build her clientele.

Dahlia pulled up to the red light and glanced over at the car with the loud system that was rattling her windows. The windows were so tinted you couldn't see who was inside. The light turned green and the driver laid on their gas, speeding off.

"You gotta be kidding me?" Dahlia spoke, speeding up.

It was the same car that had been sitting outside her grandparents' house. Dahlia remembered the paper tags on the back. She'd made sure to, just in case she ever ran into them. Dahlia tried to keep up, but the way the car darted in and out of the lanes made it hard for Dahlia to tail it.

"FUCK!" Dahlia yelled.

She no longer could see the car. She was stuck at a red light and the police were sitting on the corner, just waiting to get someone. Dahlia was pissed she couldn't find out who was behind that car window. The light turned green and Dahlia headed back to her intended destination.

Dahlia pulled up to the shop and it was jam-packed in the small parking lot that was only to be used by the shop. Everyone who rented a booth had an assigned parking spot, marked with her name.

Dahlia pulled up to her parking space and there was a car parked there. Dahlia blocked the car in and grabbed her stuff from the car. Since someone had decided to park in her space, she decided to make it hard for them to leave.

"Hey, Marlena, can you find out who's driving the white Audi that's in my parking space?" Dahlia questioned. Marlena was Chandra's younger sister who helped around the shop from time to time.

"That would belong to me," a male's voice spoke from behind Dahlia.

"Hello, Gavyn; what are you doing here? Where's your grandmother?" Dahlia questioned, turning around and looking for Ms. Janice.

"My grandmother isn't here. I came to see if you could give me a touch up?"

"Sure," Dahlia spoke, looking at Gavyn's freshly-cut hair. "But I don't see what's wrong with your hair—your line is straight, fade isn't too high or too short. Are you trying to pull a Tyrese and go bald?"

"Okay, so you busted me." Gavyn chuckled. "I actually came in here today to ask you out on a date."

"A date?" Dahlia questioned.

"Yes, a date."

"I'm not really interested in dating at this time. I actually just got out of a little situation that I'm still trying to deal with."

"Okay, let's not say a date, and consider it just hanging out. We can always use new friends."

"That is very true."

"So, what do you say? You mind hanging out with a newfound friend?" Gavyn asked.

Dahlia pondered Gavyn's invitation for a moment. "Sure, I'll take you up on your offer to hang out with a new friend."

"Okay," Gavyn said, lightly blowing out his breath.

"Did you think I would say no?" Dahlia questioned, noticing how perplexed Gavyn had seemed when she was deciding if she would take him up on his offer.

"To tell you the truth, I did. I asked your friend Traci and she told me what you just told me, that you weren't interested in dating. I asked her why, thinking she could give me some insight. She told me I should ask you myself. I gave it some thought and decided I would come and ask you myself, and pray you would say yes." He smiled.

"Well, I guess today is your lucky day."

"It is. I would have been embarrassed if you'd turned me down in front of all these people."

Dahlia turned and noticed almost everybody in the shop had their eyes locked on Dahlia and Gavyn.

"Here," Dahlia spoke, scribbling her number on the back of a receipt she'd found at her work station. "Give me a call later. I need to get set up to getting ready to help someone. Oh wait, I blocked you in." Dahlia laughed, sitting her bag down and grabbing her keys.

"Damn! Like that?" Gavyn laughed as they made their way out the shop.

"Doesn't it say reserved parking for Dahlia Willowbrook? I don't think that name suits you too well." Dahlia laughed.

"I thought that was the perfect spot to grab your attention."

"It was, because I was pissed."

"I'll let you get back to work. I hope you have a great day."

"Likewise." Dahlia smiled. *'Damn, that man is fine!'* Dahlia thought as she watched Gavyn as she backed her car up so he could move his car. She'd seen him when he first came to the shop and at Jennifer's party, but she really hadn't paid him that much attention. She'd really noticed him in Miami, and today, he was looking good and smelling even better. Once Gavyn moved his car, Dahlia pulled into her parking space and made her way back inside the shop to take the next person in line.

Chapter 22

Dahlia stood in the mirror, changing clothes for the umpteenth time, trying to figure out what she would wear for her date with Gavyn.

"Dahlia, how many more times are you going to change? Shit, you gon make my-damn-head hurt," Traci expressed, going through the clothes Dahlia had scattered all over her bed.

"Nothing looks right. I don't want to look too sexy. I told him it wasn't a date. I can't walk in the place looking like I'm trying to sleep with him."

"Then put on some jeans and a T-shirt," Traci suggested.

"That isn't dressy enough for a first outing."

"Well, bitch, I can't help your ass," Traci said, picking up her glass of wine and continuing to watch Dahlia look for something to wear.

After nearly two hours of changing clothes and nothing seeming to look right, Dahlia finally settled on a pair of distressed jeans that fit her curves just right. She paired it with a long, cotton tee and strappy, open-toe heels. Dahlia pulled her hair into a high bun. Like always, her makeup was beat to the gods.

"How do I look?" Dahlia asked Traci, turning from the mirror.

"Bitch, like you did in the last twenty outfits: cute-as-fuck." Traci laughed.

"I can't stand you. I'm being for real. Do I look real fat?"

"You look real nice, like always."

"Thank you. I need to go back on my diet and lose this-damn-weight."

"Girl, hush all that-shit-up. You are beautiful. You are gorgeous no matter the size. Beauty is not measured by size. Now go meet that man and enjoy ya-damn-self. You deserve it," Traci spoke.

"Okay; I'll text you when I get there."

"And every move you make."

"You know it."

Dahlia laughed as she got in her car to go meet Gavyn. She wasn't comfortable with him picking her up from her home because of all that had happened in the past. And she didn't need another man popping-up like Jerome.

Dahlia pulled up to the address Gavyn had given her to meet him. It was a little place in the cut, right off 3rd and La Brea. Gavyn was parked and waiting outside his car. Dahlia pulled alongside him and admired his cool demeanor. He was dressed casually in denim jeans and a nice, cotton tee that wasn't too big or too tight that showcased his chocolate, tattooed arms.

"Did you have a hard time finding the place?" Gavyn questioned as he opened the door for Dahlia.

"No, I didn't, but what is this place?"

"It's called Sip and Paint. It's a studio where you sip on wine and paint whatever picture you choose. I thought it was a nice place to relax and just talk over some nice wine and show off your creative side."

"Okay; I have never heard of it."

"I know it sounds corny. I came with my sister for her birthday and found it very relaxing. I think you'll like it."

"I wish I'd known we were painting; I would have worn something else," Dahlia spoke as they headed inside the place.

"They give out aprons. Plus, you look beautiful."

"Thank you." Dahlia blushed.

Gavyn let Dahlia pick the picture they would paint and choice of wine they would drink. Gavyn and Dahlia sat opposite each other and talked.

"So, Gavyn, why are you single?" Dahlia asked. She couldn't understand, as handsome as he was, how he was single. "Are you crazy?"

"Are you crazy?" Gavyn asked with a raised brow. "I'm single because I haven't found the right woman for me. I thought I had, but she turned out not to be the woman I saw me spending the rest of my life with. I know you said you've just got out of a situation. Why did that end, if you don't mind sharing?"

"He lied about everything, from his job and age to his relationship status."

"Relationship status?"

"Yes; he told me he was divorced. He is still legally married and also has a girlfriend with an infant child he never mentioned."

"Damn!"

"Yeah, it was a mess. Trust me, I lived it."

"Would that happen to be why you were in my uncle's courtroom?" Gavyn questioned.

"How do you know about that?" Dahlia questioned.

"I told my uncle you and I were hanging out tonight, and he told you were recently in his courtroom over some issues with your ex-boyfriend and you seemed like a very nice young lady.

"Yes, it was. I got into a fight with my ex-boyfriend's baby's mother and I ended up in jail.

She pressed charges, which is how I ended up in Wesley's courtroom," Dahlia spoke.

"Sorry to hear about that."

"It's cool; I beat the charges, thanks to your uncle. I'm leaving that drama and mess behind me."

"That's always the bigger person."

"So what did your ex do that made you change your mind about her being the one for you?"

"She grew up having a lot of materialistic things. When we started dating, I noticed she liked nice things. As her man, I wanted to provide those things for her, but when I made a career change and left the corporate world to start my own business, she thought I was crazy. She told me she couldn't be with a man who wasn't making at least six figures. I told her I couldn't be with a woman who didn't see my potential or support my goals. I helped her pack her bags. She moved in with the dude she had been creeping with, who also was my frat brother and a so-called close friend of both of ours.

"Six months later, I opened my own fitness studio. I now have four locations. She and that friend broke up a few months ago, and she has been begging to come back. She didn't see the potential, but now that I make more than her minimum of six figures. She wants to come back. I happily declined because I want a woman who wants to be with me for me, not for the money I make. Money can easily disappear. I want someone who is willing to stand by my side like I would theirs, no matter the change in money or physical appearance. I want genuine love, that old-school, nineties R&B love." Gavyn smiled. "Someone to stand the test of time."

"I bet she's hurt."

"That isn't my concern; I don't look back. I keep moving to better things."

"So tell me more about your fitness studios?"

Dahlia and Gavyn sat and talked until the painting studio was on the verge of closing.

"Are you ready to turn it in? I could go for some chicken wings," Gavyn suggested.

"Where did you have in mind?"

"There's a little hole-in-the-wall place not too far from here that has the best wings L.A. has to offer. They're still open if you want to join me in getting some good food."

"I'm down."

"Do you want to meet me there, or leave your car her and ride with me?"

"I'll ride with you. Don't try anything now. I have mace and a gun-toting grandmother," Dahlia said jokingly.

"Thank goodness I was raised by woman to be a gentleman, or hell, they'd beat my ass, so I think you're in good hands. You've met my grandmother, who also raised my mother." Gavyn chuckled as he opened the door for her.

"I hope so." Dahlia smiled as she climbed in the car.

The two made small talk on the short drive down La Brea. Just as he'd said, the place was small, tucked in the corner. If you'd never been, you'd have a hard time finding it. Reggae music blared through the speakers as Gavyn led the way in, searching for the perfect seat for them.

"Do you have a preference of where you want to sit?" Gavyn asked.

Dahlia looked around the small eatery for any available space. To be such a little spot, it was packed. "The patio," Dahlia said, pointing to the attached patio, where there were only a few people sitting around.

"Okay."

Gavyn led the way and pulled out Dahlia's seat before he took a seat across from her.

"What are your favorite wings?" Dahlia questioned, scanning the menu of the wings the place offered.

"Since I am Baldwin Hills, born and raised," Gavyn smiled, "I always get the Baldwin wings. They're my favorite, but all the wings are good."

"Hmmm, I see," Dahlia said, reading over the menu.

The place had named the wings after cities within the Los Angeles County limits. Dahlia thought it was unique.

"Welcome to Los Angeles House of Wings. What can I start you out with today?" the waitress asked.

"This is my first time here. What do you suggest?"

"We're famous for the hot wings, which are our L.A. wings. They're marinated in a secret spice and drenched with a special blend of hot sauces. My favorite is the Wood wings. They're sweet-and-spicy BBQ-flavored wings."

"I'll try those with an order of seasoned fries and a strawberry lemonade," Dahlia ordered.

"I'll take an order of the Baldwin wings, with a side order of extra sauce, onion rings, and a strawberry lemonade," Gavyn ordered. "The strawberry lemonade is the best."

"I think Hawkins Burger in Watts has the best lemonade in Los Angeles," Dahlia informed Gavyn.

"Their strawberry lemonade is good, but I think it's better here."

"We will have to see then." Dahlia laughed.

Dahlia and Gavyn were in a deep conversation, talking about Gavyn's plan to expand to more fitness studios and Dahlia's plans to open her own hair salon, as they waited for the food to be delivered. Dahlia saw the shadow of a man approaching their way, but didn't pay it much attention because there were a lot of people around and an empty table not too far from them.

"What's good, Dahlia? What're you doing out this late?" His words were slurred, and by the bottle of liquor in his hand, Dahlia knew he was drunk.

"Hey, Jerome. I'm grabbing something to eat with a friend," Dahlia looked up and replied.

"Gavyn, this is an old high school friend of mine, Jerome. Jerome, this is Gavyn."

"Hello," Gavyn spoke, reaching out his hand to give Jerome a handshake.

"What time are you going home?" Jerome questioned, never acknowledging Gavyn's presence or hand.

"I don't know. Why?" Dahlia questioned, annoyed with Jerome's line of questioning and how he was treating Gavyn. It was uncalled for.

"Call me when you make it to the house—if you're going home—I might have some information for you," Jerome spoke, hawking Gavyn as he walked off.

"What's up with dude?"

"I don't know," Dahlia replied. "I'm sorry about that."

"Seems as if he's upset about you sitting here with me. I don't mean to pry in your business, but did you two have anything going on before?" Gavyn questioned, noticing how Jerome had given him a death-stare before walking off.

"No; he's just a friend I recently ran into. He was there for me as support with the case and some other things, but that's it. We're just friends."

"The way dude just grilled you, I think he wants it to be more than friends," Gavyn informed her.

"We're just friends," Dahlia repeated.

Dahlia and Gavyn finished their wings and were enjoying the conversation when Dahlia's phone started vibrating on the table.

"You need to take that? Ol' boy calling to see if you're home yet?" Gavyn joked.

"No, it's not him." Dahlia laughed. "Excuse me. Let me take this," Dahlia said, picking her phone to see who was calling her from a Texas number.

"Hello," Dahlia said into the phone.

"This is a collect call from . . . *Shamera* . . . Do you accept?" the recording stated.

"What-in-the-hell?" Dahlia spoke, shaking her head. Dahlia followed the prompts to accept the collect call.

"Dahlia, I need you to come bail me out," Sham said as soon as the call was connected.

"Sham, I don't have any extra money to bail you out."

"I don't need your money; I have bail money. Desman will meet you with the money. I just need you to bail me out. Please, Dahlia," Sham begged.

"All right; where do I need to meet Desman?"

"He should be calling you to tell you where to meet him."

"All right," Dahlia replied.

"You have to go?" Gavyn asked.

"Yes, my auntie is in trouble. I'm sorry. Can I get a raincheck?"

"Of course; how could I turn a pretty lady like yourself down? Let me find the waitress to pay our bill and I'll get you back to your car."

"How much was my food? Dahlia questioned, reaching in her purse to pay for her food.

"Please don't insult me. I've got this," Gavyn said, walking to find the woman who was serving them.

Dahlia texted Desman, asking for the address to meet him to pick up the money to bail Sham out.

"We all ready to go?" Gavyn questioned, approaching the table.

"Yes."

Dahlia's mind was everywhere on the short ride back to her car. She didn't know what Sham had gotten herself into now. She knew it had something to do with her new boyfriend, who was in deep with the GMB, because Desman was bringing the money to bail her out. She had seen this scene play out many times before.

"You okay?" Gavyn asked, noticing how distant Dahlia had become since she'd gotten the call.

"Yeah, I'm good; just a lot on my mind. Thanks for getting me out the house."

"You're welcome. I hope I can get you out the house more often."

"I did enjoy myself tonight, thank you. I'll let you know when I'm ready to cash in on that raincheck."

Dahlia smiled as they pulled next to her car. Gavyn got out, walked around, and opened the door for her. Once she got out his car, he held the door open for her to get into her own car.

"Please let me know you made it to your destination. I enjoyed hanging with you and I hope we can do this again soon."

"I will let you know. Again, thanks, and have a good night."

"Good night," Gavyn replied. He walked back to his car and watched Dahlia pull off.

Dahlia plugged the address Desman had texted her into her navigation unit. The address looked very familiar to Dahlia. When she pulled on the block, it hit her. It was an old corner store her ex use to smuggle drugs in and out of. Dahlia knew this was confirmation Desman was selling drugs when she saw him walk out the store.

"What you doing over here? This is a heavy-traffic drug area," Dahlia said when Desman approached her window.

"Why are you always in my business? Didn't you come here to get the money to bail Sham out?"

"You know I did."

"That should be the only thing you're asking me about. Here," Desman spat, shoving the bag in Dahlia's window. Get out of here and go bail Sham out. She has shit to do," Desman said, walking off.

"Bastard!" Dahlia replied, speeding off the street.

Dahlia had already called the bail bondsman she'd worked with time-after-time to get Desman, Sham, then herself out of jail.

"What's good, Tommy?" Dahlia said, walking into the office.

"I can't call it. I've already called it in. Sham should be ready by the time you get there. You Willowbrooks have had a rough-ass-month. Who's gon be next?" Tommy laughed. "Mabel?"

"Forget you, Tommy. What was she arrested for anyway?"

Tommy rumbled through the stack of papers on his junky desk until he found the file with Sham's name on it. "It looks like she was stopped for an improper lane change and an outstanding warrant for failure to appear in court."

"Thanks again, Tommy. You always come through."

"You're welcome. Y'all need to stop getting y'all's asses arrested." Tommy laughed.

"You don't have to worry about me. I don't plan on getting arrested ever again. I can't vouch for those other two." Dahlia laughed as she walked out the bail bonds office.

She hoped Sham had already been processed-out by the time she made it to the jail because she was ready to go home and didn't feel like waiting. As always, when she got there, the station was filled with people waiting on their loved ones to be released. Dahlia headed to the front desk.

"Hi; I am trying to see if Shamera Willowbrook is ready. Her bail papers should have come over more than an hour ago?"

"We're backed up. Take a seat. Whoever you're picking up will be out once they've processed-out," the woman sitting behind the desk spat rudely.

Dahlia stared at the woman. She wanted to say something to the woman really bad, but bit her tongue and took a seat. It took over two hours for Sham to finally be released.

"Why you looking all-mad and shit?" Sham said, fishing in her purse for a cigarette.

"Because I am. I've been waiting out here for two-damn-hours. I could be at home sleep, or still on my date."

"Date?" Sham questioned.

"Yes, a date," Dahlia said as they walked out the station.

"With who?"

"You're all in my business."

"Girl, you're my niece. Now answer the question."

"Some guy I met. Now tell me who you're seeing? Because I know they have to be in heavy with the GMB. I saw the plate on the car you were driving the last time I saw you. I know for a fact that's their trademark. I also know you being arrested tonight had something to do with them. I know Desman is involved, even though he claims he isn't. He gave me over sixty thousand dollars last week and twenty thousand tonight to bail you out. So you tell me, what's good?" Dahlia questioned as they approached her car.

"Dahlia, can I talk you for a moment?"

"*What-the-hell?* Are you following me?" Dahlia questioned.

"Dahlia, how do you know this man?" Sham questioned, a frown on her face. She never took her eyes off Jerome.

"He's a friend who went to high school with me. Jerome, are you following me?" Dahlia questioned again.

"D, how do you know this-bitch?" Jerome glared at Sham.

"Wait a minute, Jerome. This is my auntie; I will not tolerate disrespect."

"This-shit's about to get real interesting." Jerome laughed. "You should have been asking her about GMB and your brother. She's fuckin' the head-nigga, but I guess that's all I am good for: helping you out with shit while you're grinning in the next-nigga's face."

"I'm not about to do this-shit with you. You are fuckin'-drunk and making an ass out of yourself. You want to talk to me? Wait until you're sober and can talk with some respect and sense. Let's go, Sham," Dahlia called out to Sham, who still hadn't broken her stare at Jerome.

"Dahlia, how much do you know about that-man?"

"He's a friend I went to high school with. I haven't seen him in a few years. Why?"

"Nothing. Just stay away from him. He's trouble."

"What do you mean, he's trouble?"

"That isn't important. Just listen to what I say and stay far away from his-ass. He's trouble. You don't need that kind of drama in your life."

"All right," Dahlia replied. "Where am I taking you?"

"You can drop me off at my parent's house."

Sham was the second person to say Jerome was trouble. Dahlia wanted to know why. Dahlia had checked her mirrors several times to ensure Jerome wasn't following her. She was going to spend the night at her grandparents' just to make sure he didn't pop-up at her house.

"You staying here tonight?" Sham asked.

"Yeah; it's late and that-fool knows where I live. I have a security system, but I'm not chancing it. I'm about to run to CVS real quick."

"I'll be gone by the time you get back. My ride is on the way."

"Okay," Dahlia said, letting Sham out and watching her get on the porch.

Dahlia pulled out, going to CVS to see if she could grab something for the headache she felt coming on. She always left clothes at her grandparents', so she knew she would have something to sleep in. As Dahlia was pulling off the street, she saw lights approaching. She hit the corner and turned off her lights. She didn't know what had caused her to do it, but she did, and to her surprise, it was the same black Lexus that had been sitting outside the house. She watched Sham get inside and the car sped off.

"What kind-of-shit are you into, Sham?" Dahlia said as she pulled into traffic, making sure to lag a few cars behind.

After following the car a few blocks, the car came to a stop. Only Sham got out.

'Who-in-the-hell is this mystery man?' Dahlia thought.

Dahlia followed Sham and the mystery man for several more stops, all at which only Sham got out.

Dahlia followed behind them to the block she had met Desman only hours ago. The car was parked and the driver shut off the lights, which was a first. This time Sham didn't get out. Dahlia's anticipation grew to see if the mystery man behind the driver's seat would get out.

Desman came walking out the storefront, a small bag in his hand. He approached the driver's side of the car. The window came down, but from Dahlia's view, she couldn't see any of the facial features of the man. Desman put the bag in the window and shook the man's hand. Dahlia could see the man's tattooed arm, custom watch, and the pinkly ring on his finger. The ring. There weren't many like that ring. Dahlia stared, almost in a shock.

"No!" she shouted. *"This can't be. D, you're trippin'! Stop getting yourself worked up,"* she thought.

When she looked back up, the car was pulling off in the opposite direction. Dahlia pulled herself together and headed back to her grandparents' to get some rest, headache medicine forgotten.

Chapter 23

Dahlia got up and went to the kitchen, where she found her grandmother over the stove whipping up her famous butter-cheese grits.

"Good morning," Mabel said as Dahlia's bare foot hit the cold kitchen tile. "Don't you come in here with no shoes on your feet. Breakfast is almost done," Mabel spoke, never lifting her head from what she was doing at the stove.

Dahlia made her way back up the stairs and quickly returned with a pair of house slippers on.

"Thank you. What brought you by in the wee hours?"

"Good morning, Granny. I had to go pick up your daughter."

"Pick her up?"

"Yes; she was arrested on a bench warrant."

"That child's always into something. That the only reason she was in jail?"

"She was stopped for an improper lane change, and when they ran her name, she had a warrant, so they arrested her."

"I'm sorry you had to bail her out. I really appreciate all you do for this family. You help us out a lot, but I want you to focus on you, Dahlia.

You have to stop running when we call. I know you never like to tell me no, but sometimes you need to. I know you want your own shop and you deserve it."

"Thank you, Granny, but last night I didn't have to pay to bail Sham out. Someone already had the money. I picked it up from Desman—"

"Desman?" Mabel questioned. "What-in-the-God's-hell is that child into? Where is he getting all this money?"

"I'm not sure, but whoever Desman and Sham are dealing with seems to have loads of money."

"Sounds like nothing but trouble. That-damn-car was by here."

"When?"

"This morning, when I went to have my morning cigarette and coffee on the porch."

"I don't think that car has anything to do with Desman, but with Sham."

"Why do you think that?"

Dahlia filled her grandmother in on what had happened that night with the car. What wasn't adding up was why whoever-it-was still coming by if they had been in touch with Sham.

'The ring,' Dahlia thought.

"Dahlia, you good, baby?"

"When the driver of the car Sham was in reached out to shake Desman's hand, the ring . . . the ring the man wore. It looked real familiar."

"Familiar? Like what? Hell, like who?" Mabel questioned, her hands on her hips, demanding an answer.

"I don't know. I think I'm just overreacting. A lot happened last night. I could be searching for stuff that isn't even something." Dahlia smiled.

"Okay; well, if you say you're okay, I am going to go with that—even though I think it's different. What do you have planned for the day?"

"Work. I'm about to shower and head to the shop. I have a few clients on my schedule today. What are you doing today?"

"The same as I do every day—dress and rest." Mabel laughed. "No, I am going to go down to the church and help them do some things around there."

"Oh, okay. What's for dinner?"

"I haven't decided yet. I will before I leave the house. I just don't know what I have a taste for right now."

"Okay; let me know if you cook before I go home, so I don't have to cook."

"Ain't that some shit."

"There's no cooking like Grandma's cooking, especially when you make these homemade biscuits. And the chocolate chip cookies with the assortment nuts. Yum!"

"Dahlia, get out of here. One day you'd better be in the kitchen doing all that. My fine-ass is getting old and tired."

"I got you, Granny." Dahlia hugged her grandmother.

"You better," Mabel said, setting a plate of food in front of Dahlia.

Dahlia and her grandmother sat and talked as they eat breakfast.

When Dahlia was done, she helped her grandmother clean the kitchen before making her way up the stairs to get ready for work. When Dahlia got upstairs, she tried calling Traci to tell her what had happened but she didn't answer, so Dahlia decided to text her.

By the time Dahlia finished taking a shower and getting dressed, Mabel was already gone.

♋•♋

Dahlia walked in the shop with a smile on her face. The shop was full of people waiting to be serviced.

"Hello, everyone," Dahlia sang.

"Hey, D, some flowers came for you. I sat them on your workstation." Chandra smiled.

"Thanks," Dahlia replied, making her way towards her workstation.

Most woman would have beamed seeing the beautiful lilies in the long, gold vase. Dahlia frowned. Grabbing the vase, she marched out the door straight to the trash. Dahlia dumped the whole vase into the dumpster before heading back inside and rushing to the restroom. She gripped the sink to hold her balance. Her hands shook. She felt dizzy. Her heart pounded. Sweat mixed with tears streamed down her face.

"Fuck!" she mumbled. She hadn't experience a panic attack in almost two years. "You got this, D; just breathe. One-two-three-four-five-six-seven-eight-nine-ten," she coached herself as she inhaled and exhaled.

KNOCK KNOCK! Someone was at the restroom door. "Is someone in here?" a voice asked.

"Yes . . . I'll be out in a second," Dahlia replied, turning the faucet on, letting the water run on her hands before splashing water over her face. She counted to ten once more, splashing more water over her face. Getting herself together as much as she could, Dahlia exited the restroom to a small line of people waiting to use it that had formed.

"Sorry, ladies." She smiled before walking off.

Dahlia made it to her station and made eye contact with Chandra, who asked with her eyes if she was okay. Dahlia simply nodded her head with a weak smile. Chandra smiled back and turned her attention back to the client sitting in her chair.

Dahlia set up her workstation and focused on what was ahead of her. Her first client was headed her way with a wide grin on her face.

"Hey, girl; what's got you walking up in here like you're floating on clouds? You found yourself a new man?" Dahlia questioned.

"Girl, hell naw. My-ass is still single and fuckin' with these nothin'-ass-niggas." Gabby laughed. "Unless that fine-ass-nigga by your car is your brother or cousin? If so, D, hook-a-bitch-up."

"Looking for me?" Dahlia questioned.

"Yeah; he's fine-as-shit, too. And, he looks like he's paid."

"Are you sure he's looking for me?" Dahlia questioned with a slight blush on her face. She hadn't recalled telling Gavyn what her favorite flowers were. Only two other men knew that.

"Yeah. He was like, 'Aye, pretty lady.'" Gabby smiled. "'You going in the hair shop?' I was like, 'Yeah.' He was like, 'You know Dahlia?' And I was like, 'Yeah; that's who's about to hook my hair up.' He was like, 'Tell Dahlia I'm looking for her.' I was like, 'Okay,' but I didn't get his name. Who is that nigga? He looks like he's paid with his fine ass." Gabby smiled lustfully. "I hope he isn't your man, because that would make me disrespectful."

"I'm not sure who it is. Give me a second, Gabby. Take down your hair. I'll be right back," Dahlia spoke, making her way outside to see who was looking for her.

She knew it wasn't Gavyn. They'd agreed he would only come to the shop when he was bringing his grandmother. Only one person popped into Dahlia's head who would bring her those flowers in that vase. She prayed it wasn't him. Dahlia made it to the shop's parking lot and froze. *It was him.* Dahlia closed her eyes and opened them again. It was him—her worst, living nightmare. It was Shad, her ex-boyfriend.

"Look at Ms. Willowbrook. Girl, you are still fine, like a classic bottle of wine. You've lost a little weight. It looks good on you. I been told you dropping a few pounds wouldn't hurt. I like it." He smiled.

Dahlia wanted to run, run fast and far away from him, but she couldn't get her feet to move. She hadn't looked him in the face since the day he'd put her in a coma over two-and-a-half years ago. She had once loved him. Loved him so dearly she'd made excuses for him every time he gave her a black eye. Every time he came home smelling like another woman.

"I see you didn't appreciate the flowers I bought for you. Lilies not your favorite anymore?" he questioned as he neared Dahlia.

The flowers were always her make-up gift. Along with a pair of designer shoes or a handbag. It all depended on the beating she'd taken.

Dahlia didn't reply; she just stared at him with a blank expression. She was hoping this was some sick dream, and at any moment, she would wake up from it. Her nostrils sucked in his signature Gucci cologne. It was a smell that use to make her weak in the knees from just the smell alone. At that moment, all she felt was nausea. She hated him. The smile that had once melted her heart scared her and made her want to faint.

"Wh . . . why are you here?" she questioned just above a whisper, frightened by his presence before her.

"You aren't happy to see me? I came to let you know I was back in town and for good. I just wanted to be the first to let you know before anyone else told you, baby. Things are about to go back to how they use to be, so just prepare yourself to see a whole lot of me, baby. And I do mean *a whole lot* of me. Don't look so sad; this is a good thing. I heard shit's been crazy since I left. I even heard you started fuckin'-with-lames who got you catching cases and shit. Don't worry, daddy is back and you know you are always welcome home."

Shad chuckled as he walked the short distance back to his running car. "You play ya' cards right this time, there might be something real special in it for you. I see you're still working at this piece-of-shit for Chandra and don't have your own. Be good and you might get blessed."

Shad smiled and sped out the parking lot, down the street.

Dahlia stood, unable to move, and watched until Shad's car could no longer be seen. She didn't know what he meant by she would see a lot of him. He wasn't supposed to be here. Dahlia gathered herself together before she made her way back inside the shop to do Gabby's hair. She refused to let him break her down. No, she was bigger than that. She was stronger. She was no longer the weak woman he use to beat on.

"Sorry about that," Dahlia said when she made it back to the waiting Gabby.

"Girl, it's fine. So is that fine-ass-nigga yours?"

"No, that's my ex-boyfriend."

"Girl, how-in-the-hell you let that fine-ass-nigga go? He looks like he's loaded-as-shit with long money."

"Sometimes money and looks don't mean much when they don't match how the man treats you. You are nothing more than a high-priced-bitch he's fuckin'. He's a walking nightmare," Dahlia replied as she draped the cape over Gabby.

"Sounds like there was a bad breakup between the two of you?"

"You don't know the half, and I really don't want to talk about it and relive the drama," Dahlia spoke, trying to quickly end Gabby's questioning of her past with Shad.

"I feel you, girl. I've had my own share of bad relationships, some I want to forget I was even in."

Dahlia heard Gabby talking, but had totally blanked her out. She couldn't stop her mind from replaying Shad's words. *'I'm back and for good.'* She didn't know what it was supposed to mean.

Dahlia had never told her family Shad was laying hands on her. When he would give her bruises makeup couldn't cover, she would stay home and avoid her family and friends. Most of the time, he gave her bruises no one could see unless she took off her clothes.

On one particular day, Shad picked a fight about Dahlia cheating. She was fed up with his lies, his cheating, and the beatings, so when he hit her, she'd called Traci and asked her to come get her. Shad had walked in as she was packing a bag. When she told him she was leaving him, he beat her some more. When Traci arrived to the home Dahlia shared with Shad, Dahlia was laid out on the floor unconscious. Shad was long gone.

Dahlia's father had ordered a hit from behind bars on Shad's life. Like he never existed, Shad had disappeared. The last anyone had heard, he was in New York. Dahlia had stayed in a coma for close to a month. When she finally came to, she'd told her family what she had endured from the man she had loved.

Dahlia was lost in her thoughts as Shad's words kept repeating in her head. *I'm back and for good.'* When she looked up, she was staring Traci right in the face.

"Hey; why aren't you at work?" Dahlia questioned, checking the time.

"I'm on lunch break. Let me see your keys; we'll talk later. Finish up your client," Traci spoke, reaching out her hand for Dahlia's keys.

"Okay," Dahlia replied, handing Traci the keys to her car.

She didn't know what was going on. She had been friends with Traci long enough to know something was wrong.

"I'll be right back," Traci said, heading back out the door.

"Gabby, give me a few moments," Dahlia said.

"Sure."

Dahlia made her way over to where Chandra was. "I'm not feeling good. I have another client coming today, a simple press-and-curl. Can you do it for me?"

"Yeah; I got you. Feel better."

"Thank you."

Just as Dahlia was making it back to her station and the waiting Gabby, Traci was coming back into the shop.

"I have to get back to work, but I left you something under your seat. Call me when you're done here."

"Okay; I'm gonna be leaving after I finish her up."

"All right."

"Traci, you good?" Dahlia questioned.

"We'll talk later." Traci smiled.

Dahlia finished up with Gabby and rushed out the shop. Just as she picked up the phone to call her grandmother, her phone rang; her grandmother was on the other end.

"Hey, Granny."

"Hey, baby. So I talked to your brother, finally. He said the money he got was a loan from a friend so I could pay the loan on the house off. He said he has been working on this friend of the both of yours' construction company site."

"I don't know anyone with a construction company. Granny, have you talked to my dad?"

"Like I told you last week, not in a few weeks. They may be on lockdown, or he's gotten himself back in the hole. Why? Is everything okay?"

"Yeah; I'm just ready to talk to him. I miss him. I'm going to try to go down there next weekend."

"That would be wonderful. He would love it."

"I know. I'm about to get into traffic and head home. My head is killing me."

"Go get some rest. Let me know when you make it home."

"I will," Dahlia replied, disconnecting the call with her grandmother.

She remembered Traci had left something under the seat. Dahlia grabbed the bag, looked inside, and stuffed it in her purse before pulling off.

Traffic wasn't so bad, so it didn't take Dahlia long to get home. Dahlia checked the mail and was headed inside when she heard footsteps.

"Can we talk?"

"Do you plan on being respectful?" Dahlia questioned, turning to face Jerome.

"I apologize about last night. I admit, I was drunk and deep in my emotions."

"That you were."

"What is it about me?"

"Jerome, I'm not understanding the question."

"I thought you weren't trying to date. Or, you just ain't trying to date me? Because you sure were all smiles with ol' dude."

"Who said it was a date? Why couldn't it just be me hanging out with a friend?" Dahlia questioned. "I actually don't have to explain myself to you."

"Can you just answer my-fuckin'-question? Is it just me you aren't trying to date?"

"If you don't know how to speak to me with respect, don't speak to me at all. I'm tired and I'm not really in the mood for bullshit. I told you I wanted us to remain friends. That is it! Just friends!"

"I-fuckin'-love you, woman! I just want to make you happy and fuck you like no man ever has. Let me be the man to make you happy."

"Jerome, please stop it. I just want us to be friends."

"Oh, I see. I'm not good enough, but that nigga Shad was?"

"I'm not about to go through this with you. Bye, Jerome." Dahlia turned and proceeded to go into her house.

"We gon talk about this right now," Jerome spoke, grabbing Dahlia by the arm. "Answer the question: Are you too good to date a nigga like me?"

"Let me go, Jerome."

"Not until you answer my question."

"If you do not want me to cause a scene, you would let me the-fuck-go right now."

"You know what? Fuck you, Dahlia! You should be happy somebody wants to fuck you. I can fuck any bitch I want, any day of the week. I don't need your-ass. It would have been a pleasure for you to be on a real-nigga's arm, but you're too use to fuckin' lame-ass-niggas. I only wanted to smash-

and-pass to the next nigga," Jerome spoke, releasing his grip on Dahlia's arm. In just an instant, his true feelings had arisen.

"I can't even say I am surprised. And you're right: I don't want to date a man like you. Been there, done that. You muthafuckas think you're God's gift to women because you think you look good and got a little money and a nice car. News flash: I got all that shit. And, I got it all on my own. I might be a fat-bitch, but you've been dying to get in between these plush thighs for years. You're a clown just like the rest of those-fools out here. Just a week ago, you were throwing cash my way and hadn't even got a good sniff of the pussy, let alone stuck the tip in. So what you can do, Jerome, is fuck off!" Dahlia said. "Now get-the-fuck off my-damn-property, fuckin' clown."

"WAP!" was the only sound you heard as Jerome's open hand connected with Dahlia's face. He had slapped her.

Dahlia was surprised. She hadn't expected him to hit her. Clutching her face, she glared at Jerome as she quickly pulled the gun from her purse and aimed it at him.

"I told myself when I woke up out that coma that another man would never put his hands on me, and Jerome, you just did . . ."

Ghetto Rose 2
Coming 2017

When they ask who I am . . .

I am a woman who refuses to let her past control her present and procrastinate her future.

I am a woman who bottled up her doubts, fears, and negative thoughts. I shipped them to God, Who replied, "My child, if you have prayed about it, why are you still worried?"

I am a woman who believes in working hard and praying even harder.

I am a woman with goals.

I am a woman who strives to inspire and aspire those near and far.

I am a woman.

You can call me Nisha, Author Nisha Lanae. I come to inspire, aspire, and entertain with words.

#iAmTheConcreteRose
#iAmTheGhettoRose